THE OUTLAWS HENNESSEY

ALSO BY BOB HERZBERG

Borderline

Sidearm

The McDermott Fifty

THE OUTLAWS HENNESSEY

BOB HERZBERG

WOLFPACK
PUBLISHING
— EST 2013 —

The Outlaws Hennessey
Paperback Edition
Copyright © 2024 Bob Herzberg

Wolfpack Publishing
1707 E. Diana Street
Tampa, Florida 33609

wolfpackpublishing.com

Paperback ISBN 978-1-63977-526-2
eBook ISBN 978-1-63977-525-5
LCCN 2024937438

THE OUTLAWS HENNESSEY

CHAPTER ONE

LORD KNOWS, I DIDN'T LIKE BEING WOKEN OUT OF BED IN the middle of the night. But Ty had a plan, and if it was to go off right, it had to be done when most folks were fast asleep in their beds. Wiping the haze from my eyes, I actually wondered why folks couldn't be robbed in the daytime when the robbers could do their jobs right and proper after a good night's sleep.

Running my fingers back through my hair, I staggered over to the closet to find some shirt to wear, and Ty grabs my arm like I was going to make some kind of life-and-death decision.

"Remember," he hissed at me, "*black*! Choose something *black*!"

I looked at him, all six feet two of him, dressed in black pants and a dark-brown shirt. Then I looked at the closet. I didn't have anything black. I didn't even have anything in dark brown, like he did.

"They're not supposed to see us, Ty," I said sleepily. "Is anyone who's not gonna see us gonna care what we wear?"

Ty raised his eyes heavenward for a second. Then he said urgently, "Wearing black is going to make sure we blend into the dark, ya damn fool! Light-colored clothes'll attract attention!"

"But if folks aren't gonna be on the street, who're we gonna attract?"

It was a good question, but Ty wasn't in the mood for logic at that point. Not with our asses on the line, he wasn't.

"Just find something, Jed. *Dark*, preferably!"

Ty was my big brother—my adopted big brother— or maybe my big stepbrother, but my brother just the same. He was just two and a half years older than me and even resembled me a little, though not totally. He had dark-brown wavy hair and brown eyes, while my hair was blonder and my eyes were dark blue. But he had my sun-darkened tan because we were both farm boys "*working the soil,*" as Easterners like to say about us Western folks. And we were tall for our respective ages too, with his age being twenty-one and a half and me a fast-growing young roughneck at nineteen. I heard from my late mom that the Tullys were of Irish stock and that would account for my height and blond hair, but my late dad said that the Tullys took some kind of side trip from the Emerald Isles to Scandinavia back in the year fifteen something or other; he didn't mention any reason for the trip though.

Both my parents were visiting kin in Montrose, which is in west-central Colorado or thereabouts, when their stagecoach overturned on a mountain pass during a bad storm and they and a whiskey drummer from Iowa and a lawyer from Grand Junction died in the fall. I remember when I was told of their deaths. I was a baby, a toddler really, and I was having a good time playing with my babysitter. She was tall for a girl her age, which I think was eleven or twelve, and she had honey-blonde hair and hazel eyes. She was responsible and mature and damn fun to be with. I think her mom was a friend of my parents. I was glad she was around when I first heard about my folks. No one actually *tells* a toddler that his parents just died, but I kind of picked things up real quick, and even that young, I realized what had happened. Only that blonde girl had kept me from going crazy while I had some endless screaming tantrums. God bless her for her love and patience. Another babysitter might've given me a whap in the face and told me to just deal with it.

The Brodys had been our neighbors, and when my folks died, they took me in. Their son, Ty, became my big brother, and no one ever had a brother as fine and loyal as he was. Or smarter. Ty read *a lot*, local newspapers mostly, and he knew words and little facts about the world I could only start to understand. Sure, we scrap and argue, but that's just what brothers—and I assume sisters—do sometimes. We both went to the little school on the edge of town and grew up on a small farm as Ty's folks, who were my folks as well now, struggled to feed us and further our education. I was still Jed Tully, but I have to say that, besides my own parents, I couldn't have had a more loving mother and father than Helen and Cal Brody. The only one I missed was my blonde *"girlfriend"* who babysat me. She disappeared from my life shortly after I became a Brody. To this day, I don't recall her name. She always loved me, and Lord knows I was crazy about her. I wondered what had happened to her, but then one thing happens, and then another, and before you know it, you grow up and forget about those folks who had once meant so much to you.

I guess just to get Ty off my back, I grabbed a dark blue shirt that already had the armpits eaten through. He didn't like my choice because he feared that the light-colored flesh under my arms, the part that *wasn't* darkened by the southwest Colorado sun, would be seen, again, by those mysterious folks who just "*happened to pass by*" in the middle of the night.

Sighing, he let me wear it, but warned me not to raise my arms during the robbery. I replied that if I raised my arms—meaning my hands—during the robbery, it would mean someone had the drop on us and we'd be under arrest so who gave a damn about my armpits being exposed anyway?

They were asleep, our folks, when we skedaddled out the window of our room and headed for town. There we were, two tow-headed farm boys who never broke a law in our collective lives, about to commit a robbery for the supposedly higher goal of *avenging an injustice.*

We took the horses out of the barn quietly. Hell, they were the only two we had, and we figured Dad wouldn't be taking any rides at one in the morning so he wouldn't know they were missing. The moon shone brightly that night, but to me it was a big ball of light illuminating our dubious journey so the whole world would see us. As I climbed into the saddle, I cursed the moon under my breath. Why couldn't it be pitch black while we're committing what some folks in the east would call a "*felony*"?

We rode at a trot, not wanting to tire the horses, especially if we had to make a fast getaway out of town.

Our Stetsons were black, their wide brims shading our faces if anyone just happened to see us on our one a.m. ride. I heard that the town marshal sometimes takes a ride around Beaumont's main street after midnight and just turns his head left, then turns his head right, guesses that all is right with the town, then hurries back to his office and gets some sleep.

In my silent prayers, I hoped so. I wasn't hankering to run into some law dog in the middle of the night, or at any other time either!

We were quiet as we rode. The dirt trail kicked up some dust from our horses' hooves and a late spring wind blew some of it up to their chests, fallen leaves following in their wake. I felt that was a bad omen, and I cursed that damn moon again for that wind. That dark blue shirt I was wearing was a thin one and the chill I felt didn't help my mood.

The town was dark and quiet when we entered Front Street, and for that I was grateful. My gratitude extended to the fact that most of the saloons were over on Vermont, a quarter mile away, but our target was Reynolds Emporium just two blocks away. We sat our horses and scanned the street.

"Got the sacks?" Ty asked quietly.

Two empty potato sacks were tied to the pommel. I lifted them slightly to show him.

"Good," he said.

"What're we gonna take?" I asked.

Impatiently, he replied, "We went over this before. I figure Old Man Reynolds won't have a cash box there; he probably lugs it home every night or deposits the money at the bank. So we grab what Ma and Pa could *use*. Foodstuffs, feed for the horses, maybe even some tool if we can carry it on our saddles." Then his eyes almost reflected the moon's glow when he said, "Yeah. There's a shiny new Winchester repeater I had my eyes on for a while. Nice to know I'll be getting it without having to pay a cent."

I looked away from him then. Didn't know exactly why, but guessed I just wanted to get it over with.

Looking down Front Street, I said, "Then we might as well get on with the avengin'."

We gigged our horses forward and arrived in front of Reynolds Emporium—which some folks justifiably called "Reynolds Gyp Joint" and watched the building as if it were ready to leap from its foundations and pounce on us. "Emporium" was a fancy word Old Man Reynolds put on the place. True, it occupied a lot of space, was a stand-alone building not linked to the properties on either side of it, with an alley on the right side and one on the left side, but it looked like just a glorified general store to me. True again, inside it had a wooden stairway with a thin railing leading up to a second-floor storage space, which gave customers a bird's-eye view of wooden barrels and crates of supplies and such, but it was no palace. The place was cleaned probably twice a month and I knew for a fact some middle-aged folks tended to sneeze an awful lot when they entered the place due to the dust coming from that upstairs supply loft.

I leaned toward Ty and asked, "The front door lock, will it give?"

"Not on Christmas or Easter or any other time, Jed. I came back here last Thursday at closing time and purposely pushed on the door after Old Man Reynolds locked it. He came to the door, raised that dirty shade, scowled at me, and yelled a muffled, 'We're closed! Come back tomorrow!' I just shrugged, gave him my stupid grin, and walked away. Could've sworn the old bastard cussed me out from behind the door, knowing full well that I'd clean his map if that locked door wasn't between us."

"So what do we do?"

"There's a back stairway in the right-hand alley that leads to that second-floor supply loft."

"Wouldn't it go to thinkin' that there'd be a sturdy lock on that door as well?"

"No, it wouldn't, Jed ol' boy, because I went up there after dark and, when no one was looking, I tried the door. It hasn't even got a lock, but it does have a chain-latch that allows the door to open a full six inches..."

"Jesus," I said, almost in wonder at the simplicity of it.

"Right as rain," Ty said, shifting restlessly in his saddle. "Put your boot against it and it'll give like a loose woman on a Saturday night."

"Kick it in?"

"No kicking! The noise'll carry. Just a firm shove and we'll be inside in two seconds."

Then, without any further words from either of us, we rode on to the alley's mouth on the right-hand side and turned our horses into it. We dismounted and tied the reins to the bottom of the worn stairway railing leading to that back door. Quietly standing there, we both looked up at the door; then we cast glances up and down the alleyway. It was quiet, with just a spill of moonlight angling in from the rooftops on either side, casting our shadows at odd angles against the building's outer wall. After tying the horses, I mounted the wooden steps and started up, Ty following. When the sixth step gave a loud creak, I halted.

"What's the matter?" he asked.

"Don't you think that noise was kinda loud this time of night?"

"The boys at the Parakeet and Queenie's four blocks away can't hear it, so stop being spooked and just get up the stairs!"

I'll admit I felt kind of foolish then. I sighed and continued up to the tiny landing outside the door. This is where Hank Beldon, the poor kid who worked for Reynolds, was breaking his back bringing barrels and crates up through here to the supply area. Hank wasn't too bright, but he worked hard. I heard he wasn't paid anything for knocking himself out for Reynolds but meager grub and sleeping in a spare room on the old man's property. Thinking about what Reynolds did to our pa, I forgot all my reservations about Ty's plan and thought, "Yeah, I'm really gonna enjoy pickin' this old man's pockets this night."

Pa was a hard-working man, but still poor. Try telling an old skinflint like Reynolds that it hadn't rained in God knows how long and with no crops growing, we couldn't pay him what we owed him. So he cut us off and threatened Pa with arrest if the money wasn't in his gnarly hands by such-and-such a time. Me and Ty had just about had it with that old crook's threats and harassment, so we decided to do things the Outlaw Way —the way the Jameses and Youngers got even—though with no shooting.

So here I was at the top stairway landing outside Reynolds's store, ready to break the seventh commandment. I turned the doorknob and pushed in so I could open it as much as the latch would allow and then press my boot against it.

It opened all the way.

We looked at each other. Then, glancing down, we saw the busted latch on the floor inside.

I said, "What the hell's goin' on?"

Ty looked down at the busted latch and said, "Maybe that kid Hank pushed open the door while rolling in a barrel and didn't realize the latch was on. Maybe he was too scared to tell the old man he busted it."

I looked back at him and said, "You're full of it, Ty..."

"Okay, smart guy, then why else is the door open?"

I knew in my bones why, but I didn't want to believe it. Someone else was here. A chill started to go down my back and made its way to the pit of my stomach. This was supposed to be a *private* robbery, not a group effort!

As if reading my mind, Ty said, "I know what you're thinkin', Jed. Somebody broke in just before us and they're here right now. Well, son, that don't make any sense! First of all, they wouldn't stick around. Second, they could've broken in any time between his closing the store at six and now."

"Then if the place is already robbed, what does that leave us?"

"We should *still* go in. Chances are the robbers didn't take the same things we're interested in takin'. It also makes it easier for us because they'll take the blame for stealing things that *we'll* take. Get it?"

I couldn't argue with Ty's logic. Still, the suspected presence of other thieves also heightened the danger element. Reluctantly, I opened the door further and stepped inside, Ty following me.

He whispered, "Close it."

There was a question in my look, and he answered, "Some jasper passing by the alley could see the open door and wonder what's up."

I closed the door.

It was dark inside, with only a spill of moonlight through the skylight giving us a vague outline of crates and barrels on either side of us. Behind the door hung on a nail was an oil lamp. Ty took it off the nail and said, "Light it. Just keep it low and away from any windows."

I pulled a Lucifer that I had swiped off Pa's dresser out of my pocket and struck it. Its blue and orange flame flashed and I lit the lamp within the wick. The path from the door was a narrow aisle with crates and barrels of different sizes on either side of us. With the lamp in front of me we advanced deeper into the space. It was just a half a minute before we heard the noise from below us. We both froze in our spots, glancing at each other, and then instinctively moving over to the balcony railing which looked out over the store proper.

As we moved forward, Ty hanging close behind me, we heard the noise again and quickly identified it as a *meow*.

"Hell!" said Ty in disgust. "It's just a cat!"

"Real funny too," I said.

"How come?"

"Old man Reynolds hates cats. Remember last November when we saw him chase some alley cat out of the place 'cause he was eating the stuff from a leaky barrel."

"Hell, yeah. He was going after it with a cleaver."

"Okay, so Old Man Reynolds isn't a cat lover. Then

what's a cat doing here when the doors are supposed to keep them locked out?"

"But the door was *open!*"

"Meaning whoever it was who broke in, the cat followed him inside."

Then we heard *another* meow coming from below us.

I said, "Sounds like a cat convention. What's got them making all that noi—"

But when I held the lamp out over the balcony railing and shined it down into the store, my heart jumped about twelve miles out of my chest. Ty gasped audibly when he looked over the edge.

There was Old Man Reynolds laying across his own counter, face up, empty eyes looking right at us, arms spread out like our Lord, with three or four scrawny alley cats eating the lower part of his face. And did I forget to mention that his throat was cut from ear to ear?

I almost dropped the lamp.

That's when a voice struck both of us out of the darkness.

"Hold it!"

We both looked off in the far corner. Someone, a young man from what I could tell from the voice and the narrowness of his hips and thin frame, stepped out of the corner and approached us. When I turned toward him, I couldn't help the lamplight shining on him. In the glimpse we had of him, we could clearly see the Colt he pointed at us. He was short, several inches shorter than me and Ty, and he had sandy blond hair and a smooth lean face. He couldn't have been older than us.

But we could see that the light was blinding him when he blinked at us and slightly turned his head.

"Turn that thing aside, damn you!"

I pulled the lamp back so the light didn't shine on him. Consequently, we were looking at a shadow, a shadow with a pistol leveled at us.

"You got names," he growled, "give 'em."

Ty was about to give his when I said, "We're not giving you anything. I don't see any marshal's badge on you."

Due to the little lamplight shining on our friend before us, I could detect a widening of the eyes, as if my remark had triggered some kind of outrage within him. Yet I also detected something else in this young gunman that came to the surface when I defied him.

He *liked* trouble.

Before he could give us any, Ty quickly said, "I'm Ty Brody and this is my brother, Jed Tully. We figured on relieving Old Man Reynolds of some supplies, but it looks like you beat us to it."

I wasn't pleased that Ty seemed to give in to this little upstart so easily, but the young man answered, "You're smart, Ty. I just woke up after bein' conked with a .45, and I'm in no mood to be riled. Not *at this time* anyway." I was right about him; he *did* like trouble. This was not just some kid who was wet behind the ears.

I indicated the corpse with my head and asked, "And what happened to Old Man Reynolds?"

"I know what you two are thinkin'," he said, "but it wasn't me that cut 'em up like that." Then his young voice deepened with rage when he said, "But I've got an idea who did..."

I said, "So we caught you at the scene. Are you going to kill us?"

The young man paused. You could see that he wasn't seriously thinking about killing us, he just wanted to unnerve us a little. He didn't, but it was an interesting attempt.

"I'll think it over," he said. "But right now we're all on the spot, so let's just leave the way we came in and act real calm when we do it. Agreed?"

He was firm, but not as hostile as when we first met. In fact, there was a sudden maturity to this kid that surprised us. The more he awakened from being hit in the head with a .45, the calmer and more decisive he seemed to get. I knew immediately that this kid couldn't have murdered Old Man Reynolds and left him down there to be devoured by alley cats. But that still didn't mean he was a harmless little lamb either.

"You lead the way," I said.

"No, Jed, you boys lead it. And put out that lamp. It makes a great target."

At first I thought he meant it was a great target for *him*, but then I realized he was talking about the towns-people who would spot it while we're leaving the scene of a crime. Still, we used the lamp to get to the door and then I blew it out and put it on the floor before I opened it. We left the place then, me and Ty in the lead and our young friend, still holding his gun, right behind us. In fact, it was pretty obvious that he had us go ahead of him, not because he was afraid we'd jump him, but because he was careful of a sudden ambush from anyone who spotted us leaving and figured to get the drop on us, and with me and Ty in the lead, *we'd* get shot, not him. Again, despite his callousness, the boy showed a certain kind of shrewdness for self-preservation you didn't find in ordinary youngsters.

We walked down the steps to our horses, both of whom looked up and started moving about restlessly.

I asked our captor, "Where's yours? Tied in front?"

I heard him snort derisively behind us.

"I ain't that stupid," he said. "I had him tied right where yours are, but Lone and the rest lit out and took him away before you boys got here."

"Lone?" Ty asked, curious. By that time, we were in the alley and untying our horses' reins.

"Okay," he replied, "enough questions." Then, with surprising speed, he took the reins out of our hands with his free hand and pointed the gun at us with the other.

"Hey!" cried Ty.

"What the hell do you think you're doin'!" I was angry but I should've known this young one would pull something like this.

He cocked the hammer and said, "Isn't it obvious? Now both of you get back to the end of the alley."

I said, "Those aren't *our* horses, they belong to our pa! He needs them on the farm!"

Did I detect a little sorrow in his eyes? I wasn't sure. But whatever it was, it vanished as quickly as it came and a hardness replaced it.

"Right now, I need 'em more! Now start walkin' down that alley, gents. I'm not foolin'!"

Ty and me looked at each and couldn't believe it. Here we were, about to get back at Old Man Reynolds for cheating our pa, and instead we were about to lose his only horses to this little thief. Reluctantly, we turned around and walked slowly down the alley, feeling like two damn fools.

As I walked, I heard behind me a foot go into a stirrup and the creak of saddle leather as his thin frame settled itself.

Then I heard him call out, no more loudly than he had to, "Sorry, boys!"

We heard him take off out of the alley and down Front Street. He was riding my horse and leading Ty's close behind him. We both ran back to the mouth of the alley and arrived just in time to see him turn down Vermont and he was gone.

"Now how're we going to get back home?" asked Ty, though the answer was pretty obvious.

"Yeah," I said. "And how're we going to explain to Pa how his horses disappeared?"

We had a lot of time to think about these things as we trudged miserably toward our home.

CHAPTER TWO

We followed the road out of town through the darkness. Except it wasn't really that dark since the moon finally came out from behind a mess of clouds and stayed more or less out in the open. The branches of the cottonwoods swayed in the wind, and I was huddled so deep in my dark blue shirt you'd swear I was this gangling two-legged turtle still in its shell. Ty was also freezing, but I guess being older and supposedly more mature, he tried to hide it and acted as if the now-biting cold wasn't getting to him at all. Springtime in southwest Colorado wasn't all it was cracked up to be, unless it was the late afternoon; then things were wonderful and warm and everything in nature looked beautiful. But in certain parts of the territory at *night* and traveling on foot in the woods wearing old cast-offs? I think I'd rather take a Shoshone torture session.

We argued during that little hike of ours. I understood Ty's rage at Reynolds for cheating Pa, but look where his attempt at revenge got us. Cold, hungry, and forced to explain to our folks how we lost their horses. The shame I felt knowing we'd have to face Pa with this bit of news made the hike far more painful than if we were merely lost. As I said before, I thought of Ty's folks as my own, and I was furious with him that we would have to come back to them now and hurt them like this.

About a half mile into the woods, I opened the ball. "You *had* to get back at Old Man Reynolds, didn't ya, Ty?"

"Shut up, Jed!"

"How's *vengeance* taste now? Good and sweet?"

He reached out then and grabbed the collar of my old shirt, tearing it.

That's all it took. We were on the edge already so I guessed it was natural what would happen next. I knocked his arm off me and then he belted me one across the jaw. I threw my right and it landed square in his nose. A slight trickle of blood came down to his upper lip and he wiped his nose and mouth, looked down at his fingers, and then roared like a savage. We quickly grappled and then went down onto the hard-packed ground, tussling and rolling over each other as if we were schoolyard enemies rather than surrogate brothers. We rolled over rocks and broken-off branches and peeled bark and pine cones and whatever else was in our path. We rolled for about a dozen yards or so, our hats coming off and our beaten-up clothes getting more ragged with each tumble.

We would've rolled on and on to the end of creation until, by instinct, we both stopped our journey a couple feet before a pair of horse's hooves.

We both saw the horse at the same time and

instantly stopped fighting. Then our heads swiveled upward and spotted this young fellow, maybe a few years older than us, peering over the pommel with amusement on his bearded face. It was ordinarily a smooth face, as I say, on the youngish side, and I had the quick impression that the beard was grown to make its wearer look older, or maybe even hide his identity. The Stetson was a little beaten-up, and his jacket and Levis had the look of hand-me-downs as well, but he was much better dressed for the brisk weather than we were. Behind his horse stood another one, its' reins loosely held by the rider.

And did I mention that the man was also pointing a Springfield carbine in our general direction?

He said, "You boys take out your problems in the strangest places."

The voice was from the area, I could tell, but there was something vaguely familiar about it, as if I had not only heard it before, but pretty recently.

We both got up off the ground awkwardly and retrieved our hats. Then we stood there and stared at him, both of us trying to determine who he was. To make sure we didn't get too close to him, the rider lightly jerked back on the reins and his mount took a couple steps away from us.

"Okay, gents," he said, and when he gestured with the barrel of the Springfield, I knew that this fellow now meant business. "What'd you do with Andrew?"

Ty asked, "*Who*?"

The rider's face got deadly serious then.

"I'm not playin' games, boys. Now you tell me what you did with him or I'll let ya both have it and you can be vittles for the wolves, suit yourselves."

From the look in his eyes, I could tell this jasper wasn't kidding. This "Andrew" must be someone special.

Angry over how things had turned out, I said defiantly, "Mister, you can take that carbine and shov—"

But Ty made his voice louder and cut mine off before I finished the sentence. He suddenly realized *why* this fellow's voice sounded familiar even though we'd never seen him before.

"He's your brother, isn't he?"

I asked, "*Who's* his brother?"

Ty replied, "Our little friend who swiped our animals, that's who."

The rider sat back slightly, a calmer expression now replacing the deadly one. I even saw a slight nod of understanding when he heard this piece of news.

Then his face broke into a grin, something I had a feeling didn't happen too often. "That's Andrew," he said. "Little brother's always puttin' one over on somebody."

"Yeah," I said sullenly. "And if we ever see him again, we'll kick his—"

Again, Ty interrupted me before we were blasted off the face of the earth.

"Who are you and how'd you get here?" Ty asked the rider. It was a bold question to ask of a man with a carbine, but Ty, forever the curious soul, wanted to know what the hell was going on. For if we did know what was going on, maybe, just maybe we could get the stolen horses back.

To my surprise, he answered him without hostility.

"We broke into Reynolds's store and grabbed what we could. Then after we rode away, I started to notice that Andrew wasn't with us. Seemed that one of our boys buffaloed him back at Reynolds's store after we all left."

Ty asked, "And the man that did the deed was named *Lone*, is that right?"

The man looked down at Ty with a kind of admiration.

"In my business, I'd say a good memory is a ticket to the cemetery, but personally, I like a man who keeps his eyes and ears open."

Shrugging off the compliment, Ty said, "So you doubled back looking for your brother, searched the store, and found nothing but Reynolds's body."

I added, "Then you saw our boot tracks in the road and followed us here by moonlight."

The rider said to us, "You boys got more brains than some jasper twice your age."

Instead of agreeing or disagreeing, Ty just looked up at him and said, "We're still waiting for you to answer my other question. *Who are you?*"

He paused for a moment. Then he raised the carbine's barrel so it wouldn't be pointed directly at us. Finally he said, "Name's Ira Toombs."

Ty stared at him then with a mixture of awe and disbelief, I wasn't sure which feeling was stronger.

Ty asked, "Ira Toombs of Leadville?"

The rider sounded bored when he answered, "Yeah..."

"The same man who held up the bank in Trinidad?"

Ira answered irritably, "It was in Gunnison. Now listen—"

"How much did you get away with, thirty thousand? Forty?"

Ira finally shouted, "Will you shut up for a minute!" Ty shut up instantly, and I kept quiet as well. Ira cocked an ear and listened. Suddenly we started to hear it too. The beat of horses' hooves, many of them, from a distance. Hell, I felt the trembling in the earth. Even the little animal and bird noises we were hearing stopped. Me and Ty looked back and saw them back in the woods, the black shadows of mounted horsemen, maybe a mile or two away from us, but getting closer as we stood there.

Ira cursed and said, "They must've found Old Man Reynolds."

I said, "But we didn't do anything." In that instant, I seemed to have forgotten our attempted burglary of the old man's store.

Ira said gravely, "You try tellin' them that. Those boys'll stretch your neck the second you open your mouths."

I then said the obvious. "We can't stay out here."

Ira replied, "First smart thing you've said. Now I brought this gelding for Andrew, but it'll be good enough to carry you two, at least for the time bein'."

Ty asked, "Where are we gonna go?"

Ira said, "You let me worry about that. You stay here, or you're dead men. Now mount up!"

He absently waved the carbine at us when he gave his order, so I figured we'd better do

as he said. Ty quickly mounted the gelding while Ira turned over the reins to him. Then I climbed up behind Ty, and we rode off at an angle that might make the posse strain to keep up with us. We sped off the trail and headed deeper into the woods. The heavy branches above us obscured the moonlight and made traveling a little rough at times, but Ira seemed to know just how to conceal himself during a chase. With thicker and thicker shrubbery around us to squeeze through, riding was uncomfortable to say the least, but these little game trails were geared for a single horse and rider to travel on, not a whole crowd of men. I tipped my hat to Mr. Toombs for knowing exactly where to go. And when the forest opened up into a clearing, he put our mounts over some rocky surfaces that wouldn't retain a track mark. Then after passing through these foothills, we hit a stream bed and followed the water flow for a few miles until it widened into a natural river, with tributaries flowing into it from both a southerly and an eastern direction. When the river got too deep, we left it and mounted its northern bank. Ty kept the gelding close on Ira's tail as if our lives depended on it, which, quite frankly, it did. It was a good thing there was a moon out that gave us just enough light. Our horses could have gone lame at any time and that would leave us at the mercy of the lynch mob behind us.

Ira looked back and apparently didn't see anyone still on our trail. When he slowed his horse to a walk, we did too.

"They're not done yet, gents," he said. "If they think we murdered the storekeeper, they'll keep on our tail till doomsday. It doesn't matter though. We're almost there."

I asked, "Almost where?"

"Our *hideout*. Except it's not exactly a hideout."

Ty said, "Listen, Toombs. Jed and me aren't going to any *hideout*. Not with those men after us. They're after you and your friends, not us."

I chimed in, "He's right. *We* didn't kill Reynolds. Why should we be part of all this?"

At that point, Ira had the carbine pointing upward, but now he lowered the barrel toward us. "Whether you like it or not, you boys *are* part of it. You saw me and you saw my brother and I can't risk you blabbing to John Law."

Ty then asked a gutsy question.

"Then what's stopping you from killing us right now?"

Ira's mouth became a grim line, as if he were fighting within himself to make a decision. Then he answered casually, "First of all, the shot would carry. Second, I'm doin' you boys a favor. You want your pa's horses, don't ya?"

If we could get Ty's father's horses back and quietly slip away, then maybe the two of us could, with little fuss, put it down to experience and forget the whole damn misadventure. Me and Ty looked at each other and we both nodded.

"All right, Toombs," said Ty. "It's your show. But could you put away the Springfield?"

Ira shook his head.

"You boys just signed yourselves a contract. This here carbine's the final signature."

Neither of us liked the analogy, but at that point we couldn't do very much about it. So with us in the lead, he took us another three or four miles west of wherever we were.

By the time we arrived at our destination, the sun was rising...

———

THE GOLDEN RAYS of a midwestern sun are beautiful to look at and to feel its warmth. But in this case, it only served to remind us of our growing hunger, since breakfast was what we would've had on our collective minds at that hour, us being early-to-rise farm boys and all.

We sat our horses outside the border of a small town. The street before us looked normal enough, a row of buildings with false fronts on either side; some stores still locked up at that early hour, even the two saloons we could spot were closed. They had probably just locked their doors. Not a man, woman or horse was on the street. A sharp gust of wind blew briefly in our direction; a final burst of bitter cold before the sun warmed the earth.

Gesturing toward the town ahead of us, Ira announced wryly, "Welcome to Fraternitas!"

I looked at him and asked, "Welcome to *what*?"

Ira replied, "Yeah, I know. Kinda a funny name for a town, but don't blame me. I think some priests or missionaries or monks, I'm not sure which, named it a couple centuries ago. Folks couldn't pronounce it, so they finally renamed it Dentonville. But the sign on the town hall still says Fraternitas. Damned if I know why..." You could see the subject was starting to bore him.

Ty, who was far more educated than me, quietly said, "I know what the word means."

Ignoring him, Ira said, "All right, gents, couple blocks yonder..."

Ty turned to him and cut him off. "You said you had a 'hideout,' but it wasn't exactly a 'hideout.' What'd you mean by that?"

"Yeah," I added, "we were kind of expecting your gang to be hiding in a cave."

Ira made a face and stared at both of us as if we were lunatics.

"A cave? Now what the hell are we supposed to do in a cave? Hunt for snakes? You boys have been reading too much hogwash from those eastern ink-slingers. They keep saying us outlaws hide in places where bears take a shit. Well, those writer fellows don't know anything about us since they never left New York. Come on, I'll show you boys our *cave*."

And with his last remark, said with barely concealed contempt, he walked his horse on down the street, bidding us to follow. Ty and me looked at each other and he just shrugged.

"We went this far," he said.

Ty prodded the gelding forward and we followed our bearded friend through the town. It seemed folks were gradually starting to wake up. A few storekeepers were beginning to open their stores, and as we passed by, they openly stared at us. Ira, it seemed, they paid no mind to. It was *us* they locked their eyes on. It both unnerved me and made me angry to be the object of their gawking. Another block of these ignorant folks staring and I was going to leap from the horse and jump one of these bug-eyed jaspers, but then, after we turned a corner, Ira finally stopped us in front of a hotel. A sign outside two second-floor windows announced that this was the Trace Hotel.

It was a four-story building amid a street of two-story structures. Oddly, a restaurant called the Pellican was right next to it, its sign misspelled with two ls. The front of the hotel looked normal enough, and I assumed that it just catered to folks who traveled through town, stayed for a spell, and then moved on. But I was wrong, dead wrong...

"Tie 'em in front," said Ira as he dismounted and started to wrap the reins around the tie rail. "I'll have a boy take 'em down to the stables later."

As we dismounted, we looked at each other over that one. *I'll have a boy take 'em down to the stables later*? "Come on inside," he said.

We entered the hotel and looked around the lobby. There was nothing special about it. It wasn't fancy, nor did it seem sleazy and disreputable. A wooden staircase led to the upper floors and at the bottom of it the desk where you register. Again, oddly, the desk clerk, a mousy little man wearing rimless cheaters and a small mustache sat in the chair. But he wasn't snoring away with his head rested in his folded arms on his desk as I've imagined most desk clerks who work the night shift. He regarded us with bright, alert eyes as we entered and not a thinning hair was out of place, nor was a lapel wrinkled. This was a man whose job was to be on the ball when customers showed up no matter what time of the day or night. For his sake, I hoped he had someone else take over when he did get tired.

"Good morning, Mr. Toombs," he said cheerfully.

Again, me and Ty and I gave each other looks. We both knew that Ira Toombs was a wanted man. Where did he rate a good morning from any representative of so-called polite society and even have his name shouted out into the open as if he were a banker, a lawyer, or a doctor?

Ira noticed our discomfort and said, "If you two stop giving each other looks like two square-heads who just got off a boat, I'm sure you'd calm down enough to have some breakfast." Neither of us protested that. Then he said to the clerk, "John, just have somebody take the horses over to the stable. They haven't eaten in a while and they're played out."

John's eyes turned bright again, and he said, almost cheerfully, "You've been traveling fast, I see. As usual."

Ira stopped and gave him a look, it wasn't pleasant.

He said, "You pay attention to the register book and keep this lobby clean and don't you worry about how I treat my animals, you hear me?"

The cheer went out of John's face and I even detected a nervous swallow in his throat before he answered, "Yes, sir."

His point made, Ira started to turn away until he said, "Oh, yeah. You see these two gents over here?"

John turned and looked at us, his big eyes blinking innocently through the peepers.

"Yes," he answered.

Ira said, "Find two jackets that fit these boys, will ya?"

"Yes, sir!"

Ty said, "Now wait a minute, we don't need—"

Ira cut him off. "Before you boys eat opposite me, you're going to look like *men*, not raggedy-ass bums!"

He was right. We were dressed in shirts that had holes in them from our various skirmishes and we were freezing to boot.

It took but five minutes before John came back with a couple denim jackets which could've come from two young ranch hands. John was a good judge of sizing us up; the coats were ideal for spring weather and they fit us perfectly. We both thanked him. He said, "You're welcome, gentlemen." Then he went back behind the counter.

"Hmm," said Ty feeling the material. "Not bad. Where'd he find them?"

"Oh," said Ira, "probably belonged to some guests who checked out early..."

We didn't pay any mind to that remark then as we would later.

Ira led us back down a hallway and with a turn to the right, we entered through an archway, its big brown curtains pulled back on either side, and found ourselves in a good-sized restaurant. In fact, it was the Pellican. The only way to enter it was through the hotel lobby, though it had huge windows that looked out into the street.

Oddly, there didn't seem to be too many patrons in the place. A middle-aged couple off in the far left-hand corner, two cowboys gobbling up what looked like a couple of steaks, and a tall, thin man in a tweedy-looking suit and white shirt with standup collar sat at a table in the other far corner. The middle-aged fellow had a few pounds on him, and his handlebar mustache looked like it could be detached from his upper lip and used to wipe the table. His wife was, from what I could see, equally well-fed, and her graying hair was piled on her head surrounding a very wrinkled face. They both glanced at us with unfriendly eyes. I didn't know what their problem was, but I never got along well with high-fallutins, no matter where I ran into them—which was rarely.

The two cowboys barely gave us a look. They probably rode for some nearby ranch and were enjoying some time off in town. Their food claimed most of their attention.

The jasper in the standup collar interested me the most though. If I had my guess, I would've pinned him down as a lawyer. He seemed to eat the eggs on his plate as if he were some big, spectacled bird, chewing daintily and then dabbing his lips after every mouthful. He seemed to be very concerned that he should actually look hungry to others in the room—or be human enough to show he liked his food. But the next thing that happened was a shock. He and Ira nodded silent greetings to each other from across the room.

Ty said to Ira, "Look, we haven't got money for fancy restaurants." Maybe Ty was being polite, but I wouldn't have called this place fancy by any stretch. Still, we figured we were white trash, and eating at restaurants wasn't an everyday occurrence for us.

"Don't worry about it," said Ira, moving into the room before we could either agree or protest.

He took a table situated against the back wall and prompted us to join him. After we sat down, I noticed that Ira may have taken a table at the back wall, but he *didn't* take the chair facing the archway, as we figured any self-respecting gunfighter would. Nope, he seemed pretty confident that a lawman wouldn't try to get the drop on him here. I couldn't put my finger on it then, but I was starting to get worried.

Ty started to say, "Listen, Toombs, we're not—"

But Ira held up his hand as a waitress in a bright apricot-colored blouse and cotton apron approached the table. She was tall, though not as much as me and Ty. Her honey-blonde hair was pinned above her ears and her hazel eyes shined brightly when she first saw us, as if the sight of me and Ty were something she could learn to like. She stood poised with a pad and pencil as she waited.

Ira said, "Hazel, I'd say three steaks, eggs, potatoes, and plenty of coffee. I'm sure these gents won't complain to that."

Hazel's eyes went from Ty's to mine. So far, she hadn't acknowledged Ira at all. Though I would say, when those hazel eyes stopped and looked at mine, "Hazel" was an appropriate name. I felt something in me then. A wave of emotion made my heart beat faster and, honestly, a stirring of another kind from another part of my body. She was definitely older than me, in her midtwenties I'd guess, but this woman was already starting to excite me and she hadn't even opened her mouth yet.

Maybe she sensed what I was thinking because her eyes just locked on mine and for a few moments didn't let go.

"Hazel!" Ira said.

I was disappointed when she snapped out of it.

"Uh, yes. I'll get right on it." The voice was pure farmland, but not Kansas or Missouri. In fact, she had a slight southern drawl, but it wasn't from the deep south. Nevertheless, one thing was for sure. This woman was a hayshaker's daughter or I was the bastard offspring of President Grant. When she moved away from our table toward a kitchen in the rear, both me and Ty watched her. She wasn't what I'd call thin, she was even matronly in a way. But I sensed she had a fire within her that couldn't be put out with all the water in Lake Michigan.

Still looking in her direction, I said, "I like the service here already."

I saw Ira look at me with narrowed eyes. The remark didn't please him, and I wondered if he was going to say something, but to my surprise, he changed the subject.

"So you two decided to relieve Old Man Reynolds of his wares, huh?"

Ty turned back to him and you could see he resented the sarcasm.

But Ira continued, "Let me tell you something. We cased his store for days. Reynolds was a crazy old man scared that any jasper was going to rob his place. When Andrew cased that store, he saw a 12-gauge shotgun under the counter and a fully-loaded Remington on the wall behind the old man's head when he was serving customers. That rifle wasn't there just for show. But while the old man was busy with a customer at another part of the store, meaning one of us, Andrew went back there and unloaded the thing hours before we hit the place. He also broke open the shotgun and pulled the shells out. By the time we showed up, Reynolds's fire-power was all gone. He was standin' there pulling the trigger on empty chambers. That's what you call preparation, boys. Givin' you that little extra edge when you're on a job."

Ty asked, "So why're you telling us all this?"

"Because you boys didn't know what the hell you were doin'. Goin' up there to rob the place because that old buzzard cheated your old man. You let anger guide your thinkin', and you didn't prepare for the unexpected."

I jumped in rather bravely. "Andrew didn't expect to get buffaloed, did he?"

Ira gave me a look, and I thought for a second that

he was going to let me have one across the jaw, but to my surprise, he gave me a wry grin.

"Yeah," he said sheepishly, "that *was* unexpected, wasn't it?"

———

THE FOOD WAS DAMN good and sorely needed. The gallons of hot coffee Hazel gave us, though, did not please me as much as her just being there. As I looked up at her, she didn't face me, but I knew she could feel me staring at her. Hers was a tough job, and it wouldn't have surprised me if she also doubled as the kitchen help, sweeping the floors, washing the dishes, and cleaning the ovens. The strands of her honey-blonde hair were coming down and falling in her eyes. She lamely strove to push them back behind her ears as she looked down and served us. At one point our eyes met as the hair fell over them again and I could see that farmgirl's face of hers turn bright red. She quickly averted her eyes and finished pouring the coffee.

"Will that be all?" Her question was directed at Ira.

"For now," he replied. The way we had wolfed down our food, he probably wasn't sure whether we'd ask for seconds.

I noticed Hazel was very deferential to him, but I got the impression she'd rather be with us.

Or was I hoping longingly she'd just want to be with *me*.

She eyed both me and Ty yet again and then went back to the kitchen. I didn't look at my companions until the kitchen door swung closed. When I did look at them, though, Ira was staring at me.

"You got ideas about the waitress?" he asked.

I noticed he didn't use her name; maybe he wanted to call attention to her lowly station, I'm not sure.

I answered in a surly manner. "So what of it? Did you stake a claim on her?"

He kept his eyes on me and didn't answer at first. Then he said, "You're a might young for her."

Ty said casually, "They all gotta grow up sometime."

"Yeah," said Ira, "but this time, it might stop him from growin'..."

I glared at him, sensing a direct threat. I was ready to get up and challenge him when the tall gent who had nodded to him earlier approached our table. He looked at both me and Ty as if we were bugs and basically focused his attention on Ira. Again, like Hazel and John, the hotel clerk, this man spoke to Ira with some respect.

"Ira," he said, nodding hello.

"Jessup," Ira replied in return.

"Just came back I see."

"Yeah. Had to turn back and fetch my brother. You didn't happen to see him, did you?"

"He's with Finch and the others down at the house. He brought in two horses."

Ty and I tensed when we heard that.

Ira must've sensed our excitement, but he ignored it and asked, "How long ago?"

"Maybe two hours," answered Jessup. "He was looking for Lone—"

"I'll bet he was."

"I heard your last one didn't go so well."

"We got enough to keep us warm in the winter..."

Then Jessup's eyes took in both me and Ty and his

face showed some worry, as if Ira were talking out of turn.

"Don't worry about them," said Ira easily. "Them's is fellow badmen. You're free to say whatever you want in front of 'em."

Ty and I were not crazy about the *fellow badmen* crack, but we wanted to find out about the horses, so we let it ride.

Jessup's look didn't hide his contempt for us, but he went right on anyway.

"Some of the boys have been talking when they rode in."

Ira casually rolled himself a cigarette and lit it. "Is that so? Pray tell what've they been talking about, Hiram?"

I could tell that Jessup didn't like to be called that, especially in the light manner that Ira had just done. But he answered him anyway.

"Somebody got a little wild and left a corpse behind."

"Well, you can't expect us to take him with us, can you?"

Jessup was starting to boil at Ira's being flip. I could see the veins in his neck above the standup collar pulsing like little snakes about to pounce.

"This is no laughing matter, Ira."

Then Ira looked up at him seriously for the first time during the conversation.

"No, Hiram, it isn't..."

"Things can't go on like this much longer and you know it."

Ira just stared at him and didn't answer.

Ty and me looked at each other and the worry on

our faces said it all. *Just how many corpses are these boys responsible for anyway?*

Finally Ira answered, "Appreciate your opinions, Hiram. Now you were leavin', weren't ya?"

Jessup grimaced and said, "Things like this can't be *ignored*, Ira."

For the first time, Ira raised his voice. "You worry about adding figures and we'll worry about what we do on the trails, ya hear?"

Jessup's narrow face stiffened and he backed away from the table. It was plain to see that he could Ira just so far.

"See you later at the ranch, Ira," he said, and marched out of the restaurant as if he had just been dismissed by his superior officer, and he wasn't happy about it.

After I saw him leave, I suddenly noticed that Hazel had entered the room and was pouring coffee for one of the cowboys. Then, as if sensing that I was gazing at her, she looked up at me. Unfortunately, that's when she missed the pour and the cowboy whose cup she was filling screamed and leaped up as if he was having a hotfoot. Only it wasn't his foot that was getting hot at the moment.

His companion rocked back in his chair and laughed.

Hazel was in a panic, maybe because this happened right in front of Ira, I wasn't sure. She was apologetic and her hands came together in a begging pose, hoping that the scalded man would forgive her.

He didn't. He roared, "Stupid bitch!" Then he backhanded her across her right cheek. The knuckles of his meaty hand alone must have hurt Hazel because she fell back across the next table, which was unoccupied.

I saw Ira and Ty start to rise, but I beat them to it. I shot across the room and hurled myself into that cowboy's midsection before anyone could blink. We both went down and rolled under the table, our Stetsons coming off and our blood boiling as we swung at each other. I gave him some good punches in his wide, meaty face, but he hurt me as well. His fists were jabbing my ribs as if they were knives. We rolled over and he was on top of me, straddling me and letting me have it in the face with both fists. I fought back, and my long arm-reach served me well. I got to bloody his nose, but he was starting to work on my right eye, forcing me to close it and turn my face away.

I felt a pain in my feet and ankles and I realized that someone was kicking them. Then the pain stopped and there was more commotion from above, since I was under a table getting my lights punched in, I couldn't see what was happening. Then I heard the sounds of fighting and even a chair crashing down on something. Meanwhile, my face was getting smashed up as I lay there.

I tried to get his massive weight off me, but it was like having a bull elephant on top of you. For all I knew, he was probably crushing my kidneys, but there was little I could do about it. Then, as I was starting to lose consciousness, the cowboy's head was suddenly pulled back by the hair and a cocked gun pressed into his temple.

Ira said, "Fun's over, Ed."

Ed reluctantly lowered his fists and awkwardly shifted his weight off me. He rose off the floor as Ira released him and stood back. My face was throbbing in pain, but my body felt a wave of relief after that big ox got the hell off of me. Gradually, I crawled out from under the table, every bone in my body on fire, and I rose dizzily.

I saw that Ira had holstered his gun. Then I turned and saw that Ty was getting up as well, maybe in as much pain as I was, I wasn't sure. Both he and the cowboy's friend were hatless and Ty had some bruises on his face. Both had been fighting and the other man had the leg of a chair in his hand. It looked like he had smashed the chair over Ty's head but only hit part of his body instead. Ty was holding his left shoulder painfully.

Hazel was watching all of us fearfully. Her beautiful face had a bright red mark on the right cheek and her eyes were red with tears. Was she crying for herself, or were they for me? I'd like to think the latter.

Ira glared at Ed. I saw that he was angry, though the rage was not in his face so much as in the taut moves of his body, and it seemed a huge effort for him to keep from exploding.

"Ed," he said, "you and Jack make yourselves scarce for a few days."

Ed picked up his hat and said sullenly, "I don't see why. That little bastard started it, Ira—"

Ira reached out and grabbed the front of Ed's vest, his hand shooting out like the strike of a rattler.

"You're not hearin' well, Ed," said Ira, "I said take off! Hit the high country for a few days."

Ed started to protest, "But what about our share for the train job?"

"You'll get it when you come back. You can trust us."

Maybe I detected a little irony in Ira's last comment.

Then he shoved Ed away and looked at Jack. "You hard of hearin' too?"

Jack picked up his hat and he and Ed quickly left the restaurant, but not before Ed gave me a murderous look.

Ira turned back to us. "You boys all right?"

"Sure," said Ty, "I get chairs broken over me every day."

"You're lucky he just got you in the shoulder," said Ira. "I've seen Jack Foster break quite a few heads over the years."

Angrily, I asked, "Aren't you going to ask about Hazel?"

I could see her start to hold up a restraining hand to me, but the words were already out of my mouth.

Ira turned to me and said, "I already saved your face from a good beatin', don't push it, Jed."

Out of the corner of my wounded right eye, I noticed that Hazel looked up then. She was staring at me again. The look on her beautiful face was part compassion for me getting my eye busted to part surprise that I risked said eye—and other parts—for busting to defend her.

Grudgingly, it seemed, Ira faced Hazel for the first time and asked, "How's the cheek?"

She took her attention off me and replied, "I'll get over it, Ira..."

"Fine," he said, sounding like he didn't care one way or the other.

The old distinguished-looking couple came over. I didn't know where they were during the fight, but I could imagine them cowering in a far corner somewhere while Ty and me were getting clobbered.

Both of them looked at us with some contempt. The woman spoke first.

"This is outrageous conduct, sir!" She had spoken to Ira, who had probably been accused of many things, but never of *outrageous conduct*. Then her husband spoke.

"Sir, if we didn't have to stop here on our way to visit my wife's sister, we would've given your *establishment* a wide berth!"

He said *establishment* as if it were a disease. But at the time, I didn't understand what a *wide berth* was, and visions of a fat woman giving birth came to mind.

Ira glared at them both, never saying anything. Again, he didn't *have* to say anything; his rage was obvious. In fact, it was this look that caused the two high-fallutins to leave the room but fast. As they passed beneath the archway, I noticed them put some speed into their step.

Letting the tension flow out of him, Ira looked at Ty holding on to his shoulder and said wearily, "I'll take ya to the doc."

Ty looked at him sullenly and said, "Thanks a lot." Ira glanced at him. Amazingly, he let it slide. Then he said to Hazel, "Take him to the back and have Bessie give him something for his eye. Come on."

Ty had just enough time to give me a questioning look before he followed our outlaw host out of the room. Through the large window, I could see the two head down the street, presumably toward the stables where our horses had been taken.

Staring at the two as they disappeared from view, I started when I felt Hazel's hand on my shoulder. I turned to look up at her and saw those beautiful hazel eyes gazing at me.

"Thank you, Jed."

Since she was the first female I ever fought over, I didn't rightly know how to respond.

I finally blurted out, "My pleasure!"

She grinned at me then. It was a smile that shined across the room, the kind only a gal raised in the farm country could have; that is, after all the chores have been done. Her right cheek was bright red, but as I stared at her, even the bruise seemed to fade and her complexion was again strong and alive and her lips full and beautiful. I was breathing fast, and I felt that my heart was about to jump out of my chest. Then, when her honey-blonde hair suddenly fell in her eyes, I reached up and pushed it back. Still smiling, she took my hand off her hair and gently squeezed it.

Then she said, "I think we'd better do something about that eye."

———

LIKE HAZEL, Bessie worked in the restaurant, but by the sight of her apron, which was far dirtier than Hazel's, I could see that she worked mostly in the kitchen. She looked like she was about my age. She was also a little on the tall side, and it seemed that her tied-up dark-brown hair kept falling into her eyes every two seconds. The heat of the place might have been getting to her too. Sweat glistened on her forehead and cheeks.

When I entered the kitchen, she looked up at me and her blue eyes held me for about a second or two before she noticed my black eye. Quickly her interested expression turned sour and she angrily tossed a dishrag on a counter. I correctly guessed my appearance didn't please her. She came up to me and, with surprising strength, shoved me down into a chair near a carving board. Then she stared at my eye like she was about to pluck it out.

Finally, she grabbed a large carving knife, quickly cut off a slab of beef, put down the knife—for which I was thankful—and then smacked me in the eye with the damn thing so hard, it might as well as been Ed punching my lights out again.

"Ow! Did ya have to slam me so hard?"

Bessie leaned back and gazed at me frowning. "Sorry," she said, definitely not meaning it. Her brogue was thick and her blue eyes seemed to become as sharp as needles.

Again, pretending to apologize for her roughness, she ended up putting the knife in deeper.

"Didn't mean to slap it on so hard, but I don't do this kind of work on young ruffians every day. Perhaps if it happened more often, I could refine my technique."

Hazel stood off to the side, watching us.

"Ed Plummer slapped me, Bessie. And Jed got his eye busted standing up for me."

Bessie faced me again, and for a second or two. I actually thought there was some kindness in her sour puss. But the moment I spotted it, it was as if a light had gone out in her and she reverted to hostile form.

"Perhaps he wants a medal for his bravery," she said irritably.

As I held the meat against my wounded eye, my other one glared at her.

Still looking at my face, she said, "An angry one too he is. Lord Jesus, I bet if you had a mind to, you'd like to take my head right off, wouldn't ya, ya young hellion?"

I didn't reply. I just glared at her as if she were a cockroach beneath my feet.

Then she answered her own question. "And I can promise you, it'd be the last thing you'd ever do."

Her work done, or perhaps having said her piece, she stood erect, wiped her hands on her apron, and walked out of the kitchen.

Hazel came over and put her hand on my shoulder.

"Don't let her get to you, Jed. She's not as mean as she lets on."

Though I was falling for this lovely woman, I somehow couldn't believe she'd be that naive.

I said wryly, "I bet before she left County Cork, she ate broken glass."

Hazel smiled at me. She just *knew* I didn't mean it, even though I most definitely did.

Then her smile disappeared and she looked at me with some worry.

"Saw you with Ira Toombs. You ridin' with him?"

I knew what she was asking. She figured that me and Ty were two young hardcases joining up with Ira to rob banks and stages.

"Would it matter to you if I was?" I asked.

She didn't hesitate.

"Yes, it would."

It was mid-morning and I thanked God the restaurant was empty at this time. I sat there with the body part of some dead cow on my wounded eye and told her from the beginning how Ty and me got into this mess.

At the end of my story, she backed away from me and stared, putting her hand on her mouth. I even heard her gasp.

I asked, "What's wrong?"

She shook her head and didn't say anything, as if she was too emotional to speak. Her eyes were moistening with tears.

Then she came over and took me in her arms, hugging me tightly. I lifted my arms and embraced her. I felt wonderful there, her arms around me and me looking up at her, that face just above mine. Her hair was down in her eyes again as she was crying happy tears. I pulled my head back slightly and looked up at her beautiful mouth. Slowly I prepared my lips for the kiss I knew I was going to plant on her.

Then she pulled back out of the embrace and looked down at me, stroking my hair gently.

Her voice full of emotion, she said, "I never thought I'd see another Tully again..."

I sat up then and stared at her. I didn't recall ever having given her my last name.

Her eyes scanned my face, enjoying my youth, my being a strapping, healthy lad of nineteen, but certainly not looking at me as a potential lover. In fact, she was looking at me as if I were her kid brother. But that was impossible. I was an only child. I know I was.

She said, "I don't expect you to remember me..."

Again, she was wrong. I'd remember this lovely woman if she were in a crowd of a hundred people. But what was she driving at?

"Your folks probably didn't ever mention me..."

I suddenly sat up straighter. I stared at her hard now.

"I don't know how to say this," she started to say.

I said evenly, "Hazel, I ain't much for riddles, so you might as well come out and say it plain."

She walked away from me then and faced the opposite wall for what seemed like the longest time but was just a few seconds.

Then she turned around and said, "I'm your big sister!"

The steak slipped out of my hand and slapped hard on the floor.

———

BESSIE HAD WALKED in and harshly announced that the restaurant had a customer and what was Hazel doing jawin' with me and other such complaints that seemed part of her ornery nature. A hot mug of coffee was suddenly shoved into my hand and she ordered me to sit at some table outside and out of her way as she went about preparing some meal in *her* kitchen. As for Hazel, she just smiled at me sweetly and quietly went out to serve the customer.

I took the mug and started to leave the kitchen. But when I turned back to give Bessie a dirty look, I caught her staring at me. In that couple seconds I looked at her, I didn't see any scowl or dirty look or bitterness of any kind, just a curiosity in her face as she gazed at me. But as soon as she saw me looking at her, she spun around and busied herself with cleaning the range on the stove. I didn't think much about it then.

Don't tell me I'm *her* brother too! God help me if I'm related to the likes of *her*.

Quietly, I went into the restaurant and sat at a table, watching Hazel's body as she hustled back into the kitchen with some dude's order. Only now I started to feel ashamed for having done so. The man at the center table was dressed spiffy enough, handsome gray suit, standup collar, string tie, derby, which was off at that point and on a chair. He was reading some newspaper, probably from one of the bigger cities. He had a carpetbag on the other chair. He was about in his twenties, and he seemed full of energy; his coffee cup shook as he seized it off the saucer, practically spilling it. Was he wound up or just nervous for some reason, I couldn't tell which.

As I sat there and sipped my coffee, I thought about what she had said. *Big sister*! No, that was impossible, it couldn't be!

After a few minutes, Hazel returned with a plate of steaming food and more coffee. She served him and then, as he nervously lifted the cup to his lips, she glanced at me and smiled. It was a warm and pleasant smile, but it was not the smile of a young woman for a young man, it was the smile of a big sister for her younger brother. I returned her smile wanly and even managed a little wave. She returned to the kitchen. I had liked watching her move from one place to the other, and suddenly I found that I couldn't and lowered my eyes.

Then I found myself looking at the dude. Again, he seemed jumpy. He devoured his meal as if it should've been eaten yesterday. When Hazel came back in to see if he wanted anything else, he asked her a question. I was too far away to hear it, but I caught the name Hennessey.

After he asked his question, I saw that Hazel suddenly froze where she stood. Her rosy complexion seemed to turn pale—or maybe it was the overhead lamplight running out of oil and casting shadows on the room. I couldn't hear what her answer was, but it was quick, for right after she gave it, she about-faced and went back into the kitchen. The dude just stared after her. Then he lifted his coffee cup to drink, but I noticed now that it was definitely shaking in his hand.

I just sat there staring at him, or as much staring as I could with one partially closed eye.

Then he abruptly got up, grabbed his derby and his carpetbag, and went to pay his check.

After he left, Hazel returned, only this time her apron was gone, her shoulders were draped in a shawl and a little hat of some kind was atop her head.

She said, "Another girl will take my shift for a couple hours. I think you and I should take a walk..."

CHAPTER THREE

WE WALKED SLOWLY DOWN THE BOARDWALK, PEOPLE passing us as we went. They had seen Hazel and hardly gave her a glance. It was different with me. They had never seen me before and their eyes went to me suspiciously. We crossed the street then, avoiding an occasional rider and passing buckboard.

As if by mutual consent, neither of us had said a word since leaving the restaurant. As far as I was concerned, I considered it her show and was waiting for her to start the conversation. Then, after we left the business district and the streets got more tree-lined and houses were few, she spoke.

"Your father was in the war many years ago..."

I looked at her. I knew that Dad was in the war. He was at Chancellorsville. Lucky to get out of it with all his body parts from what I gathered. But this was only from what I was able to piece together years later. As a child at the dinner table, I heard of his war service and the names of the places he fought, but that was about it. When he and Ma got on the subject of the war, he always got a faraway look in his eyes, his face absolutely still as he seemed to look at something across the room that wasn't there. But those times were few and far between. He didn't like talking about the war or what he did in it. Except for a few snatches of quick conversation, mostly from Mom, you'd think that my pa never wore a uniform in his life. But what did his being in the war have to do with Hazel?

"Your pa was a youngin', maybe as old as you. He was a hero." She shyly looked at the ground for a bit as we walked. Then she faced me and said, "This was years before he met your mom. After Chancellorsville, a year later in '64, he was with Phil Sheridan when he marched through the Shenandoah Valley. Your father fought at places like Fisher's Hill and Cedar Creek. Sheridan's orders were pretty plain. Destroy every piece of livestock and burn all the grain in the Shenandoah Valley. Not kill the civilians, just destroy the South's ability to make war by burning its sources of food. My mom was a simple farmwife. Her husband had died some time before the war even started. Maybe 1860 or so. When your father showed up, he was going to burn her barn and she came after him with a Henry rifle. She was about to shoot him, but he said there was nothing personal, he was just following Sheridan's orders. She said she understood, then suddenly she started crying. She dropped the rifle and your dad just doused the torch in a bucket of water by the well. She told me he took her in his arms then and comforted her." She stopped and looked at me. "You've got to understand. She was without a man for four long years. She was very attractive. I like to think I take after her."

I knew how I felt about her, but I didn't reply.

Then she said, "I was born nine months later..."

I stared at Hazel, too stunned to speak. She watched my face then and saw pretty plainly how I was taking it. Therefore, instead of dwelling on the details of her birth, she decided to continue with her story. It was then that she resumed the walk.

"After the war, with nothing left, we moved to the Midwest. Kansas at first, then Colorado. She had male friends here and there, but she never married again. Then at a town dance where she was hoping to meet someone, she spotted your parents. She introduced herself to them and your father remembered her right away. He was glad to see her and he introduced her to your mom as an old acquaintance from his hometown. There was good feeling all around. My mom was even over for dinner a few times and she brought me along. I was a young girl and your folks showed you off. You were just a toddler and I played with you often. You were the cutest little boy."

My memory went back to that time. I remembered the girl now, blonde-haired, hazel-eyed, and tall for her age. She was a sweet angel of a girl who was always playing with me. She'd be rolling around on the ground with me and playfully lifting me up in the air. I'd reach out with my little hands and touch that pretty, smiling face of hers, or playfully pull her hair into her eyes as she laughed. I was an only child and I remember loving this girl even then. What a wonderful friend she was to a lonely little boy. I looked forward to her visits, especially when she was babysitting me. But then one day, not too long after she comforted me when my parents died, she stopped coming. I never saw her again.

No one ever knew how broken-hearted I was.

Hazel stopped and faced me. She looked at me seriously.

"One day at the house...well, I was at the school-house near Kidd's Creek. You know the one?"

I nodded, having gone to that schoolhouse myself years later.

"Anyway...my mom told me that your pa dropped by...without your ma. At first it was just a friendly visit. But then...my ma wasn't very clear on the details, but one thing led to another and my mom took your dad upstairs..."

I may not have been too bright, but Ty did tell me a few things about sparking with women that I *didn't* learn in that little schoolhouse at Kidd's Creek.

"She was a lonely woman, just like she was back at the Shenandoah Valley. Your dad came by and...well, I will say that your father was a gentleman. He didn't force himself on her."

I stared at her then, not knowing what to say. As I gazed into those hazel eyes, thinking back to the wonderful, loving playmate I had as a child, I barely realized that tears were welling up in my eyes.

I asked her, "Why didn't you come back?"

"We wanted to take you in after your folks died, but my mom knew it was hard enough to feed even one child without a man in the house. She wasn't sure she could support *two* children. We were happy when you went to live with the Brodys; they're fine people. And I remember Ty from school. But my mom was heartbroken over your dad's death. Beaumont had too many memories for her—and I guess for me as well. After all, he was my father too. So we moved away. It wasn't until we settled here in Dentonville that she told me the whole story."

"Your mom, is she still alive?"

She replied, "No. She died a few years ago and I had to fend for myself."

I said with emotion, "I loved you then. But after you went away, I made myself forget about you..."

"Are you sorry you found me?"

I managed a grin even as tears started to roll down my cheeks.

"What do you think?"

Then she was crying, though they seemed to be tears of joy because she was smiling also. Then we hugged each other tightly.

I never had a big sister...

―――――

We felt a spring breeze and a few fallen leaves blew back along the residential street we were on. We were silent as we walked, each in our own thoughts. I looked at her as she quietly faced the ground. This was country and there wasn't any boardwalk. What was going on behind those lovely eyes? Did she really enjoy reuniting with the little brother she hadn't seen in so long? Or did our touching reunion complicate things for her? She seemed to be quiet for an awful long time, even though it had just been a couple minutes since we embraced.

Then I broke the silence with a question that was as surprising to me as it was for her.

"Hazel, who was that man who asked about someone named Hennessey?"

I looked at that wonderful face and saw the freeze

come over her, just as I saw it on her face when the dude had mentioned that name.

She paused before answering. "I don't know who he was, Jed."

I don't know why, but I found myself pressing on. "But why did he ask you about someone named Hennessey? You froze up like he pointed a gun at you. Kinda like now when I'm asking about it."

Hazel stopped then. She smiled at me, picked up my hand and squeezed it affectionately.

"You're a curious little fellow, Jed. When I'd visit you at the house, you were always curious about every little thing there was. One day, we found a garden snake under the porch and you wanted to reach out and touch it. I had to stop you and pull you back. Your pa eventually killed it."

I said, "You probably saved my life." Of course, I was just guessing. I was not an expert on snakes.

Still, she blushed when I said it, looking more beautiful than ever. Oh, why did she have to be my *sister*.

But I did take issue with something she said.

"But I'm not a *little fellow*."

"Sorry."

"I can take a punch or two."

"I saw that today. You're not a child anymore."

"All right then. Who's Hennessey?"

Hazel's face fell then, as if that very name disturbed the hell out of her.

Then she looked at me as if she was about to answer, but a horse galloping up to us stopped her. We looked up and saw a tall ramrod of a cowboy staring down at us. He didn't say anything, he just narrowed his eyes and gave us both a hostile look. The eyes were piercing and black, like an Indian's. The mouth was small, like a tiny black worm, and the high cheekbones and tanned face made me think that this jasper might actually *be* Indian. I wasn't about to ask; his expression dissuaded me of that notion. Then I glanced at Hazel as she looked up at this cowpoke and right away, I saw the fear. Hell, I couldn't miss it.

Then he spoke, a deep but sharp voice that cut off the ends of words like hatchets. I could tell that this man didn't waste either words or gestures that he didn't have to.

"Who's he?" Obviously, the question was directed at Hazel. It was neither friendly nor even cordial. He acted as if I wasn't there.

Hazel looked up at him, her beautiful eyes suddenly full of fear.

"He's a friend, Lone..."

Suddenly I wasn't her brother anymore, now I was a *friend*. But then again, this arrogant man didn't exactly look like he was going to sit his horse and be patient enough to hear Hazel's story about our reunion.

Again, acting like I wasn't there, he said, "Get rid of him. I'll see you later tonight."

My blood was starting to boil and I let him have it.

"Get out of here," I said, glaring up at him.

Lone stared down at me for a moment, perhaps too surprised that anyone like me spoke back to him. Then his lips widened into a nasty little smile; wicked, knowing, and hostile all at once.

Suddenly he rode forward and his boot struck me full in the face knocking me to the ground. There was no warning to the attack and the pain was sharp and throbbing, the left side of my face hurting like a mule's hoof just walked on it. As I fell, I heard Hazel cry out. She bent down to me and her loving hands were all over my face as she cradled my head in her lap.

I had stars in my eyes at that point and couldn't see Hazel looking up at the man on horseback, but at least I heard her, her anguished voice full of terror and her eyes filled with tears.

"Lone, please! He's just a *friend*, nothing more! I'll see you tonight, but *please* don't do anymore!"

Lone. That name that Ira Toombs mentioned earlier.

There was a pause after Hazel's plea, as if the man on horseback was taking his sweet time considering it.

Apparently it worked, because I heard the clip-clopping of the horse as he rode on past us down the street. My vision cleared then, and I turned my head (still in Hazel's lap) to look after the man, but he was gone.

Her face streaked with tears, Hazel said, "I'm so sorry, Jed!"

As she helped me to my feet, I said, "Sis, you got some strange friends."

After we both got up, she felt the side of my face. "Are you all right? I thought he broke your jaw."

I felt it and experimentally moved it around. It ached like hell, but it didn't fall off or anything.

I asked no one in particular, "What the hell's wrong with the folks in this town?"

Hazel said, "They're not bad people, Jed. It's just—"

She stopped then, like she was too ashamed or afraid to say anything else.

"Just *what*?"

Hazel didn't want to answer, but in a way she did. Looking me in the eye, she said, "Get out of here, Jed.

Get hold of Ty, get your horses, and get the hell out of here!"

I stared at her, partly in fear, but other parts were pure orneriness.

"Not without you!"

Hazel then hit her hand against her side and irritably looked up at the sky as if God were giving her some trouble she sure as hell didn't need.

Then grasping my shoulders, she again looked me in the eye in a now-accustomed big sisterly way. "Lone Hennessey is not someone to fool around with!"

"So *he's* the Hennessey that dude must be looking for! I can see what a hardcase he is. This is easy. We just turn him over to Johnny Law and your problems'll be over."

Hazel stared at me then with great love but also great aggravation, as if she couldn't believe that any kin of hers could be this stupid. Shaking her head, she said, "Oh, Jed, dear Jed, you're so naïve!"

My eyes narrowed as I stared back at her. *Naïve!*

I was about to argue with her until another set of horse's hooves sounded close to us. I tensed even before looking up, half-expecting this Lone character to clip me again with the toe of his dirty boot.

To my surprise, the young man on a tan-colored sorrel was Andrew, the short young man who robbed us of our horses.

He grinned at us and said, "Well, well, look who I see takin' a stroll with our Hazel! Where'd ya find 'em? We've been lookin'—"

He didn't get a chance to finish. I reached up with both my hands and pulled him off the saddle. He fell to the ground heavily. I was about to lean in and lift him to his feet for a punch when he pulled his gun, stopping me in my tracks.

"Okay, Jed!" he said angrily. "I understand you bein' pissed off, but don't you dare lay a hand on me again! You got that?"

I was breathing hard and was pretty angry myself. I said bitterly, "Put down that hogleg and I'll show you how much I care about you and your damn warnings!"

Hazel stepped in then and said, "Stop it, both of you!" Turning to the youth on the ground, she said, "Andrew, Jed just had a run-in with Lone."

Getting up off the road, Andrew smiled gravely and said, "So that's why he's on the prod. I wondered where he got those bruises."

I added, "I also got my eye busted by some jasper called Ed."

Still pointing the gun, Andrew's grin widened as he said, "Must've been Ed Plummer. Heard he was around."

"It was," Hazel said.

Andrew looked at me with new admiration. Holstering his gun, he said, "Well, Jed, looks like you've been rubbing shoulders with tough men." He said "tough men" as if I had never met any before in my life. "I've got to hand it to ya. Both of them would've killed you as soon as spit, so you're lucky to still be alive."

His compliments calmed me down a little, but I wasn't going to be his friend, not until I straightened something out.

"Where'd you put our horses?"

"That's why I'm glad I found you. I found Ira and he took your brother to the doc to fix his shoulder. We'll meet them there and we'll all ride out to where we got your horses."

I noticed then that Hazel gave Andrew a pleading look, as if she didn't want him to take me on this trip. He ignored her and reached up with a friendly hand to grasp my shoulder.

Smiling at me, he said, "The doc's not too far away, but I'm afraid the sorrel won't take a tall hombre like you."

Hazel said to me, "I've got to get back to the restaurant, Jed. Later on, just...stop in before you leave town."

Somehow, I couldn't face the thought of leaving my sister, not again, not after so many years. Still, uppermost in my mind was her safety, as well as the company she keeps.

"You're not gonna meet with *him* tonight, are ya?"

Her eyes briefly went to Andrew, and it was obvious she didn't want to talk about Lone Hennessey in front of him. Instead, she looked at me and said quickly, "I'll see you later." Then she moved on down the street, quickening her pace as she walked.

"Come on, Jed," Andrew said as he mounted his horse. "Let's go see how Ty's doin'..."

CHAPTER FOUR

THE DOCTOR'S HOUSE WAS A FEW BLOCKS AWAY. ANDREW dismounted and tied the sorrel to the tie rail in front. It was a one-story frame house with a small porch and a front yard covered with dead grass. As we mounted the front steps, out of the corner of my eye, I thought I saw a movement on the ground. It was then I caught sight of the rat's tail slithering under the end of the porch.

I got real worried then. If this was the way this sawbones treated his property, what was he doing to Ty?

Andrew led the way. After we entered, I noticed the musty smell. There wasn't much in the way of upholstered furniture, and what I saw, a moldy-looking couch, a couple chairs, looked ancient, with dust caking on the wooden armrests.

I asked, "Maid's day off?"

Andrew smiled wryly and said, "We don't have Doc Elder around 'cause of the way he keeps his house."

His statement made me curious. Something told me then the *we* he was talking about was not necessarily the citizens in town.

We entered through an archway into the doctor's office. Ty had his shirt off and it looked like an old man with wisps of crinkly gray hair around his ears was wrapping a white cloth tightly around his left shoulder and across his right rib cage. He turned around and looked at us with a sour expression on his wrinkled face.

"Sure," he growled, "the more the merrier. I love workin' before an audience."

Ira had his arms folded and was leaning against the doctor's small wooden desk. He looked bored, but he became alert when he saw my face. Ty was clearly shocked.

"Jesus, Jed!"

Elder turned back then and gazed at me as well.

"Well, what happened to you, young man?" Then he turned to Ira and said, "You bringin' me more customers, Ira?"

Andrew said, "He had a run-in with Lone."

Ira said grimly, "He's lucky."

Ty said, "*Lone*? You mentioned that name before."

Andrew said, "You don't want to know, friend."

Doc Elder stood up and said, "All done. Keep that shoulder straight, young man. It'll hurt less and heal a lot faster."

Ty got off the table and put on his shirt, jacket, and Stetson.

"How much is the bill?"

I saw the doc's eyes go to Ira, who responded by shaking his head.

So Elder said to Ty, "Forget it."

Clearly happy he didn't have to pay a bill he didn't

have money for anyway, Ty walked up to me and scanned my face.

"You all right?"

"I'll live," I replied. In reality, it hurt like hell.

We all got out of there and assembled on the porch.

I saw Ira huddle with his brother and talk in lowered voices. But I caught the words *Dover House*.

Ty came over to them and they separated and faced him when they saw him approach.

"All right, boys," he said, "Jed and me have gone through hell this morning and we've seen a little more than we ever wanted to see, including a dead body. So let's just get our pa's horses and we won't bother you again."

The two brothers gave each other looks. Then Ira said, "We could give you two other animals."

Ty shook his head and said, "They're good stock. They take to the plow as well as the saddle. Anyway, you think my pa's not gonna notice the difference? I appreciate what you've done for us, but I think me and Jed better get back home. By now, our folks have found out that we're gone and are probably worried sick about us."

Again, the brothers gave each other looks, then Ira shrugged. "Suit yourself." He said to Andrew, "Go to the stables and tell Pop to give you one mount. They could ride double till we get to Dover." He sounded as if he was annoyed with us when he said that last sentence.

Andrew got on his sorrel and left.

Now it was our turn to give each other looks.

"Dover?" said Ty. "Where's that?"

Ira answered, "A little place outside town."

"How far?"

Ira said irritably, "What is this, a quiz in school? You

want your horses? We've got to go to where they are. Take it or leave it."

We weren't too happy with that answer, but what else could we do? One thing was for sure, something was making me think that the Toombs boys were on some fishing trip, and after they cast the line, Ty and me bit, and now they were reeling us in...

———

WE WERE RIDING EVEN FURTHER out of town and the trail took us out into some open country. The cottonwoods that had been thick and plentiful on either side of the trail slacked off as we climbed one of the foothills that ringed the area. It was tough going for the nag that Ty and I rode, with me in front and him seated behind me, but it was better than going up this incline on foot. Of course, the Toombs brothers had excellent horses and navigated the steeper patches pretty easily. No one had said anything all during the ride, but I was sure that Ty was thinking the same thing I was: Where were these two outlaws taking us?

After the incline leveled off and we were on flat ground again, Andrew rode his sorrel up to our right-hand side. As we rode, I looked down at him since he had a shorter mount and was himself smaller in height than we were. He was keeping pace with us and I wondered why. It wasn't long before I found out.

"Hey, Jed, I was just wonderin' something."

I gazed down at him and said, "Yeah, what was that?"

"How come you got so friendly with our Hazel all of a sudden?"

I didn't answer right away, but the question tensed me up, as if he was going into forbidden territory.

When he saw that I didn't answer, he continued, "What's the matter? Cat got your tongue?"

I replied, "I don't know what you're getting at."

"Oh," he said, in a bad imitation of me, "you don't know what I'm gettin' at. Well, I'll explain it to you. Our Hazel is—"

I cut him off. "*Our* Hazel?"

Andrew seemed to realize that he might have said something out of turn. He looked away for a moment and pressed his lips together as if I had irritated him. Then he turned and looked up at me. There was something sparkling in his eyes, as if a switch had been suddenly turned on.

"You know that Hazel is seein' Lone Hennessey, don't ya?"

I looked down at him and didn't answer. Now *I* was getting annoyed. I could feel Ty starting to tighten his arms around my waist, as if preparing to restrain me.

Andrew continued the egging-on. "You don't have any, um...what they call *designs* on her yourself, do you? I mean, we've all seen that gal and how pretty she is. We watch her when she moves around that restaurant and we watch her bendin' over and all, and we all agree she's kinda hot stuff just made to be—"

I broke out of Ty's grip and leaped out of the saddle squarely on the shorter man. I plowed into him and the two of us hit the ground with a loud thud, throwing up a thick cloud of dust in our wake. Our Stetsons flew off and the two of us were rolling around in the dirt punching and kicking as the three horses near us stopped.

During the fight, I heard Ty say, "Can't you stop 'em?"

I caught snatches of Ira's reply while I was getting my head punched in.

"Let 'em get it off their chests. Andrew hasn't had a good dust-up in days..."

We rolled around on the ground slugging each other for all it was worth. I had to say, despite the fact I was a good foot taller than Andrew, that little rooster was one tough fighter. With my left eye half-closed, he was gamely working on my right and even clipped me on the nose a couple times. After we broke free of each other, while I was still on the ground, he rose up quickly —being so short, he didn't have much distance to go to get to his feet—and kicked me in the face with his boot heel. The impact of the blow rolled me over on my stomach. After getting kicked in the face an hour ago by Lone Hennessey, I've got to say that this blow wasn't as hard. Still, I wouldn't want to feel it again.

As I started to push myself off the ground, the little bastard threw himself on me and put his left arm around my neck, tightening the hold right away. Then, as if that wasn't enough, he threw his other arm around my head and his spreading fingers were clawing my already bruised face as if he were trying to tear it off. I was in this painful position for a while, his fingers starting to dig into my eye sockets.

Angrily, he said, "I *told* you not to lay a hand on me again, didn't I?"

At that point, it was pretty much impossible to answer him. Instead, I sifted my fingers under the vise-like arm around my neck and heaved forward with all my body weight. I bent over fully and his slight body flew over my head and crashed onto the ground heavily. I heard him grunt in pain then, but he was far from finished.

He shot off the ground like a jungle cat springing at some prey and plowed his small but very hard head into my breadbasket. It knocked the wind out of me and my stomach felt like it was hit with a sack of rocks. I flew back with his head still in my stomach, but when I tried to regain my balance, I found out to my horror that there wasn't any road behind me. During our battle, we hadn't realized that we had traveled to the edge of the hill. We flew off the road and tumbled down over crags and broken ground for about thirty or forty feet or so, I couldn't be too accurate at that point. During the tumble down, the sounds of running water were coming to me, but there wasn't anything I could do at that point.

However, we didn't roll into the nearby stream, but stopped just a few yards short of it. We broke away from each other after we hit bottom ground, me once again ending up flat on my stomach, my face inches from a sandy dune. As I lifted my head up, Andrew was upon me again, leaping on my back and pinning me to the ground with my face in the dirt. Then, after grabbing fistfuls of my hair, he pushed my head deeper into the dirt. I tried to push him off, but despite his slight size, he was heavier than I imagined—or maybe he took his fighting more seriously than I did. In seconds, my eyes and mouth were full of dirt and my breathing was cut off. When he pulled my head back up, I was coughing harshly.

Sitting on my back and still holding onto my hair, Andrew said, "Give it up, Jed! You hear me?"

When I didn't answer, he again pushed my face into

the dirt, a little longer this time. I was starting to see stars as I was choking to death. I shut my eyes and mouth and clamped my teeth to keep the county's soil from going down my windpipe. I thought I was going to suffocate in the next five seconds when the weight was suddenly lifted bodily off my back and to make sure I didn't get my air cut off again, I rolled onto my back and leaped to my feet.

As I stood there, I saw that Andrew was still in a scrapping mood, but his arms were pinned back by both Ty and Ira.

Wryly, Ira said, "You know, Jed, I'm getting awful tired of pullin' people off you."

"All right, Ira!" shouted Andrew, trying to calm down. "You boys got the upper hand. All right? You can let me go now. I swear I'll be good."

Reluctantly, after Ty and Ira glanced warily at each other, they let him go.

That's when Andrew swung up at me with his right. Figuring he would do something like that, I leaned back, and the small but hard fist flew before my face without touching me. But then I responded by punching him hard in the eye with my right, then following up with a haymaker to his mouth with my left. The blows dropped him to the ground between Ty and his brother.

As we all looked down at the little man, him holding onto his bleeding mouth and gazing up at me sullenly, he then did a funny thing.

He laughed. Me and Ty looked at each other, but the laugh didn't seem to surprise Ira, who had apparently experienced his brother's swings in mood before. Andrew just rolled around on the ground, laughing long and loud. It was a weird high-pitched cackle too, and an awful lot of it coming as it did from such a small fellow.

He reached out and said to Ty and Ira, "Help me to my feet, boys. It's all right, I won't do nothin'." Ty paused, but Ira immediately helped Andrew to his feet. I stepped back and started to ball my fists.

Still feeling his jaw, Andrew smiled at me and said, "You're more of a hellion than I gave ya credit for, Jed. Ya never gave up, not once."

He didn't offer his hand, but as he walked by me, he affectionately gripped my shoulder and then climbed up the hill, his brother following him.

Ty came over to me and put his hand on my face.

"How are ya, buddy? Does it hurt?"

He got his answer when he heard me wince.

"Sorry."

"It's all right."

"Hell, Jed, why'd you get mad when he started ribbing you about that waitress? I mean, what is she anyway? She's just someone we met for two seconds who served us food. That's the second time you almost got your head busted open for her. I mean, what is she to you anyway? You got a crush on her or somethin'?"

I looked at him and didn't answer. I just stood there with my wounded eye and my dirt-caked and bruised face staring back at him. Maybe seeing that it was useless to keep talking about it, Ty said gently, "Go put some water on those bruises." Then he turned around and climbed up the hill.

I stood there and gazed up at them briefly, then turned around and went to the stream. It wasn't very big, just about a dozen feet across, with a good amount of water crashing over its mostly rocky surface. It wasn't deep either. A man could take a walk through it if he wanted to and could be guaranteed not to have the water flow over his boot-tops.

I tiredly went over to the bank and then went down on my knees. Bending over, my face peering over the clear running water, I reached in, got handfuls of it, and splashed it hungrily all over my face and eyes. The coolness felt good on my battered face, especially my left eye. Better than any steak, in fact. I just stayed there for a couple minutes and splashed and splashed, the water refreshing and healing all at once.

And then, after I had run my hands back through my dirt-caked hair with handfuls of water, I looked up and suddenly saw it. My eyes widened and I fell back onto the ground, giving a short scream while I was at it. I never saw anything like it in all my days, and it chilled me down to the bone.

There, caught onto a jutting rock in the other side of the stream, was the head of the dude I had seen back at the restaurant, the nervous one who had been asking Hazel about the Hennesseys...

CHAPTER FIVE

THE OTHERS HEARD ME AND TURNED TO LOOK AT WHAT I was gaping at.

Ty said, "Jesus Christ!"

Andrew slapped his dirty Stetson against his side and then put it on. But instead of being surprised, he just looked up at his brother, who stared at the head and didn't say anything. In fact, the sight of the head hanging there with a slightly detached left ear caught on the point of the jagged rock, a good supply of cool, clear water rushing over it, made Ira look angry. As I stared at the thing, I saw its eyes wide open, as if the man who had once possessed them was scared to death. I'd never forget those eyes the rest of my days. They were brown and filmed over, the skin on the face gleaming wet and deathly pale, the hair straggly and soaked. Instead of walking straight up, I practically backed up the hill, going forward, yet always turning back to that awful sight. Once I reached the top, I picked up my Stetson and put it on, but then I couldn't help looking out onto that stream and seeing it still hanging there staring at us.

Then I jumped out of my skin when a shot was fired from close behind me. I turned and saw Andrew with his gun smoking. Then I turned in the direction of what he had been aiming at and saw the head, its detached ear that hooked around the jutted rock now totally shot off. With nothing to hold it, the head continued down the rushing stream, bobbing and tumbling along the water as it made its journey due south, and eventually out of our sight.

I said to Andrew, "What'd you do that for?"

As he holstered his .45, he answered, "Don't want it to stay there till the end of creation, do you? In the direction this stream is goin', it'll empty out into Little Bear Lake and then probably out to sea where no one else'll ever spot it again." As if that settled the discussion, he turned and put his foot in the stirrup of the sorrel standing behind him.

Ira followed his brother's lead and also mounted, but I saw the look on his face, and he said nothing, again. I saw the rage within him, as if it was very close to coming out.

Ty and me just looked at each other. Then, as if there was nothing else to do, we mounted our horse and followed them down the trail.

———

IT WAS another fifteen minutes or so before I spoke to Ty, him holding on behind me as we rode down the trail. No one had said anything till then, and I carefully looked ahead of me before I spoke. I saw the two brothers about ten or so yards ahead of us, riding side by side, but not saying anything that we could hear.

Still facing the trail and watching the Toombs boys ahead of us, I said, "Ty, there's something fishy here."

With just the right amount of sarcasm, he replied, "Oh, you think so?"

Ignoring the tone, I said urgently, "Ty, that poor man whose head we saw in the stream back there...I saw him when he was alive!"

There was a pause then, with Ty probably gaping at me before he spoke.

He said tensely, "Are you sure about that?"

"I don't know too many men that have had their heads cut off. I think I'd recognize one when it happened."

"I don't believe it. You've got to be mistaken."

"I wish to God I was, Ty..."

He didn't say anything for a couple moments. Then he asked, "Where'd you see him?"

"He was in that hotel restaurant."

"Are you *sure*?"

I was starting to get pissed. "Yes, I'm sure! Stop asking me that!"

I might have been a bit too loud at that point because I noticed the two brothers ahead both look back at us. I made myself smile wanly at them and they turned around.

I continued in a harsh whisper. "Yeah, I'm sure it was him. He was there after you left with Ira. I didn't see him until after that little bitch, Bessie, put a steak on my eye in the back kitchen. He had a carpetbag; figure he was already staying at the hotel. He was new in town, asking Hazel how he could find the Hennesseys or maybe one of 'em, I couldn't tell which, I didn't hear him clear enough. And one more thing, he was nervous as a cat."

Ty cut me off. "Wait a minute. Did you say *Hennesseys*?"

I paused, wondering if I said something out of turn.

I answered uncertainly, "Uh...*yeah*."

He just stared at me for the longest time with his mouth open. Finally, he sighed and said, "I hope it's not who I think they are."

"All right, who are they?"

"You don't read the papers, Jed, so you don't know, do you?"

I said sullenly, "Stop rubbing *that* in, Ty. I know I don't keep up with events like you do."

Ty faced the trail then. Quietly he said, "Reading a newspaper about them is one thing. Meeting 'em face to face is another..."

———

BY THE TIME our horses stopped somewhere back in the trees, it was already early evening and the sun was starting to set. Again, we were getting hungry, but by this time, we figured to just pick up the horses and get the hell out of the territory fast.

I asked, "Why're we stopping here in the middle of the woods?"

Ira didn't answer. He just said, "Just follow us and try not to make too much noise doin' it." He sounded as close to being on edge as I've ever seen him up to that point.

We walked maybe a few hundred yards or so and came out into a clearing. Now we looked up and saw the house a short distance in front of us. It was three stories topped by an attic and slate gray against the darkening sky. The upper floors were almost carefully hidden by the branches of tall sycamores reaching out and practically clinging to the higher window frames. In fact, a harsh wind blew at that point and the ends of those very branches scratched persistently at the wooden shutters high above. With clouds passing overhead in a dark sky, the sight threw a chill in me that had nothing to do with the weather.

Andrew said to us, "Gents, welcome to the Dover House!"

Ty stared at him and said, "Dover House? I thought I heard of this place somewhere before."

"Yeah?" said Ira. "Where did you hear about it?"

Ty answered, "A few years ago, this wealthy family named the Dovers owned this property. The papers said they owned property in a lot of places, and I guess they used this house like all the others as just someplace to stay until they got tired of it and then moved on to the next one." He stopped and looked up at the house, pausing before he spoke. When he did, he faced Ira and said, "There were four of 'em, the old man, his wife, a grown son, and a little girl. Then one day, maybe five years ago, according to the Colorado papers anyway, the Dovers disappeared. Every one of them. Looked like the earth swallowed 'em up."

Andrew turned and faced him. I noticed then that he brought his right hand up and rested it on the butt of his holstered gun. I faced him as he did so, wondering if my jump and my arm-reach were long enough to stop him.

I'll say this, I don't think I ever admired Ty as I did at

that moment, facing down both Toombs boys as he said his piece.

"So what of it?" asked Andrew. His surliness seemed to be growing as he faced us.

Ty answered, "So now you boys are here. Kind of a big house for just you two. Landlord know about it?"

Ira stepped forward and put a restraining hand on Andrew's shoulder. Then he said, quietly and without fuss, "No big secret, boys. The Dovers disappeared, and we don't know what happened to 'em. But in the meantime, the house was empty and me and Andrew moved in. It was just sittin' out here with no use to anybody and we were able to buy the property from the heir up in Glenwood Springs. Want me to produce the deed?"

Ty and me relaxed then, and Ty even looked down a little shamefaced and smiled.

He said, "Sorry, Ira. After remembering about the Dovers, I just thought it looked kinda funny you boys staying here..."

"Yeah," said Andrew wryly, "hilarious..."

Then Ira said, "All right, boys, let's circle around quietly to the stables on the left. And try not to make too much noise while you're at it."

Ty and me tensed up and looked at each other.

I asked, "Why're we supposed to be quiet? Aren't our animals in *your* stable? Especially since you say you own the place."

Ira heard me raise my voice when I asked the question and the look he gave me was ugly. Something was wrong here.

It was verified when we heard the metallic cocking back of a hammer and we all turned to the front of the house.

The man standing there had his face in shadow, but I knew that low, harsh voice.

"You back for more, boy?" Lone said to me.

The gun wasn't held on the Toombs boys as it was on me and Ty. They weren't too surprised to see Lone either. They weren't smiling when he showed up, and they didn't greet him, they just stared at him. The look on Ira's face especially revealing that we had almost gotten away with something, but we were foiled at the last second.

"Inside!" commanded Lone Hennessey, the wave of his pistol backing him up.

We walked past him, and as we did so, Lone punched me in the back of the head with his free hand.

I whirled at him and he stuck the barrel of his gun practically into my teeth.

"Lone!" Ira said.

The half-breed just glanced at him and then smiled at me, a wide, wicked smile that said who was in charge. Seeing that Lone was going to hold off another attack, I turned back and lightly shoved Ty ahead of me before he would've gotten shot defending me. We marched through a lawn covered in dead grass. Standing on a stool off to the side of the lawn was a wash basin filled with, I assume, icy water, since nights were still chilly that time of year.

We mounted the front steps and stopped at an old wooden door. The porch was kind of seedy looking, though I couldn't tell very well in the fading sunlight. A few chairs were strewn about, including one that was overturned. I imagined something made the person seated there stand up in a hurry, or perhaps there was some ruckus. A wooden card table near the overturned chair answered my question. Maybe somebody who had sat there had cheated at cards. I wasn't sure.

Ira said gently, "Just go in, Jed..." Though angry with me for being loud enough to alert Lone that we were outside, the half-breed's attack might have pulled him over to my side a little. I also noticed that the Toombs boys placed themselves behind Lone, just in case.

I turned the old brass doorknob and pushed the door open, entering a foyer with a musty smell. Lamplight shined in from the living room through the archway on our right. I looked ahead and a huge staircase spiraled up and turned to the right above the living room and led upward to the rest of the house. Some paintings were on the wall, or should I say *had* been left on the wall, since I noticed several empty spaces where paintings used to be. I made a quick guess that the better paintings were either sold for their value or destroyed outright. The paintings that were left seemed to be of depictions of the War between the States, with Confederate soldiers prominent in most of them, and usually in some victorious pose or another.

Lone didn't have to tell us to go into the living room since that's where we heard all the voices coming from. We passed under the once-impressive archway and found ourselves being stared at by the surliest group of hardcases I ever saw. And seated at a small rolltop desk in the far corner of the room, as if he were an outsider who was not part of the inner circle, was Hiram Jessup. When we entered, he had been scanning some papers and looked up at us through the wire-rim glasses perched on his nose. The look wasn't friendly, which actually fit in perfectly with those of the dozen or so wild-looking young men who sat on a huge couch or various cushy chairs glaring at us.

I glanced down to my right and saw a disheveled cowboy sitting in a couch with torn upholstery. He looked up at me with bloodshot eyes, an open whiskey bottle at his elbow.

Lone said to the group, "I found these two outside with Ira." For some reason, he didn't bother to mention Andrew. I looked at the little man and his anger was plain for everyone to see.

A young fellow rose from his seat by the fireplace and stared at us. His range clothes were dusty and his black Stetson was lightened by age and the elements. His face was not as hatchet-like as Lone's, but close. The eyes were small and reminded me of a rat's. It wouldn't have surprised me if he could see in the dark. He came over to us, moving like a cat, his boots never once making a sound.

"Nice of you boys to show up," he said wryly. "We're still waitin' on Severin."

Andrew said with a wide smile, "Awful nice of you to care about us, Finch."

Finch looked at the little man as if he were a disease.

"Heard about you bein' buffaloed by Lone back at that store. I'm sorry the townspeople didn't find you and lynch your sorry butt for killin' that storekeeper."

Andrew's face twitched slightly, but he kept his smile when he said, "I didn't kill him, Cousin, but I didn't expect the chief to tell ya that. Thanks for the best wishes anyway, I won't forget 'em..." Those last words were said with some bitterness. Ty and me kept our mouths shut tight and just watched and listened.

Finch's eyes then went to Ira, who he probably felt

was the more mature of the brothers. "What about it, Ira? Where's the money?"

Ira said, "You know I rode back to find out what happened to Andrew."

"Yeah?" said Finch. "You sure you didn't stop by some hollow tree to remove the money and split it with Sev?"

With feigned patience, Ira replied, "Yes, Clay, I'm sure."

Lone had the cold iron of the gun barrel in my back so hard it hurt.

He said, "Any of you boys curious about these two?"

Finch finally looked at us for the first time, the money now secondary in his thoughts. He looked at us oddly.

"Albeit. Who are they?"

Before anyone else could answer, Ira blurted out, "They want to ride with us, Clay."

Ty and me fought the impulse to openly deny what Ira just said, but some well-honed survival instinct on our parts kept us quiet as mice.

Finch gave us a quick appraisal and said, "All right, they're young and they look fit enough, but do they have a stomach for it?"

Ira said, "We've lost four men in the past month, Clay. You yourself said we need new blood."

Finch rubbed his chin thoughtfully and said, "I did say somethin' like that, didn't I?"

Lone complained, "Now wait a minute! I didn't hear anything about these two wanting to join us!"

Andrew gave Lone a big smile and said, "Don't worry, Lone, this is one time the white-eyes kept their ears to the ground and the redskin didn't."

Angrily, Lone turned his gun from my back to Andrew, but the little guy pulled his own .45 so fast it was a blur. Ty and me stepped out of the way as the two of them angrily stood near the archway pointing their guns at each other. The others in the room didn't move, nor did they seem upset. Apparently, witnessing this kind of standoff was not new to them.

Lone growled, "Don't push me, white trash. I eat little girls like you for breakfast."

Andrew just glared back at him and said, "Go ahead, Lone, why don't you tell me about your mama doin' some bluecoat in the backroom of a fort for two dollars."

Lone gave a roar and fired just as I clobbered him in the back of his huge head with the cowboy's whiskey bottle. As the glass splinters and the leftover whiskey flew about, Lone's bullet went over Andrew's head and harmlessly went through a wall.

Everyone was absolutely still, they just stared at me as if I had sprouted wings. Only the drunken cowboy moved; he shouted something about me swiping his whiskey and tried to get up from his seat, but he rose too fast and the move caused him to dizzily fall back into the chair.

Andrew's tight-lipped expression changed to one of surprise, then a huge smile in my direction.

With admiration, he crowed, "I said you were you a hellion, Jed!"

Even Finch said, "That was some quick thinkin', kid, but the chief isn't going to thank you for it. In fact, you better grow a pair of eyes in the back of your skull from now on."

At that point, Ira said, "You see, Clay? Shows they've got what it takes."

I resisted the impulse to glare at Ira. *We're goddamn farm boys, not robbers and killers!*

Still, as if answering Ira, Finch said, "We haven't seen everything they could do. How do we know that they won't go runnin' back home to their folks the moment things get too hot."

Holding in my anger, I said, "My folks are dead."

Ty added, "And my folks are poor people from the backcountry. We took Jed in after his folks died."

Finch's eyes almost lit up when they heard that.

"You're *brothers?*"

"That's right."

"My folks were also poor. It's not easy breakin' your back sixteen hours a day on crops that don't grow and then owe some jasper more money than you ever make in ten years just to keep it goin'..."

Finch stared at us both for a few more moments, as if he had come to some quiet understanding.

At that point, Jessup whipped off his spectacles and got up. "You're not seriously going to let them into the gang, are you?"

Finch barely glanced at him when he said, "You get back to your corner, paper-pusher."

I saw Jessup's face; it was getting redder and redder as he stood there.

Finally, he shouted, "Damn it, Finch! You boys are getting too big for your britches already! That man in the store in Beaumont. Then that journalist from that Telluride paper."

Ty and I looked at each other; we had a feeling we knew who they were talking about.

Ira cut in. "Hiram's got a point there, Clay. We were out by the stream that flows into the Little Bear. We all saw something swimming in it and it wasn't a trout."

Finch didn't say anything for a moment.

Then he finally replied, "No big deal, Ira." Casually, he took out the makin's and rolled himself a cigarette. "Just some jasper says he wants to join us, but what he *really* wants to do is get the goods on the notorious Hennessey Gang." This last sentence was said with a twinkle in his eyes and a little playfulness in his tone. He lit his cigarette then and blew out some smoke toward the ancient ceiling. Then the twinkle disappeared and something hard came into his face when he said, "He just met with an accident."

I couldn't help blurting out, "An accident?"

Finch looked my way and replied, "Sure, kid. That reporter fella was doin' fine until his head suddenly got detached from his body..."

He let the words lie there and me and I'm sure Ty felt chilled to the bone when he said it. The men around him in their couch and plushy chairs, though, laughed derisively when they heard it.

Then Finch flicked ash on the tattered rug and took a step forward to stand in front of me. He was only a couple inches shorter than me, but when he looked into my eyes and searched them for any sign of fear, I could see that here was a man who felt that his way was right and you'd never convince him otherwise. As his small eyes bore into mine, he finally asked, "Does this talk frighten you?"

I stared at him and tried to keep the fear and revulsion out of my face. I don't know how I did it, but I thought I sounded convincing when I said, "No. You just did what you had to do, that's all..."

I could feel Ty's eyes on me, and I had a feeling the Toombs boys were staring at me too.

The silence was broken by loud snoring from the drunken outlaw down at my right from whom I swiped the bottle of whiskey. Finch looked down at him with contempt. Then he walked over and brutally kicked his stretched-out legs. The drunk cried out and leaned over, painfully feeling his legs. His bloodshot eyes looked up at Finch with some fear.

"If we had a pigpen here, Mart," Finch growled, "I'd make you sleep outside with your own kind..."

There was more cruel laughter from the other outlaws seated around us.

Jessup broke into their laughter with his voice, loud and piercing and furious all at once.

"Big men every damn one of you! It never occurred to you that when Oscar Frenwick doesn't report back to his newspaper, maybe they might send out someone else to find out what happened to him?" He walked into the circle of outlaws, rage plain on his long, bony face. "No! That never occurred to your kill-em-all-and-hell-with-the-consequences attitude! And now you want to take *these two*...these two *farm boys* into the gang!" He practically spat out farm boys in a way I didn't like at all. Then, his eyes on Finch, he said with disdain, "I'm so glad I'm not from your branch of the family!"

"Yeah," said Finch, with some resentment. "You proved that by changing your last name to Jessup. Hennessey's a good name, Uncle. You should be proud of it!"

"Proud?" Jessup shook his head as if he were talking

to a child. "Yeah, you're a Hennessey all right. You're as stark, raving mad as the rest of them."

Finch just stared at him. He didn't look angry, but standing just a few inches from him, I could feel the rage starting to form.

He asked sarcastically, "Anymore pearls of wisdom, Uncle Hiram?"

"Yeah," he answered defiantly. "Your folks should've left you on Bob Ford's doorstep!"

Having one's folks considered a few notches *below* a man that many outlaws think of as a traitor and back-shooter might've been going too far. Finch's face trembled and his hand went to his holstered gun. He was starting to lift it when Ira shouted, "Clay!"

Finch paused, his eyes still on Jessup with a look that could kill weaker men. Amazingly, the staid book-keeper kept his own gaze steady, glaring back at this outlaw boss with his own brand of defiance. For a moment, I was actually starting to admire this curt, stuck-up man.

The silence in the room, even from the outlaws who only watched the scene with a mixture of wonder and amusement, was suddenly broken by the sounds of horse's hooves outside. Then a tall and hefty young man in dusty range clothes pushed in the front door without knocking and tramped into the living room. His face, especially the small eyes and set of the jaw, instantly reminded me of Finch. In fact, everything except for the size, he was taller than him by a half dozen inches and had a wide chest and big stomach as well. It turned out he *was* Finch's brother, but whereas Finch was lean, this man ate his fill as well as seconds. The size difference might've also been (as we learned later), because Ma Hennessey didn't exactly sleep with Pa *all the time.*

"We got troubles, Clay."

Finch recovered his sense of wry humor to reply, "No foolin'?"

The young man glanced briefly at me and Ty, not having seen us before, and then his eyes went down to Lone's unconscious form on the ground.

Finch said irritably, "The chief's takin' a nap, Ben. Now what's up?"

Catching his breath, he faced the outlaw boss and said, "I found Sev."

"Where?"

"Saloon in Telluride. He looked like he was drinkin' up his share of the robbery money."

Finch asked cautiously, "*Just* his share?"

Ben answered, "I don't think so. He was drinkin' all night. Had a couple of tarts on his lap and givin' out money like it grew on trees. But—" He hesitated.

"But *what*?"

"Sev was boasting. You know how he gets. Give him a bottle and he talks a blue streak." Then the young man said apologetically, "I'm sorry, Clay. He's our brother and all, but—"

Finch gave him a dismissive wave of his hand, as if Ben's concerns for insulting the family were unimportant, though he reacted a bit differently when his uncle was tearing it down.

He asked, "Can ya lead us to 'em?"

"If he's still there, sure."

Finch turned back to face the other outlaws.

"I need two more of ya to ride with me."

Then he turned and faced me and Ty.

"And you two as well."

Ira said apprehensively, "We'll go along too, Clay."

"No," said Finch. "Not you or Little Sure-Shot over there either." By the look on Andrew's face, I could tell that he wasn't crazy about being compared to Annie Oakley. Finch continued, "These boys want to join up and I want to see what they can do without the Toombs boys backin' 'em up."

Ty and me glanced at each other uncertainly.

Then Finch faced me and Ty.

"If you boys have any ideas about riding off once we hit the trail, remember it'll be four against two and you're not getting any guns until I say so. And if *that* doesn't convince you we mean business, remember that head you boys found floating in the river..."

CHAPTER SIX

THEY GAVE US TWO MOUNTS THAT WERE OBVIOUSLY *NOT* Ty's father's horses.

We were both pretty tired, but there was nothing we could do. We mounted our geldings and Finch and a few other hardcases, including the big one named Ben, mounted theirs. Then, on Finch's command, we rode off down the trail we had used to get to the Dover House. The Toombs boys just stood on the front porch and helplessly watched us ride away.

As our group rode, me and Ty saw that we were basically surrounded, with Finch and Ben in front and the others riding close behind us. If we did have a mind to get away from these men, it looked like we'd just have to take our horses and merely fly over them.

But I kind of gave up *that* idea...

Feeling pretty nervous about the whole thing, I quietly asked Ty, "Do ya think we have a chance to—"

But he quietly cut me off with "Talkin's not a good idea now, Jed..."

I quickly shut up.

The moon above shone its light down on us, making it much easier to navigate our mounts in the growing darkness. After an hour, trees around us slacked off and the trail opened up somewhat. Then our horses started to climb some hills deep into timber country. The cool spring night chilled us at first, but only temporarily. This was because the tension Ty and me were experiencing kept us pretty warm; in fact, sweat was actually dampening my dark blue shirt and practically soaking through to the Levi jacket I was wearing over it. After we topped one of the foothills, the ground leveled off and we hit another trail. After a quarter to a half mile, we spotted a crudely drawn sign that announced that we were only two miles from Telluride.

As we rode, I noticed Finch talking to Ben and occasionally nodding as the younger man was, I guess, answering all his questions. Then I saw Finch unconsciously grip the butt of his holstered gun, lift it slightly, then allow it to drop snugly back into the worn holster.

It was as if he were preparing it for some future use...

———

THE TOWN of Telluride was not one of the biggest in Colorado, but big enough.

It was big enough for the townsfolk *not* to notice us as we rode in.

I couldn't rightly say that too many families were out on the streets at that hour, but their absence was more than made up for the various cowboys, either loafing around the porches of the false-front buildings or in the saloons, of which I counted a half dozen on one block. If there were any other businesses open in Telluride at that hour, it must've been behind closed doors.

As we rode, we saw two cowboys, now hatless, rolling around in the dirt, punching away at each other as the other men around them cheered them on. I wondered what could've caused the argument. It was probably over whose gun was shinier...

I had heard Ben say the word Kings to Finch and he nodded.

Now, two minutes after Ben had said it, we drew our animals up to the front of a saloon with a typically gaudy sign that said *KINGS*. We all dismounted and tied our horses to one of the few open tie rails near the swinging doors. Ty and me stared at the front of the place, neither of us had ever seen a big saloon before, and were kind of speechless that we were in front of one now.

Finch looked at both of us and said, "Poor farm boys don't usually have a chance to see a place like this, much less go inside. Well, now I'm giving you that chance."

The outlaw wasn't sarcastic when he said it. In fact, he even sounded sympathetic to us.

Then, switching his attention back to business, he turned to the others and said, "Stu, you and Frank get around to the back door and cover it. The rest of us go in the front."

The two men disappeared down a nearby alley and the rest of us just pushed through the swinging batwing doors and went inside. The odor of whiskey and cigar smoke hit me all at once, and I had to mentally stop myself from gagging. If Ty felt the same way, then he hid it much better than I did.

The men at the crowded bar were elbow to elbow. A large mirror hung behind the busy bartenders as they served what I'm sure was a rancid swill. Finch scanned the long room through the thick, smoky haze until Ben tapped him and pointed over to the far left. He was pointing in the direction of some dancehall girl seated pretty comfortably in the lap of some laughing cowboy, beer or maybe some other drink spilled all his open vest and calico shirt.

Finch led the way and we all followed him up to the table. As we approached, we also saw a second man seated there as well, but his attention was taken up by another woman in some low-cut dress nibbling on his earlobe as he laughed. Open bottles, some empty, a couple half-full, were all over the table, with cigarette or cigar burns clearly seen on the wood, along with spilled liquor.

I'd *never* seen that much of a woman's skin out in the open in my life up to that point. I stared openly at these women, my fascination growing as we got near them.

Ty noticed immediately and quietly said to me, "Jed, if your eyes get any bigger, they're gonna pop out and roll onto the floor..."

I relaxed then. But one of the girls, a redhead sitting on one cowboy's lap, stopped nibbling his ear and then gave me a scan I'll never forget. She was looking at me like a wolf staring at a calf caught in some barbed wire, her smile filled with pleasure and probably a little animal hunger as well. The cowboy didn't like her looking at me that way at all.

A very pretty brunette was sitting on the other cowboy's lap. They were both laughing and hugging each other when Finch leaned over and quietly said to the brunette, "You were with Severin earlier today." It wasn't a question, but a statement of fact.

The cowboy whose lap she was adorning looked up at him with half-open, but still angry eyes.

"Who the hell are you?"

Finch's eyes settled on him briefly, then they went back to her.

"I won't ask you a second time. Where did Severin go?"

The man put his hands on the brunette's waist and shifted her body off him. She then stood up and stared at the two as the cowboy reached down to the gun in his holster. Seeing this, she started to back away.

That's when Finch ordered, "Stay where you are! You're not goin' anywhere."

Angry, the cowboy said to Finch, "Get the fuck out of here, you little rat."

Finch, still leaning over, just stared at him but didn't make a move.

The cowboy growled, "Son of a bitch..." Then he lifted the gun out of the holster.

But just then, Ben, who placed himself behind the cowboy, suddenly grabbed his gun arm and yanked it back. In the next instant, Finch drew his gun and walloped the cowboy across the forehead, his Stetson flying, brim-first, into the face of the other cowboy. It was so quick; it was as if I was watching some well-oiled machine at work. The now-unconscious cowboy slipped off the chair and fell onto the dirty, drink-covered floor, his head bleeding profusely. The other cowboy was feeling his lip, which had just been struck by the sharp brim on the other's Stetson. The brunette Finch was asking questions of stared at him now with some fear.

The redhead who was still sitting in the other cowboy's lap had her eyes open wide, but not with fear, but with a kind of wonder, as if she had thoroughly enjoyed seeing Finch pistol-whip the other man. She was the same one who had been eyeing me like a slab of prime beef. Seeing her cowboy bleeding from the lip and now thoroughly meek, she shifted her beautiful form onto the empty chair the other cowboy vacated. Sitting with his unconscious body practically at her feet didn't bother her. Some of the patrons near us stopped talking and watched us, but the ones at the bar or further away continued to laugh and drink and have a good time, unaware, or maybe just not caring, what had happened at our table.

Finch didn't exactly point his gun at the brunette, but he didn't turn it away from her either.

"Ready to talk?" His harsh whisper was like the hissing of a snake.

The girl, her brown eyes widening enough for a bug to fly into, nodded vigorously and her words tumbled out in seconds.

"He left us earlier in the day. He said he was gonna go back to his room and sleep it off." Her southern drawl was hard to miss.

Finch asked, "Where's that?"

"The Angel House. It's right outside town, maybe a half mile. You can get to it by going up the street yonder. Uh, north I guess." She was trying to be helpful, maybe so Finch and the rest of us would disappear faster.

After getting his answer, Finch's already small eyes shrunk to little slits. He asked quietly, "Did he give you any money?"

She paused, her eyes wide and blinking in fear.

Then they unconsciously looked to the other girl, as if she were looking for help in how to answer the question.

The redhead looked up at Finch and smiled like a cat—that is, if cats did smile that way.

She said resentfully, "That one was cheap, mister. He didn't give us nothin'!"

Finch gave a slight nod. I don't think he believed her for a second.

Then, without a word, he left us and went over to a door in the back, which I guessed led to some office. We saw him knock on it. Finch had either been there before or he somehow knew exactly where to go if he had a problem. After a moment, a stout man in a dark gray suit opened it and we clearly heard him cheerfully say, "Clay! Haven't seen you in a coon's age! Come on in!" After the man happily shook Finch's hand, he ushered him inside, then closed the door.

Meanwhile, me, Ty and Ben stood patiently at the table. At that point, the cowboy, his lip bleeding, stared at us with some fear. Then he made a move to get up.

Ben shoved him down with his huge, meaty hand. "Where do you think you're goin'?"

The man meekly slid back into his seat without giving an answer. Then he nervously poured himself a glass of whiskey and downed it fast.

The brunette saloon gal whom Finch asked questions just stood at the table, almost afraid to make a move. The redhead stayed seated, but her eyes were all over me. She gave me a smile that was both friendly and wicked all at once. It was not as if these women weren't attractive. The one who was standing was five feet eight or so, with her dark-brown hair pinned up and her brown eyes wide as pools. Her long, sleek, white neck fairly glistened in the above harsh light. It was obvious her work kept her indoors a lot. Her shoulders looked soft and her waist was narrow; the red dress she was wearing tight enough around her to make her breasts stick out— but then, what did I expect from a saloon girl, the look of a church mouse? The other one was a fire redhead with gray eyes and a long tongue, which I could see for myself since she obscenely licked her lips while staring at me.

I was almost thankful that her undressing me with her eyes was cut short when the back office door opened and the boss waved his hand at us and called us over. Ben ordered, "Come on, folks." And so, we all started toward the office door, even the drunken cowboy.

Then, at a signal from the boss through the open door, Ben turned around and shoved the cowboy away.

"Not you. Beat it."

The cowboy blinked his eyes at him, then almost gratefully turned around and sped out of the saloon.

We all squeezed into the back office. It had a file cabinet and a rolltop desk, which the saloon's owner sat behind. Finch was seated in a chair before the desk, a whiskey glass in his hand and an open bottle near him. It was obvious that he and the saloon owner were old friends.

Suddenly, one of the two girls, the brunette, blurted out, "Is anything wrong, Mr. Crowley?"

Crowley's eyes went to his lap as if there were cigar ashes on it. Then he looked up and said to the two women, "I'm sorry, Jill."

Jill responded with, "Sorry? Why? Uh, I didn't—"

Crowley said, "Sorry for both of you girls. But we're not making as much money this month as we'd like. I'm going to have to let you two go..."

The other one, the one who'd been ready to eat me alive with her eyes alone, then got angry. She looked at him incredulously. "What?" she said. "This place is making money hand over fist and you're letting us go?"

Crowley clasped his hands on his expensive checked vest with cravat and shrugged, trying to look innocent.

"Why is this happening *now*?" asked the redhead.

Crowley sighed and said, "Sherry, you're just making this harder."

Sherry took two steps forward. She was standing practically above Finch now.

She started to point at him when she said loudly, "We were doing fine, and then *he* comes in here, snaps his fingers and you fire us!"

Crowley frowned at her. "Now, Sherry, you're starting to cross a line. Clay Finch Hennessey is my friend. And an honored guest. I told you girls why I have to let you go. Mr. Hennessey didn't influence my decision in the slightest."

After hearing the name *Hennessey*, I saw Sherry back away slightly from Finch, as if he suddenly had chicken pox. Then, backing up against the wall, Sherry's normally pale complexion got very red and she cursed at Crowley. My god, she about hurled every curse in the book at this outwardly calm, fat man in the expensive suit. He looked up at her frowning and then his eyes went to Finch, who nodded so subtly I barely saw it.

Then Crowley rose from behind the desk and went around it. He walked over to Sherry as she was still heaping venomous curses at him. Suddenly he exploded, slapping her with his big, meaty hand again and again. He did it I don't know how many times, the violence from him all the more frightening from this short, fat man who looked like he was far more comfortable adding figures than beating women.

Ty and me stared at the scene with revulsion, and I tried to step forward to stop it, but Ty grabbed me around the shoulders and held me tight in his iron grip. In my head, I knew it might be death to interfere, but as a man I couldn't just stand there and watch this saloon owner beat a woman.

After the first hard slap, which resounded around the small confines of the office, Sherry stopped cursing and cried out piteously with every blow. Then she backed up against the wall and gradually slid down it, her face bright red from both the slaps she was taking and her tears. In fact, her face almost matched the color of her hair.

She was now down on the floor at the bottom of the wall, sobbing convulsively as we all looked down at her.

Breathing harshly, Crowley looked at her and I was surprised to see sadness in his face, as if he had regretted beating her.

Then, as if *he* had been the one who was hurt, he asked her, "*Why* do you make me do this, Sherry? Why!" He turned away from her. At first, I thought he was disgusted with his own violence, but then I turned back to look down at her.

I was shocked at what I saw.

Her tear-streaked face, now bruised from Crowley's slaps, was looking up at us, but the tears had suddenly stopped. And instead of pain and sadness, she was grinning wildly. I had never seen anything like it in my life;

neither did Ty. Her eyes were large and filled with some kind of joy, her expression clearly excited. I shook my head as I looked down at her. Then I looked at the others. Crowley was leaning against the opposite wall, holding onto the knuckles of the hand he was using to slap Sherry as if his fingers were going to fall off. Finch was watching the scene with all the interest of a man watching a blacksmith shoe his horse. The others weren't very surprised either, even Jill didn't seem too surprised at what just happened.

Finally recovering, Crowley got off the wall, went back around to his desk and sat down.

He sounded tired when he said, "Now, Mr. Hennessey tells me that you two owe him some money."

As Sherry remained on the floor enjoying herself in that position, Jill said, "But that man who was with us... Severin? *He* kept giving us all this money. How did we know it belonged to Mr. Hennessey?"

Finch kept silent, letting Crowley do all the talking.

"You girls didn't know who the money belonged to, true, but you both possessed it and you'll return it to Mr. Hennessey right now."

A clearly panicked Jill looked around as if she were some trapped animal, her eyes then settling fearfully on Sherry sitting up on the floor and feeling her cheek with a big smile on her face.

"But," Jill faced Crowley and hesitated. "But after Severin left, we went over to the Birdcage and put all the money down on the roulette wheel."

Crowley sighed again, only this time, it was an angry sigh.

"And just *why* did you girls decide to go to the Birdcage down the block when you could've gambled at the roulette table upstairs in *my* establishment?"

She paused, fear returning. Finally she asked timidly, "You won't take this wrong, Mr. Crowley?"

He shook his head.

"We heard from some customers that the gambling tables at Kings are crooked."

Crowley didn't say anything, but I saw his eyes get smaller and his nostrils flare like an angry bull. His right hand balled into a fist.

Now Finch took over. He turned around and asked Jill, "You lose *all* of it?"

In fear, she couldn't answer verbally, so she just nodded vigorously.

Finch paused for a moment and none of us dared make a sound he decided what course to take. Then, in a surprisingly controlled voice, he said, "All right, girls, this is what you're going to do. You'll both go up to your rooms and pack your clothes. Don't take more than ten minutes. A couple of my boys will be waiting downstairs for you with a buckboard. You both have just been fired. So you're both going to come with us and...work off your debt. If either of you has any idea of backing out of this deal or maybe contacting the law, then I promise you that your bodies won't be found for months..."

From the floor, Sherry growled, "Drop dead!"

Finch just looked up at Ben, and the outlaw stuck his boot out and kicked Sherry in the stomach. She cried out and doubled over, writhing around the floor.

From behind the desk, Crowley said, "Clay, don't do that anymore. That's what she *wants*..."

Finch nodded as he stared down at her. She was breathing fast, and even managed a smile.

He said, "Havin' her around is going to be interesting..."

———

THE TWO WOMEN lived in a room above Kings. Finch's men were covering the back and front entrances, including the windows. It looked like this debt was going to be paid one way or the other. Ty and me waited in front with Ben and a tall, lanky outlaw called Stu. Finch was not there at the time, but I heard Ben mention to the other man that he was paying a friendly visit to the marshal so there would be no interference during this obvious kidnapping, or, for that matter, when Finch and his boys confronted Severin.

Again, Ty and me wondered just what kind of influence the name Hennessey had in this territory.

As the other two were off to the side leaning against a brand-new buckboard being pulled by two beautiful stallions, I spoke quietly to Ty.

I asked him, "What do you suppose our folks are thinking now?"

Ty looked at me with some sadness on his face. Hanging around these killers, we were both wondering if we were ever going to see our home again.

He replied, "They probably reported our disappearance to the marshal. And *that*, Jed, will indirectly be our finish."

"How do you figure?"

Ty paused as he scanned the streets, his right hand

on an upright post. He looked like he was tired and he needed sleep. I knew how he felt.

"When Marshal Clell finds Old Man Reynolds's body with his throat cut from ear to ear, and then hears my pa telling him that you and me disappeared in the middle of the night, they're gonna put two and two together and figure we killed him because of the way he treated our pa. Hell, that posse in the woods that saw us with Ira came to the same conclusion. They obviously found Reynolds and tied us in with Ira Toombs and Reynolds's murder."

"That posse was some two hundred feet away and lookin' at us through trees and shrubbery..."

"Then *why* did we suddenly disappear from home just around the time they discovered Reynolds's body?" He shook his head sadly. "No, Jed, in the eyes of Johnny Law, we're as guilty as Ira Toombs and the gang he rides with that did the deed."

"We can tell 'em the truth."

Ty stared at me as if I were some escaped lunatic.

"Sure," he said sarcastically. "Tell 'em we were just breaking into Reynolds's store to steal from him and just happened to find his body with his throat cut from ear to ear. And by an amazing coincidence, the Hennessey Gang who really killed him, decided to rob the place *just before we got there*! Try again, Jed..."

"But we can't *ride* with these boys! They're goddamn killers!"

"And that's why we're gonna have to ride with these boys! *Because* they're goddamn killers! We've seen their work up close, *twice* yet! I don't know about you, Jed, but I have no intention of having *my* head floating and bobbing along some stream that leads into the Little Bear River!"

"So we stay?"

"For now. Play it by ear. Look for some opportunity to get away when they're not lookin'..."

We were both quiet then, each in our own thoughts. Suddenly we heard footsteps on the wooden stairway steps a few feet off the entrance from Kings. The two women were now wearing dresses that covered their flesh far more than the flimsy garments we'd seen them in before. Shawls draped their slender, milk-white shoulders and hats were tied around their chins. They were coming down the steps carrying moth-eaten carpetbags that had seen better days. With the town's deputies already covering the exits around Kings, this freed up a couple of Finch's men to follow the two women as they descended the steps.

I also noticed they weren't helping them carry their bags.

None of the men by the buckboard helped them in, so Ty stepped forward and held out his arm for the brunette, Jill. She saw that none of Finch's men were helping them, and when Ty offered his arm, she looked up at him with large brown eyes, obviously surprised. After a moment, she saw that he was far more of a gentleman than the men he apparently was riding with and she gave him a little smile. I was sorry that Ty did that. Now Sherry stood on the walk with her bags and stared at me, waiting for me to duplicate Ty's chivalry with her, a prospect I did *not* want.

But after Ty helped Jill into the buckboard, Ben lumbered over and picked up Sherry in his arms. She screamed, though in irritation more than in fear. Then the big man roughly threw her in the back next to Jill. Landing on her stomach, her hat came off and her hair got mussed in her eyes. Then Ben picked up her bag and threw the thing on top of her. She cried out when it hit her back—she was lucky there wasn't anything heavy in it—and she let loose a string of curses at Ben. To his credit, he ignored her and signaled the men in the front seats. The driver took the reins and the other sat next to him with a long gun. Ben and Stu already tied the men's horses to the tie-gate and with a shake of the reins and a cluck of the tongue the buckboard moved forward. But as it traveled down the street, Sherry, still on her stomach, and with her red hair still in her eyes, watched me hungrily, her tongue moving slowly around her full red lips. She was still staring at me until they all turned the corner and were out of sight. I was breathing fast as I stared back at her, and after they disappeared, I tried in vain to calm the stirring in my pants.

Ty said, "That redhead sure wants you, Jed..."

Suddenly full of confidence, I said, "Yeah, but I'm not sure I want her."

"Oh really?" Ty said with some skepticism. "You'd better get rid of that third leg then..."

Embarrassed, I cleared my throat and tried not to look down. *Geez, was it that obvious*?

Ty said, "I could see the two of you. Smack her around and she'll be your best friend."

I shivered a little when I thought of that scene back in Crowley's office. Good God, how did that girl get that way?

Curious, I walked over to Ben and asked where they were being taken. At first, he looked at me as if I were a bug on his shirt sleeve. Then he answered, "Dover House..." I knew he wasn't going to say anything more to me, so I just nodded and returned to where Ty was standing.

Ty said, "Doesn't talk much unless Finch tells 'em to, huh?"

"He said enough. They're being taken back to the Dover House."

"That's good for us. So now it's just Finch, Ben and that man named Stu."

"Better odds when we try for a break."

Unfortunately, Finch was coming toward us, his business with the marshal apparently finished. He said to us, "Just like that honey-chile said, Angel House is right outside town. So get your animals. We'll be goin' in through the front door..."

This was a break for us. If we could sneak out the back entrance...

But then, as if reading my mind, Finch said, "The back entrance will be covered by the marshal's deputies."

At that point, I couldn't help asking, "The marshal's deputies are helping you?"

Finch turned to look at me. With a little smile, he said, "Sure, kid. These law-dogs make little as it is. I'm just helping 'em supplement their income, that's all..."

I didn't exactly understand the phrase supplement their income, but I had a good idea it was something crooked.

I asked, "Will there be trouble at the Angel House?"

Finch looked at me, and I almost detected a little warmth in his eyes, as if he appreciated my interest in what we were about to do.

"Severin won't give us trouble. It's the folks who run the establishment who might interfere. Ya see, Ma Hamlin and her boys run the place. Ma's girls are pretty popular in these parts and the marshal's on Ma's payroll. But she's been a bit tardy with payments lately.

"So he's letting us pay her establishment a little visit..."

———

THE PLACE WAS a two-story house about a half mile outside the town limits. Looking at it after we dismounted, we could easily see that the outer walls were painted totally in dark red—reminding me of blood. Then I figured it wasn't supposed to be blood at all, but instead scarlet, as in the practice of sin. It was also distinguishable enough for any randy cowpoke to at least take a second look and be pleasantly surprised at all the girls who worked for Ma Hamlin. For a tired cowboy on the trails, that red house must've been a welcome sight. An oasis in the desert that is, depending on what kind of desert you've been in...

We had pulled up way off the trail and tied our mounts to some cottonwoods, but we could still see Ma's place from where we stood. Finch had sent Ben to go around back, and in a couple minutes, he returned and gave Finch a full report.

"The deputies are there. Two of 'em keeping an eye on the back exit."

Finch listened and nodded. Then his eyes went to the building and he silently watched the front for a while. Finally he broke his silence.

THE OUTLAWS HENNESSEY   103

"Ma and her boys know me like the back of her hand. And you boys have been to Ma's also…"

Then his eyes settled on me, the callow-faced youth of the bunch.

"But they never saw Jed…"

Ty spoke up. "Now wait a minute, Finch. He's a little too young to be in the middle if something happens. Why don't I go?"

Finch's eyes went to Ty and stared at him for the longest time before he replied, "Two reasons. One is, it looks perfect. He's young and it looks like he just wants to sample the women for the first time."

"What's the second reason?"

"'Cause I want it that way…"

He wasn't smiling when he said it either.

Finch was backed by Ben and Stu. Ty couldn't say anymore. Then the outlaw boss looked at me, his eyes sullen but alert. He was all business now.

"You walk in the front. You tell 'em you want a woman. Tell 'em it's your first time."

I nodded uncertainly.

Then he switched gears and a twinkle came into his eye. "By the way," he asked, "*is it your first time*?"

I paused and eyed my dirty boots for a moment. Then I quietly nodded.

I almost felt Ty's embarrassment at me having answered this outlaw's question. Standing near us, both Ben and Stu started to giggle. If they didn't have to be quiet, I'm sure they would've laughed a lot louder.

Then, to my surprise, Finch cut them off with, "Shut up!" The two suddenly stopped and looked appropriately ashamed.

"Go ahead, kid."

"What'll you boys be doin' after I get into the place?"

"Let us worry about that..."

———

I WALKED over to the big red house trying to swallow my fear. Somehow, I felt that I was being used as cannon fodder and I didn't like it. But then again, they had Ty back there too. Finch didn't actually threaten to kill Ty if I didn't do as he said, but after what I've seen, I wouldn't put anything past these boys.

I mounted a few wooden steps and got to the red door. I knocked.

The door then whipped open and a pistol with an extra-long barrel was stuck in my face. The hammer was cocked and it looked like in the next second it was going to come down and blow me all to hell. For a moment, my heart leaped in my chest. But then a strange thing happened. I started to get good and angry. This is the second time since back at the Dover and Lone Hennessey stuck a gun in my face, and I didn't like the feeling.

The hand that held the gun was gnarled and bony and so was the face behind it, the eyes black and tiny. A battered slouch hat sat on top of the oddly shaped head; chewing tobacco filling the slit of a mouth as the juice dribble down his chin. He was tall, though not much taller than me. Then the tobacco stopped moving and slitted mouth moved.

He said, "You want somethin', boy?"

I stared at him, surprised at his high-pitched voice.

He glared at me then and aimed the barrel toward my right eye.

"Your eyes look like they're poppin' out of yo' head. An' in two seconds, I'm gonna shoot one of 'em out."

I stared back at this ogre and in a move that surprised even me, I reached out and shoved his gun hand upward and the hammer went down. The shot was loud in that doorway. The wood at the top chipped and splinters rained down on us as we struggled over the gun.

Then, with his free hand, he reached out and covered my face with his long, smelly fingers, blinding me and almost making me wretch at the same time. I took my right hand off his gun arm and punched him solidly in the face. He stumbled back through the doorway into the house. Unfortunately, he didn't let go of the gun. The stumble back gave him enough room to aim it at me and again cock the hammer.

But before he fired, an old woman's voice shouted at him. He stopped then, uncocking the hammer, and looking off to the side. I stepped into the house then and saw a fairly big woman come down some rickety stairs and walk up to me on gouty legs. Her face seemed as big as her body and she had cherry-red hair, though I suspected it was a wig.

She eyed me up and down and said, "Well, now, you're a tall strapping young man, ain't ya?"

Instead of answering her, I glanced up at the stairs and saw three women leaning over a worn wooden railing watching me. I just stood there and suddenly my throat was dry. They weren't wearing too much. And though one or two of them might have been pretty in better light, they seemed to be either too thin or too fat. They also didn't look much younger than forty, if I was any judge. And like Ma Hamlin a couple feet away from me, they were looking at me like they wanted to devour me.

She asked, "What's your name, son?"

I almost cringed at being called *son* by this woman, but I told her anyway.

"Well, Jed, you come here to sow your oats?"

I was going to answer her, but the ugly man with the gun was glaring at me and I didn't know what he was going to do next.

Seeing me staring at him, she said, "Oh, don't let Cliff get to ya. He hasn't been the same since the Shoshones worked on him 'bout twenty, maybe twenty-five years ago." Then she leaned close to me and raised herself up to my ear on her tiptoes. Deciding she was close enough without Cliff hearing us, she whispered, and loudly at that, "The red niggers cut off his privates..."

After she saw the disgusted look on my face, she laughed loud enough to have the echo bounce off the ceiling. I glanced at Cliff and saw the mean look on his ugly face that said to me he heard every word.

"Oh, don't take it so hard, Cliff!" Ma Hamlin's raspy voice shouted. "So your manhood's some trophy in a Shoshone squaw's tepee, who cares? We all love ya!"

Cliff looked mad enough to bust a gut. The gun tightened in his grip.

But Ma Hamlin couldn't care less. Ignoring him, she turned to me and said, "Which one were you figurin' on havin'? And uh, by the way, you ever have a woman before?"

I looked down at her and was about to lie when three tall men came in through the open front door. A couple of them looked up at the bullet hole in the ceiling of the doorway as they went under it.

The tallest one looked at me, then at Ma. He asked, "What happened, Ma? He givin' you any trouble?"

I guessed these three were the fat woman's sons. They were tall, rugged-looking, and as tanned from the outdoors as she was pale from being in dark rooms and creaky old houses in the middle of nowhere.

Answering her son, she said, "No, Verne, he just wants to feel like a man, that's all."

Verne and the other two grinned at me, looked me up and down, and laughed. All of them had their guns tied down and their jackets drawn back. I just stood there and seethed in frustration. I wanted to take all of them in my hands and beat them to the usual bloody pulp. But I had no doubt that if I made a move, I wouldn't live to make another one.

Ma Hamlin looked up at me then, and I saw right away that she was now all business. She said, "It's two dollars for fifteen minutes. At the end of the fifteen minutes, Cliff comes for you whether you're finished, you haven't started, or you're in the middle of dippin' your wick. So...two dollars in advance."

I stared at her and thought of Finch and his men outside. Jeez, how long was this game going to go on? With the three hardcases, as well as Cliff and the women looking at me, I reached into my pocket and gave her the money. I didn't have much left after that.

She took the money and gestured up to the three women looking down at me from the balcony.

I surprised myself then by asking her, "Is this all the women you have here?"

Ma Hamlin chortled then, a kind of loud cawing

noise I'd never heard from anyone before. "Oh, ho, ho! Randy rooster, ain't he? Want to do all three up there and then try the fourth one?" She smiled leeringly at me, her tongue at the edge of her teeth. I felt disgusted by her, but she told me what I wanted to know.

There was a fourth woman at the Angel House, and at that moment she was off in some upstairs room with Severin.

Verne walked up to me then and again looked me up and down, sizing me up.

The arrogance in his smile made me tense up, something I'm sure he saw right away.

"Where you from, boy?"

I stared right back at him and didn't answer.

"I asked you a question!"

Ma Hamlin said worriedly, "Aw now, Verne, he's just a boy—"

Ignoring his mother, he said, "You got a tongue, boy? Now talk!"

Again, I didn't answer. I didn't like the bossy questions or his arrogant manner. Suddenly he punched me in the side of my face so hard it knocked me off my feet. I fell to the floor, hat rolling off somewhere and my mouth practically tasting the fibers of the tattered rug when my face hit it. I heard the other two outlaws, as well as Cliff, laugh.

I rolled onto my back and sat up, glaring at him.

Ma Hamlin shouted, "Verne!"

But he didn't hear her or maybe he didn't want to. He looked down at me and then drew his gun.

"Okay, smart boy," he said, "Why're you here? And where's your horse?"

Ma Hamlin said, "What?!"

"That's right, Ma. He didn't tie a horse outside. How'd you get here, boy? Drop from the sky?"

Of course, my horse was back in the trees with Ty and the others.

I continued to keep my bleeding mouth shut as I glared up at him. The longer I refused to say anything, the angrier he got. He cocked the hammer of his gun.

Ma Hamlin put a fat hand on her son's wrist.

"Verne, you don't have to kill him! He's just a boy. I'm sure he's just here for a girl, that's all!"

"In a pig's eye!" he said.

Verne shook her hand off and faced her for just a moment, but it was long enough. Angrily, I swung my foot, hooked it around his left leg, then pulled. It was hard enough for the leg to fold under him. Caught off guard, he cried out and fell forward. But just as he hit the floor, his gun fired. I started when I heard the shot, but then I noticed that he stopped moving. Apprehensively, I shoved his body over and saw his gun arm folded under his body. Blood had spread all over his stomach.

When Ma Hamlin saw her son dead, she screamed.

The others started to move toward me and lifted their guns.

But then Verne's brothers turned toward the open doorway and the man closest to it raised his gun. A flurry of shots was heard from outside and the man fell, dropping his gun to the floor.

Ma Hamlin screamed again at the death of her second son.

Then Cliff and her third son fled across the room and disappeared behind a door beneath the stairway. I looked up from the floor and saw the women scream and scatter back to whatever rooms they had been in. Then Ma Hamlin, self-preservation winning out over grief, followed the other two through the door, her waddle more obvious the faster she moved.

Not knowing what was going to happen next, I reached out and yanked the gun out of Verne's dead fingers. I held it in my hand and looked at it for a second, my fingers wrapped around its walnut butt, not sure exactly what I wanted to do with it.

Finch and the rest came through the doorway with their guns drawn, smoke rising out of the barrels. Ty came in on their heels and quickly spotted me still lying on the floor. He went over to me.

"Jed! You all right?"

I answered glumly, "Just the usual knockin' around I've been getting lately…"

Ty helped me to my feet. Then he looked at Verne's body and indicated him with his head. "Is he…"

"Yeah, he's dead."

Then he saw the gun in my hand and his eyes looked into mine with a question.

"No," I said, "I didn't do it. It was an accident."

Ty looked back at the doorway nervously and he got closer to me so no one would see the gun. "Put it away quick!" he ordered. "It might be our ticket outta here."

Quickly, I shoved it into my waistband and let my jacket cover it.

I looked past Ty to the open doorway and saw Finch standing there with his gun before him, his eyes searching the room. Without him telling Ben and Stu, they fanned out with drawn guns, Ben taking the right and heading for the door under the stairs and Stu going to the left and headed for what we assumed was the kitchen and the back entrance beyond. Finch took the stairs, quickly climbing them to the next landing. Ty and I gave each other knowing looks. *Now's our chance.* But in our moment of hesitation, a burly man wearing a deputy's star appeared with a drawn gun and stood in the doorway. Not only did his presence stop anyone from leaving, but it destroyed our hopes of getting away from the Hennesseys.

In fact, the deputy, thinking we were part of the gang, shouted to us, "I got it covered here, boys! Y'all better back up Finch!"

Ty and I glanced at each other and then, with little choice, moved toward the bottom of the stairs and started to climb them. We went up the steps slowly, but with some kind of purpose since the big deputy was watching us as we ascended. Idly, I wondered if he noticed that in such dangerous surroundings, we didn't have guns in front of us like everyone else who broke into the place, and I felt vaguely self-conscious about not drawing the gun I had in my waistband just to look like I *belonged*. In fact, as we got to the first landing, out of the corner of my eye, I saw Ben double back, enter the foyer and then mount the stairs after us. Apparently, his search came up empty and he decided to back Finch's play. Unfortunately with him now behind us, we had no choice but to follow Finch wherever he went.

Finch was about a landing ahead of us. In fact he already had made it to the second floor and with some inborn sense of direction headed to his right down the hallway, as if he instinctively *knew* what room Severin was hiding in. I could only guess that he'd been in the place before, that he knew what kind of woman met

Severin's tastes, and that he knew exactly what room she'd be in.

As if verifying my guess, he stopped outside an old wooden door and kicked it open, the impact of his boot breaking a cheap bolt and busting the door's upper hinge. With his Colt before him, he leaped into the room, his eyes darting around.

Me and Ty were already a few feet behind him in the hallway. With Ben behind us, we were forced to go forward and soon found ourselves standing in the open doorway watching Finch enter deeper into the room and look around. We all saw a young blonde woman cowering against the room's far corner, covering her nakedness with a meager house dress—and I do mean meager—with a scared look on her face. She wasn't half bad looking, but in that moment looking attractive was clearly the furthest thing on her mind. Her hair was in her eyes and fear darkened her face. Finch's sudden appearance scared her. With all the noise and the gunshots from below, I wondered why she didn't have the time to try to escape with everyone else. I then realized it was because she was interrupted in her duties and didn't have the time to get away before Finch burst her door in.

This also meant that Severin was nearby, not having had the time or the opportunity to get away either.

Finch glanced at her. She was a young woman frightened out of her wits—if indeed she had any—and already knowing it was useless to ask her where he was. In fact he already knew to turn toward the closet behind him. But in that second or two that his eyes saw the blonde, the closet door that was slightly ajar burst open and from my point of view I saw a gun barrel protruding from it. A man's hand had already cocked the hammer and was about to fire.

Still standing outside the room, I instantly shouted, "Look out!" Then I drew the gun in my waistband and fired into the room directly at the hand holding the gun. However, since I wasn't what you'd call *the fastest gun west of the Pecos*, my shot went wide, even in that short distance and the bullet went through a chest of drawers only a couple feet away from the naked blonde cowering in the corner.

The closet door swung open suddenly, and we saw the man. He was young, but he had the hooded eyes of someone very old, or possibly hungover. He quickly threw his hands up since he now realized that guns were pointed at him from another direction. Finch was turning around anyway, so he was just in time to heed my warning and see my bad shot. Quickly he extended his gun arm and the barrel touched Severin's head. The young man dropped his own gun and gritted his teeth under the pressure of the cold, steel barrel pressed against his forehead. Finch had the hammer back and we could see the knuckles of his hand were white as they were wrapped around the trigger guard. The look on his face was pure stone. It must've been one hellacious second there when Severin thought it would be his last.

Tensely, Finch said, "I don't know why I shouldn't blow your fucking brains all over this chippie's room. For all the shit you put me and the boys through lookin' for your sorry ass..."

With his trembling hands raised and suddenly ready to burst into tears, Severin closed his moist eyes tightly and implored, "Please, Finch! I—I didn't know it was you! I thought it was Verne and the others!"

Then all of us looked down at him and the ugly smell hit us a moment later. Ty and me witnessed this and were appalled. He and I may have been farm boys and not hardened outlaws, but we were ashamed at this fellow's lack of manliness. At that moment, we were practically on Finch's side as he grabbed the man by the front of his shirt and, with his gun still pointed at Severin's head, led the way out the door and pulled his prisoner along with him. Me, Ty, and Ben parted like the Red Sea as the two passed us and Finch continued to pull him down the hallway. When they got to the top of the stairs, I knew what Finch would do. Still holding onto him, he planted his left boot on Severin's stomach and shoved him. The terrified outlaw quickly toppled down the stairs and didn't stop until he hit the first floor.

The burly deputy below at the doorway watched this impassively. We all saw that after Severin hit the dirty floor he just lay there in a twisted position.

Then, as if he suddenly noticed it, with his own gun on me, Ben grabbed Verne's Colt out of my hand and held onto it. Then he approached Finch at the top of the stairs.

"Ya know, Finch, maybe you hadn't oughtta done that. If he's dead, he can't tell us where the money is."

I had a feeling people didn't always say things like that to Finch Hennessey, but to his credit he nodded slowly. He was furious, but I noticed his face was calm as he shoved his brother down the stairs. He knew that what he had just done was wrong, that is, from the point of view of a professional outlaw. Where lots of money was at stake, you don't knock off the one man who could lead you to it—at least, not till he led you to it *first*. But Finch had let his anger get the better of him. He didn't shoot Severin dead, but he might have done something just as bad.

Then, as we looked below, it was with some relief that we saw the broken body at the bottom of the stairs start to move. Groaning painfully, he attempted to sit up. That's when the burly deputy moved forward and roughly lifted him up to his feet.

Pointing his gun at Severin's head, he looked up to Finch and asked, "Want me to kill 'em?"

Decisively, Finch answered, "No. Leave him to us..."

———

BEN DRAGGED Severin's now-unconscious body out into the night and tied him to his horse, belly down. Stu had his gun on Ma Hamlin's back as he shoved her before Finch and the burly deputy. Two other deputies stood back as they held onto Cliff.

With his arms pinned back, Cliff's ugly face was still defiant, as if he'd like to take all of us on.

Putting away his gun, Finch looked at me with an expression that wasn't unkind. Without smiling, he put his hand on my shoulder and said, "Thanks, Jed. You saved my bacon all right."

I didn't know what to say. I had a feeling Clay Finch Hennessey wasn't a man who said thank you or expressed a kindness very often. Without smiling, I just solemnly nodded. Perhaps realizing that he showed more emotion in front of his men than he should have, he quickly took his hand off my shoulder and turned back to the matter at hand.

He asked the two deputies, "What happened to Vic?"

Vic, I gathered, was Ma Hamlin's third son.

One of the deputies answered, "We ordered him to drop his gun, but he kept shootin' at us. We had to kill 'em..."

Glaring at Finch, Ma Hamlin bitterly said, "Murderer! You and Marshal Taylor! You both killed my sons!"

Finch just looked back at her, not caring to answer.

But Ben said, "Your sons were trash and got what they deserved!"

Ma Hamlin replied with a string of curses, and as she spat them out, her tears increased until she bent over and hit the ground on her knees. Her body became racked with sobs as she kneeled on the ground.

Indicating Cliff, one of the deputies asked, "What do we do with him?"

Finch was about to tell them until I said, "Wait a minute."

Everyone, including Ty, stared at me, but my reply was only for Finch.

"Tell them to let go of his arms..." Finch looked at me for only a moment, then he nodded to the deputies and they let Cliff go. I stepped before him knowing what he'd do.

Glaring at me, he suddenly swung his right fist straight toward my eye. But I blocked the blow with my left arm and punched him square on the already crooked nose. Then I followed up with a hard punch which plowed deep into his stomach. He doubled over and crumpled painfully to his knees beside Ma Hamlin. In fact, he quickly lost his lunch. Or dinner—I wasn't sure which.

Finch stared at me, as did Ty, who looked as if he hadn't seen me before. Then Finch said to the deputies, "Tell Taylor I appreciate your help. You might as well take those two and lock 'em up." He then looked at the house and said, "I'm sure you'll find another woman with another stable who can put this place to some kind of use."

Ty then asked, "That's right. What happened to all those women?"

The burly deputy answered, "Fled for the hills with what little they had on their backs. They didn't know whether we were gonna arrest 'em or kill 'em."

Finch walked over to the horse Severin was tied on. He lifted Severin's head up by the hair, and though he was unconscious, he spoke to him.

"Sev, we're takin' you back to home sweet home..." Then he unceremoniously dropped the head and walked over to his horse.

Ty stopped and stared at Finch. At first, I didn't know why, but at that point I didn't think it mattered.

There were too many men around to try to make a break, so once again we were riding back with our hosts whether we liked it or not...

CHAPTER SEVEN

THIS TIME WE AVOIDED TOWN AND THE DEPUTIES SPLIT off somewhere on the trail and headed back there with Ma Hamlin and Cliff—for her, one of them had to go back to town to get a buckboard, since she was too fat to get on a horse. We rode on to the Dover House. The night winds blew a little less this evening, becoming more like a refreshing spring breeze. We rode as we did on the way in, with *someone* always riding in front of us as well as behind us. This time, Ben and Stu were behind us with the unconscious form of Severin tied to his horse, and Finch and the other men leading the way, us in the middle.

Ty waited a good while until it looked like Finch and the other riders were way ahead of us before he spoke to me.

"Jed," he started.

"I know what you're gonna say, Ty."

Ty shook his head cynically.

"Shit, Jed!"

My eyes indicated the others in front of us and he

calmed down, or at least lowered his voice. I noticed Finch's head then turn to the side briefly, as if he were cocking an ear. Hearing nothing but the night breeze, he turned his head back to the trail.

Quietly but firmly, Ty said, "You had a gun in your hand! At some point later on when their attention was on something else, we could've gotten the drop on 'em and got the hell away from 'em! Maybe even with Pa's horses."

"There's no guarantee we would've gotten away. I have a feeling these boys would've opened up on us for laughs."

"And you *saved* Finch's life!"

I was quiet then, as I tried to think why I did that. Actually, when I went back on it in my mind, I knew that it was one of those decisions you make in a split second. You don't think and you don't sit back and reflect, there's no time for that, you just see someone else's life in danger and you just *act*.

I asked him, "Would you rather I let Severin kill Finch?"

Then Ty did a strange thing. Instead of replying *yes*, he paused, as if he suddenly wasn't sure of his answer.

"Well?"

Ty sighed and then said, "No, I guess I couldn't say I want him dead."

"Yeah," I said, watching Finch ride ahead of us. "He kinda grows on ya, doesn't he?"

With his eyes on the back of the gang leader's head, Ty said, "Yeah, I'll admit that. It's not a weak man who can take a bunch of killers and ride herd on 'em as easy as he does."

"True enough."

"All right," Ty said thoughtfully. "We agree Finch Hennessey's the boss. And despite they're watching us like hawks, it looks like he kinda likes us too. You saving his life probably made you as well as me look good in his eyes. In fact, as long as we're here, we're going to need him and probably the Toombs boys to watch our backs from the wilder members of the gang. You agree?"

With my eyes on the trail, I nodded and said, "I certainly do, big brother."

"Good. Then let's keep playing this crazy little game by ear..."

——————

THE DOVER HOUSE came into view like a giant sentinel in the middle of an already spooky forest. The same branches were scratching the same upper window shutters and the barn with Pa's horses had the same wooden bolt across it as we saw before.

That's when a huge shadow sprang up from the right and reached out for me with long arms and clawing hands. Instinctively I pulled my booted foot out of the right stirrup and kicked the shadow hard in the chest. I heard a grunt of pain and it hit the ground with a thud.

A spill of moonlight revealed Lone Hennessey lying back on the ground, but only for a moment. With a roar, he got back up and leaped for me again. But before he could complete the leap, Ty, still sitting on his horse, yanked his boot out of the stirrup and kicked Lone right in the face. We heard Lone scream in pain and fall back on the ground again. This time he didn't get up.

Then we heard the clicks of two Colt hammers being uncocked. I looked at the front porch and saw Ira and Andrew Toombs standing there in the shadows with their guns out. After a couple moments, seeing everything under control, they holstered them.

Finch looked at them he didn't have to ask the question.

Andrew said, "You know what a long memory the chief has. We had an idea he was gonna ambush Jed. So just like a damn Indian with all the patience in the world he waited in that grove for hours to make his play."

Finch asked, "Anybody give him a drink?"

"Nope. And that's a fact."

Finch dismounted and said angrily, "Got enough troubles. I don't need to worry about him too."

The Toombs brothers looked at each other. Then in the darkness they saw the other horse, the one with Severin tied to it.

Ira said, "You got him."

"Yeah," Finch said, his anger growing. "We got him. And three men died because of him."

Andrew asked, "Anyone worth killin'?"

"Just the Hamlin boys. No one's gonna miss them. But that mother of theirs might make a stink."

"So what? If she says something on Taylor, that's his lookout."

"And if Taylor says something on us, that's *our* lookout."

"But he can't squawk about what happened here—"

Finch cut him off loudly. "Enough of this jawbonin'! Let's take him upstairs."

Ira paused and then indicated the unconscious Lone lying on the ground.

"*Which one?*"

Finch looked back at Severin, then at Lone Hennessey.

"*Both* of 'em!"

ONLY A FEW MEMBERS of the gang were around. We were told that most of them were in town drinking or getting into some such other mischief.

Ben and Stu had their hands full, dragging the tied-up Severin upstairs. Then they did the same thing to Lone, though his body was much heavier to drag up the steps and the two men grunted loudly on the way up.

Finch brought us over to a small room on the ground floor. There were two moldy mattresses against the wall. Whether they had bedbugs on them, I didn't know.

"Gentlemen, your room for the night..."

Ty said, "Uh, listen, Finch, we kind of..."

Finch quietly interrupted, "No, Ty. Let me say something. You boys see how we work and maybe that might not be your way of doin' things, but it works for us. I don't know of any gang that doesn't get a little out of hand once in a while. We're not gonna get the love and admiration of a lot of stupid people—like they give the James boys. But we're kinda strict about loyalty here. You ride with us, it's a lifetime deal. But you're both gonna see more money in one day than our poor daddies plowin' the fields ever saw in ten years. Now it's been a long day. Right now, you bunk here. Get a long sleep, you boys need it..."

He didn't wait for us to say anything further he just turned around and left the room as if he had seen too much of us for one day.

At that point Ira and Andrew appeared in the doorway.

"A room of your own," said Andrew, looking around. Then he faced us and said with a grin, "He likes you. And Finch Hennessey's a man who doesn't take kindly to just *anyone*."

Ira said, "He's right. What'd you boys do to get this kind of treatment?"

Ty answered, "Jed stopped Severin from shooting Finch."

Both brothers looked at each other, surprise on their faces.

Andrew asked me, a twinkle in his eye, "And what possessed you to save our dear leader's life?"

I just shrugged my shoulders and looked away.

Ty asked them, "Why? Don't you like him?"

"Let's put it this way—He's *family*..."

"You guys are also Hennesseys?"

"Another branch of the family. The ship that had the Toombs clan sailed from Ireland to America a few years *after* the Hennesseys."

Ira added, "So Finch and the others are our distant cousins."

Andrew said, "Sometimes we think they're not distant enough..."

Ira paused before he added, "What Andrew means is, he and I try to work a little quieter..." Then he looked at his younger brother and said gravely, "Well, I like to think *I* do anyway." We saw Andrew look away briefly. It was the first time I had ever seen even a hint of shame come from this young hellion.

Then Ira faced us again and explained, "We're a bunch of wild boys—you've seen what we do and how we act. To be in our business, whether we like someone or not isn't what's important. It's the fact that we all know that Finch Hennessey could do anything any of us could do, but ten times better. He knows that if he didn't swing a big stick, we'd eat him alive, or anyone else who tried to run herd on us. And I never a met a Hennessey who didn't want to be top dog in the pack. His side of the family's got a long bloodline, accent on the blood part..."

Warming to that subject, Andrew said cheerfully, "Heard that back on the old sod, the Hennesseys used to hang those fancy Limeys for fun. They didn't care whether they were overseers or soldiers or whoever."

Ty said, "And in this country, they own the marshal and the deputies of Telluride, and who else? The judges? The whole court system of the town?"

"Try the county..." said Ira.

I could see Ty's eyes widen slightly at that remark. I was a little taken aback by it myself.

"The *county*? You mean the Hennesseys give the county sheriff his marching orders too?"

Ira answered wryly, "The Hennesseys always shoot high, boys. I can't say some big shots in Denver will dine with us, but they'll make sure no one interrupts us while we eat..."

Ty and I let that one sink in.

Stretching, Andrew said, "Well, it's getting late. I'm

goin' to town to find some fillies to dip my wick in. Night, boys..."

I noticed that Ira didn't say that he was going to go with him, but then he always seemed less impulsive and more restrained than his little brother.

Both of them started to turn away.

"Wait!" said Ty.

They stopped and looked at us.

"What about our pa's horses?"

Ira said plainly, "We had our chance, but Lone gummed up the works."

"But what better time than to try it in the dark?"

He answered patiently, "Because not everyone's asleep, that's why. So if you make a trip to the stable and try to grab 'em tonight, they're gonna catch ya. And Finch may like you two, but if you pull a fool stunt like that after the day he's had, he's gonna be mad. And mean as me and Andrew can get, even *we* don't want to be around when that happens..."

Andrew said, "Anyway, you'll be goin' to town tomorrow with the other boys. If you play your cards right, you might make your break then—without your pa's horses."

Ira added, "But if you stick with us, you'll be able to afford a *whole string* of ponies. Enough to work twenty farms." Tiring of the conversation, he finally said, "Just go to sleep. Things'll look different in the morning..."

And without waiting for a reply, he left the room. Andrew just gave a quick grin, then followed him out.

Ty went over to the door and closed it. Then he faced me.

"Tell you the truth, Jed, I'm too damn tired to make a daring getaway."

"So am I. Lord knows what our folks are thinking right now about what happened to us."

"Lord knows what Johnny Law is thinking right now about what happened to us."

"Yeah…"

"I'll take the mattress on the right. Looks like it's got less bedbugs…"

CHAPTER EIGHT

Ty was right. My mattress had more bedbugs, or at least I couldn't imagine it having any more than it had. I could swear I did more scratching than sleeping.

But when I did sleep, I slept happy because I dreamed of Hazel. "No," I said to myself, "No! I can't believe that beautiful doll is any more my sister than Lone Hennessey is Sitting Bull." The dream I had of her was certainly not that of a young man for his sister, I can tell you that! One good thing about the morning, we would ride into town and I'd be able to see her. Maybe, just maybe we'd get a chance to ride off with her and leave the Hennesseys for good.

I turned over, threw off the moldy sheet and looked to the other mattress. Ty was snoring loudly, which for him meant he was sleeping peacefully. The bedbugs must've left his mattress and jumped over to mine.

I rose groggily and left the room, closing the door behind me.

It was then that I heard a sharp noise.

Curiously, I started down the hallway toward the

sound. Then I heard it again. Some sharp impact, but this time followed by a cry.

It took all of two seconds to find the wooden door on the right where the sounds were coming from. Approaching it, I put my hand on the knob, turned and opened it. You could've hit me in the face with a switch and I couldn't feel any more startled.

Tied to a chair in the center of the room was Severin, his mouth bloody and his bruised right eye almost shut. Ben was towering over him, the knuckles on his right hand, which was balled into a fist, literally dripping blood, though I couldn't rightly say whose it was. Finch was seated on a worn upholstered chair smoking a cigarette. Another outlaw was off to the side, an old lash in his hand; apparently he was waiting his turn when Ben was through. All of them turned toward me when I opened the door. It was pretty much a sure thing they all saw my look of disgust. I quickly stepped back and slammed the door. Lord, I never felt so sick, I wanted to vomit out my guts into the next century and beyond.

I moved quickly down the hallway, past the foyer and out of the house, leaving the front door wide open. As I did so, I heard footsteps coming up fast behind me. I went down the steps and, for the second time in as many days, let out my supper—this time on the front lawn, which didn't matter because it was all dead grass anyway.

After I was through and I wiped my mouth and started to rise, I felt a firm hand on my shoulder. I turned around and it was Finch.

I wrenched my shoulder out of his grip and stood back. The look I gave him was *not* friendly.

"Take it easy, Jed."

"Take it easy!"

"We were just teachin' Severin a lesson, that's all."

"A lesson! I'm surprised he's still alive!"

His face hardened then, and he said angrily, "Listen, kid, you keep carryin' on and you won't be."

I stopped and stared at him, suddenly sobered by the fact that I was starting to morally indict a killer who was well-armed and standing just two feet in front of me in the middle of nowhere. One quick bullet in the head and I'm just another burden for one of his boys to bury out in the woods with no questions asked and no one around to mourn for me but Ty.

And then *he'd* be put in the grave next to mine.

Reluctantly, I forced myself to calm down.

"Why were you beating him?" I quietly asked. "I mean *really*?"

"Really? The bulk of that money from that old man's emporium is missing, that's why. Ben made the mistake of having Sev hold a locked cash box while he went outside and pulled the horses around to the back door. Sev was the last one riding with that box, and when we spotted a posse some distance in the woods, we split off in several directions. Sev disappeared with the box and we knew what kind of man he is."

"Unreliable?"

"Let's put it this way. I'd sooner trust Satan with a Gatling gun than that low-rent, drunken little rich boy..."

I looked at him oddly, not understanding the *rich boy* part of it.

Finch continued, "Sure, he might've given it all to those two saloon tarts who gambled it away, but even if we never see that money again, he's gonna pay for spending what rightfully belongs to *all of us*!"

Looking at him then just proved what I saw in him before: It was *his* way or none at all.

I asked, "Well, if he's such a drunk and you don't trust him, why is he with you?"

"Long story. And I don't particularly feel like going into it right now."

I looked down at the toes of my scuffed boots, suddenly feeling ashamed.

"Sorry, Finch," I found myself saying, surprising myself. "Guess you have a right to ride herd on your men..."

Finch stood back and studied me. I don't know if he was amused by me or starting to understand my point of view.

"Maybe you'll work out after all," he said.

———————

As we rode to town, I told Ty of the beating of Severin and the encounter outside the house with Finch.

"You avoided another close one, Jed. I don't know how many times we can duck the bullet with these guys..."

"Long as we're able, I guess."

"But there's one thing about your talk with him that bothers me."

"What's that? My sayin' I'm sorry to him and him goin' 'I think you'll work out after all'?"

"No. That's not what bothers me."

"It doesn't?"

"Well, I know you're not serious and you had to say what you did to stay alive."

I thought about that one. Then I suddenly found myself defending my apology to Finch. "How do you know I didn't mean it?"

"You mean you really *were* sorry you started to indict him for beating up Severin?"

I paused. "Well—"

"Well *what*?"

I didn't know how to say it.

Finally, I blurted out, "It's *his* gang, Ty! He can run it the way he wants to."

Ty stared at me as we rode.

"You mean you can understand his men beating the hell out of another man. A man who was tied to a chair and couldn't defend himself?"

I looked at him, my mouth partly open as if I was about to answer him, but I couldn't. I couldn't explain just *why* I was defending Finch.

And then I thought of the look on his face when he said that the stolen money from Reynolds's store belonged to *all of us*. This was a man who'd stop at nothing, and people who'd stop at nothing were downright dangerous. In fact, that was the reason I agreed with Finch that he was right and I was taking Severin's beating all wrong, because if I didn't agree, *bang!*

I decided to change the subject, quickly.

"All right, you tell me why there was something that I told you about the whole thing that bothered you *more* than me telling you about the beating."

The trail ahead widened and the road to town came into view. The spring breeze got suddenly chilly.

"It was what Finch said to you about Severin. Maybe he said it when he didn't have his guard up."

"What's that?"

"He called Severin a 'drunken rich boy.'"

"Yeah, I remember that. I thought it was strange too."

"Yeah..."

"But maybe he was referring to the money Severin ran off with after the robbery."

"Yeah," said Ty, deep in thought. "Maybe..."

———

It was mid-morning by the time we rode into town.

The only one missing was Lone. I didn't know for sure where he was, but I heard Ben comment to Finch that he hoped Lone didn't break through his ropes. I can only imagine this was the Hennessey way of allowing one of their own some time to cool off. I also remember Finch's question to Ira if Lone had had anything to drink. Perhaps keeping him away from town and its many saloons was a good idea. With a bottle in his paw and me and Ty in his gunsights, there's no telling how crazy he'd get.

Without Finch telling them, the gang headed for the Trace Hotel and Pellican restaurant next door. Since they usually rode with us in the middle, we had no choice but to go with the group. Personally, I would've gone there anyway if only to see Hazel again.

We all dismounted at an already crowded tie rail and tied our horses. As Ben was passing me and headed toward the hotel's door, Ty asked him, "Hey, Ben, do you know what happened to those girls from Kings?"

Ben stared at him for a moment, as if no one was allowed to interrupt him as he's on his way to breakfast. Still, he answered, "They're back at the Dover doin' various *chores*."

"We didn't see them at the Dover."

"Well, you boys were on the first floor. What they were doin' was takin' place upstairs." He gave a little smile, as if he was letting us in on a little joke. Then, without waiting for Ty or me to respond, he entered the hotel.

It was then I noticed Ty look concerned.

I asked Ty, "Why are you asking about the saloon girls?"

Ty shrugged. "I don't know. Just wondering what happened to 'em..."

"Well, that Sherry looks like she can take of herself."

"And what about Jill?"

"I don't know. What about her?"

"Just wondering. She doesn't seem half as crazy as Sherry."

"How do you know?"

"I *don't* know," he answered. "There's just something about her. She seems more decent and down-to-earth than that redhead."

"She's also pretty. I'm sure you didn't miss that."

He paused before he replied, "No, I didn't..."

I put my hand on his shoulder and said, "Well, listen, brother. I may be a young beanpole of nineteen, but I know for a fact she's not the kind of gal you can bring back home to your ma."

Ty looked at me and asked, "And how do you know *that*?"

"Look at where we found her—some dirty saloon.

Now how can you be in a nest of snakes and not act like one?"

"What about us?" he pointedly asked. "*We're* in a nest of snakes, and we're forced to act like them..."

I paused, thinking about that one. When I didn't answer him, he just went inside.

————

AFTER WE ENTERED THE HOTEL, we found Ben placing the mousy little desk clerk named John in a headlock while another man was yanking his left arm behind his back and with his other hand, was drawing a tiny circle over his bald head with a black pen. A spilled inkwell lay nearby on the front desk. Several of the outlaws were laughing at the little man's distress. They easily dragged the smaller man out from behind the front desk and forced him to face the restaurant.

A third man, a tobacco-chewing cuss who seemed to spit juice with every other step he took, passed under the archway into the restaurant for about a dozen feet and drew his gun. Then he turned and faced the struggling clerk with a wicked smile on his reddened face. The smile looked wider with his cheeks bulging with tobacco.

I glanced inside the restaurant. The place was full, and patrons were horrified at the spectacle. Then I saw Hazel and Bessie serving them, with Hazel at the far end of the room and Bessie not far from the archway. From the separate places they stood, they also stopped and stared at the scene.

Me and Ty were angered by what we were seeing, but several outlaws standing in our way blocked us from interfering. And when we tried to push our way forward, we were roughly elbowed back by the outlaws. Finch just stood off to the side. Again, he seemed bored, as if he were thinking *boys will be boys*, and all that nonsense. The Toombs boys also didn't do anything but watch. I had a feeling getting their breakfast was slightly more important to them than a man getting his head shot off.

Then Bessie, her face an angry mask, plunked her tray down on the nearest table of a shocked middle-aged couple and rushed over. With strength I didn't know she had—I wondered if *she* did—she shoved the tobacco-chewing outlaw out of the way and went right over to the others. He fell to the floor noisily knocking back an empty chair. Rushing up to the three men, Bessie was able to yank the other man's hand off John's arm and then push him away. He fell back against the hard wood of the front desk. Then, facing Ben, she shoved him hard in the chest to get him off of John, but the big man stayed where he was, with the clerk still trapped in his headlock.

By then, the other man recovered and reached out with his long arm, grabbing a fistful of Bessie's pinned-up hair. With her head yanked back, she screamed and reached back for the outlaw's hand. The other hard-cases were laughing at this scene anyway, except the laughter seemed even louder this time.

I don't know what Hazel or the Toombs boys or Finch or Ty or anyone else was doing at the time, and I didn't care. I roughly shoved the cluster of outlaws out of my way and rushed forward. When I got up to the group at the front desk, I came in swinging and my left fist connected with the jaw of the man grabbing Bessie's hair. Releasing her, he fell back hard against the front desk, again, but this time, he slid down to the floor, temporarily stunned.

Angrily, Ben tossed the little clerk out of his way and faced me, his huge fist raised. I put my hands on Bessie's shoulders and shifted her out of the way so I could fight back, but then a loud gunshot was heard from the restaurant and a corner of the front desk was chipped by a bullet. At the sound of the shot, and without thinking, I found myself putting my arms protectively around Bessie. It took a couple seconds before I realized what I was doing, but then it took a couple seconds more before I realized that she was not only letting my arms remain where they were, but she was putting her own arms around me as well.

We both looked up and saw the tobacco-chewer, now off the ground, aiming his gun directly at us.

He spat a wad of the awful stuff and said, "Say the word, Ben, and I'll put one in both of 'em!"

Everyone stopped what they were doing, patrons, outlaws, John cringing near the floor, Ty, who had run up to us, Hazel, me, Bessie, the whole place.

The only one who moved was Finch, who slowly walked up to the tobacco-chewer, unhesitatingly yanked the gun out of his hand and backhanded him full in the face. Then, he slapped him with his open palm and backhanded his face again as his arm swung back. The tobacco-chewer gave a painful swallow, having just disposed of his last gob of the stuff down his food pipe. He stared back at Finch less in anger than in fear and defeat.

Still glaring at him, Finch said loud enough for all to hear, "Now I don't know about the rest of you, but

I'm *hungry* and I want this bullshit stopped! Ya hear me?"

No one answered him, but they sure as hell obeyed him. The cluster of men in the foyer broke up and started to head for the tables. Ben and the other man who rose from the floor gave me dirty looks and they also went inside.

Then Finch roughly shoved the gun at the tobacco-chewer and sarcastically said, "Here, Arch, you might need this!" Arch took it obediently and meekly holstered it.

While she was still in my arms, Bessie looked up at me and our eyes locked for just a moment. Her hair was now down around her ears and her blouse was disheveled. In that second or two, I saw something else besides anger and resentment in those usually sharp blue eyes. I saw a vague look of gratitude. But then, even as her mouth started to widen into a weak smile, something came over her and she pulled out of my embrace.

Looking away from me, she said, almost resentfully, "Thank you."

As I stared at her, I could see that she was avoiding my eyes.

With equal surliness, I replied, "Anytime."

She responded curtly, "That won't be necessary."

"I'll remember that the next time something like this happens again."

Bessie's eyes flashed angrily and she looked up at me for the first time since she pulled out of my arms. She looked like she wanted to devour me, but she restrained herself admirably.

Then I left her with her rage and followed Ty into the restaurant. Whether she stayed where she was and glared at my retreating back or went into the kitchen to fix her hair, I didn't know and didn't care.

As we headed inside, he asked me, "What was *that* about? You just saved her butt."

"She has it in for me," I said sullenly. "Damned if I know *why*."

I tried to sound like I was dismissing her resentment toward me, but deep down I felt kind of hurt. I started to wonder just what I had done to make her hate me so much.

Ty said irritably, "Getting so a man can't rescue a damsel in distress anymore without them getting pissed off about it."

"You could say that again..."

He didn't say it again, but then it didn't matter.

Hazel came up to me and embraced me tightly. At least *someone* was grateful!

After we hugged, she held me at arm's length and said, "I'm glad for what you did for Bessie."

"Yeah," I said to her, "but *she's* not!"

"That's because she hates outlaws, Jed. She's always hated them ever since—"

Suddenly one of the gang called, "Hey! How about some service!"

Great timing. Despite my own resentment against Bessie, I *was* curious to hear the rest of what Hazel had to say. Reluctantly, she pulled away from me and started to walk toward the outlaw's table all the way at the other end of the restaurant.

The restaurant may have been full of people before, but it wasn't for long. Hell, I never saw such an exodus from an establishment as I did then. Finch and the boys didn't have to search for tables; the patrons suddenly wiped their mouths on napkins and quickly vacated them. Husbands, wives, sons, daughters, the well-dressed and the not-so-well-dressed, called for their checks, put on their hats, and took to the door, of course, giving us an open aisle as we entered.

Hazel had to quickly pull out her checks and see which person had what. Distracted, she started to another table until she passed one where Ira and Andrew were at. It wasn't them that gave her a problem, but the outlaw who was already seated. Andrew had already sat down and Ira was about to sit next to him when Hazel started to pass them. That's when the outlaw seated on Andrew's other side reached out with long fingers like talons and gave Hazel's right butt-cheek a big squeeze.

She screamed and jumped, almost dropping her pen and her checks.

Still standing, Ira quickly lifted his booted foot and kicked the randy outlaw full in the face. The impact knocked both him and his chair over onto the floor. The others stared at this, some rising out of their chairs.

Then Ira leaned down and grabbed a fistful of the outlaw's shirt in his trembling fists. With a mean look I didn't see on his face too often, he said angrily, "Didn't you hear what Finch said, Riley? He said to *stop the bull-shit!*" On "stop the bullshit," he roughly shoved Riley back onto the floor and rose to his feet. Riley didn't like being manhandled, but he liked tangling with Ira Toombs even less, and as he felt his bleeding jaw, he back-crawled away from him and went over to another table. Then Ira sat down next to Andrew in the seat Riley vacated.

I looked at Hazel then, and I was shocked to see her

staring at Ira with a weak little smile. Was it my imagination or were those beautiful eyes of hers starting to
well up in tears?

But if Ira was making a show of defending Hazel,
you wouldn't know it from him. Rather coldly I thought,
he faced the table and started to unfold his napkin. For
all we knew, he had kicked the outlaw aside so that he
could have his chair and sit next to his brother.

I looked back at Hazel. Disappointment crossed her
face as she headed for the table of a middle-aged couple
ready to head out the door without paying.

At least there was something left on their table that
interested me and Ty that the couple neglected to take
with them as they hurried out. A newspaper.

Both of us headed fast toward the table and, as an
outlaw was about to sit at that spot Ty put his hand on
the chair and used his body to block him from sitting
down while I swept the paper off the table. It was
perfect teamwork in action, but the outlaw didn't appreciate it. He shoved Ty hard in the chest, causing him to
stagger back against another table, almost stumbling
into Hazel as she was cleaning it. Angry, I stomped hard
on the toe of the man's boot with the heel of mine. He
cried out and reached for his holstered gun.

"Hey!" shouted Finch. "Are you boys deaf too? Sit
down!"

The outlaw gave me a surly look and then walked
over to the far end of another table and sat down.
Ignoring him, Ty and I took our seats. I noticed then
that Finch was careful enough to sit in a chair where he
had a commanding view of both the front window
which looked out onto the street and our tied-up horses
and the restaurant's archway which led into the hotel.

After we all had noisily sat down, Hazel recovered from the ass-grab and whatever disappointment she may have felt about Ira and went about taking our orders. But since Hazel was so busy, Bessie came right back out of the kitchen to help take the orders. Her hair was pinned back up and her blouse was more or less back in place, but her apron was as dirty as it was before.

I was still a little angry at her, but when she started to pass by, I couldn't help asking her, "You all right?"

She stopped and said curtly, "I'm fine, thank you."

What did I expect? "Just askin," I said lamely.

"Thank you for your courtesy, but I was doin' all right until you intervened."

Outraged, I turned to stare at her and started to say something, but then she quickly scooted down to the other end of the table before I could get a word out.

I was boiling mad, but when I looked at Ty, I quickly forgot my anger.

He had ignored Bessie and me and was reading the front page of the newspaper. When I looked at him now, his brow was furrowed and his mouth a grim, straight line.

I didn't like it.

The paper was practically crumpled between his fists and if it didn't look like the weight of the world was on him, at least it was a few continents.

Concerned, I said, "Ty?"

Without a word, he shoved the crumpled newspaper toward me while he stared into his coffee cup.

I took the paper and found a certain article headlined, MURDER AND ROBBERY OF BEAUMONT STORE OWNER.

Oh boy, reading this was not going to be easy.

Robbers broke into Reynolds Emporium on Front Street last night and cut the throat of Cyrus Reynolds, 66, and reportedly escaped with thousands of dollars which the owner kept hidden in a locked metal box beneath the counter. It's not certain exactly how much was stolen, but Reynolds's wife told lawmen that her husband didn't trust banks and always kept the profits from his store, as well as other investments and securities, always within his reach. The empty box was found later out on the street with its lock broken and the money gone.

Marshal Tom Clell later cast suspicion for the crimes on two young men, Jed Tully and Tyrone Brody, whose folks reported them missing the morning after the robbery. The marshal said he knew the young men harbored resentment against Reynolds for threatening to seize their parents' farm if bills for the sale of feed and equipment were not paid up immediately. Their participation in the robbery and heinous murder was verified when Clell and his posse clearly saw them escaping on horseback in the woods outside town in the company of the notorious outlaw Ira Toombs, a member of that bunch of robbers and cutthroats known as the Hennessey Gang. The posse opened fire on the desperate trio, but they escaped along the river. Trackers are still hunting the murderers and Marshal Clell vowed to have the two young men captured as soon as possible. It is not out of the realm of possibility to predict that County Judge Theodore Harding will sentence the two young hooligans to the hangman's noose at the end of their trial.

I dropped the paper on the table and felt as morose as Ty.

"Marshal Clell," I said bitterly.

Ty added dryly, "Never trust a man with three *ls* in his last name..."

"Yep."

Ty looked at me then and pointed at the crumpled newspaper. He asked, "Well, what do you think about *that*?"

Without looking at him, I sadly replied, "I don't know, hooligan. I just don't goddamn know..."

CHAPTER NINE

WHEN HAZEL GOT TO US TO TAKE OUR ORDERS, SHE could tell that something was wrong. To explain why our faces were long enough to touch the floor, without a word, Ty handed the newspaper up to her.

"Better read it in the kitchen," he said quietly to her. "Don't want anyone around here to look at it."

"That is," I added, "if they can read at all."

Hazel nodded and took the paper—and our orders—back with her to the kitchen.

When trays filled with plates of steaks and potatoes and eggs and gallons of black coffee were carried to our tables by both Hazel and Bessie, I noticed that not only was Hazel looking sad, but, amazingly enough, so was Bessie. A few times as she was serving us, I found her looking at me with sympathy. But then some outlaw made a demand for service and she had to scoot over quickly to his table.

As Hazel put down our plates, not that either of us were very hungry at that moment, and mugs of coffee, she whispered to me and Ty, "Another girl will come in in another twenty minutes and I can take a break then. Meet me in front of Sadie's Hat Shop a few doors down from here."

Then she continued down to the other tables without missing a beat. It was then I noticed Ira looking at us when he saw Hazel pause a little longer at our end than usual. I wondered what he was thinking. To look like I hadn't noticed his curiosity, I quickly started eating my food. Ty ate his as well, for despite our mutual depression, we found ourselves famished and devoured everything on our plates and drained the coffees. Ty and I had to endure the Hennessey Gang's bad table manners, like belching, spitting and loud belches which could be heard in Nevada.

When we were through and everyone rose at one stage or another from their chairs, instead of going to the outhouses in the back, Ty and me slipped out the hotel's front door and in less than a minute, found Sadie's Hat Shop.

She was there waiting for us. She was still wearing a white waitress getup, but she had her shawl over it and her little hat was atop her head.

"Thank God I was able to get you boys away from them!"

I looked back toward the hotel. Luckily, it seemed that two of the gang had gotten into some kind of argument and before you knew it, they were slugging each other and soon rolling around in the street as the others cheered for either one or the other. Finch watched them looking bored stiff. That's when I saw Hiram Jessup leave the hotel and come up to Finch. I noticed that the surly paper-pusher didn't eat with us earlier. As the two men were rolling around in the dust and spilling blood, Jessup said something to Finch and then the two disappeared back into the hotel. Watching the crowd, I saw Andrew, as well as the others, cheering on the fight. Only one man wasn't: Ira Toombs. He was standing on the sidewalk, watching us in front of Sadie's.

Before Hazel could say anything else, I stopped her and said quietly, "Ira's watchin' us like a hawk."

Hazel said, "Let's take a slow walk."

Ty added, "In the opposite direction."

"Well, they can't think we're running out on 'em. Our animals are still tied up back there."

In mutual agreement, we went down the boardwalk and the noise of the fight and the cheering fell away as we talked.

"I'm sorry," said Hazel.

"What have you got to be sorry about?" asked Ty. "You didn't break into Old Man Reynolds's store right after the Hennessey gang robbed it. We did."

I cut in, "Don't get mad at Hazel! She was only saying she was sorry we're in this fix."

Ty said sincerely, "Sorry, Hazel."

"That's all right, Ty. I wish I could do something for you boys."

Ty said, "Well, unless you can get Marshal Clell to back off having us shot on sight..."

"Never trusted that law dog," I said sullenly. "Reynolds always had him in his back pocket."

"Yeah, I think the old man gave him discounts or something."

"What Ma and Pa are probably thinking of us now..."

Hazel said, "I don't think they think any less of you

and Ty. I always remembered the Brodys as wonderful people."

That's when Ty stopped and turned to stare at her.

He asked, "You met our folks?"

I said, "Look at her again, Ty. That blonde girl who used to babysit me when I was a kid."

Ty stared hard at Hazel as she stood there, a bit ill at ease under the scrutiny.

He said, "Take off your hat."

She untied the little hat and took it off, patting her hair down after she did so.

Still staring, Ty finally said to her, "I don't believe it. *You!*"

She gave a wan little smile and nodded. "Um-hm."

I said, "Yeah, after so many years."

Ty said to me, "And you had the biggest crush on her too!"

Suddenly he realized what he had just said. As Hazel was reminded of my affection for her, she got all uncomfortable and looked at the ground.

Ty started lamely, "Um, well, anyway..."

Partly to alleviate her discomfort, I blurted out, "You don't know all of it."

Ty stared hard at me and asked, "What's that supposed to mean?"

"We'll talk about it later. We have other problems right now."

"I'll say. You and me are wanted men." He gestured back at the Hennesseys. "To the law, we're no different than they are."

"And that means we can't go back, can we?"

"Unless you want a posse to shoot us or face the hangman."

"We're dead either way."

Hazel said sincerely, "There *must* be some way to prove that you weren't involved in that killing or the robbery."

"Sure," said Ty wryly. "All we have to do is capture the gang. And I don't know about you, little brother, but I value my head bein' attached to my body."

Hazel looked at him strangely and said, "*What*?"

"Forget it," I said. "It's too awful to repeat."

Hazel suddenly took my wrist and squeezed it. Deadly serious, she stared at me and said, "Jed, are you saying that they...they *mutilated* someone?"

Me and Ty gave each other looks.

"*Decapitated* is more like it," he said.

Though still holding onto my wrist, she faced Ty and asked, "Who was it?"

"Some reporter for a newspaper in Telluride. He figured he could infiltrate the Hennesseys. He was wrong..."

I piped in, "You know 'em, Hazel. The nervous one you served the other day asking about how to find the Hennesseys."

Hazel let go of my wrist and thought back. "Oh, yes, now I remember...*Jesus*! No wonder he was so scared. His boss probably insisted he take this assignment."

"Yeah, his last one."

Hazel then turned to me and asked, with growing desperation, "One thing I've got to know, Jed. Did the Toombs brothers have anything to do with the killing? Did *Ira*?"

I paused and stared at her, wondering why it mattered so much to her if the Toombs boys were responsible for that reporter's horrible death, especially Ira.

Ty cut in with, "You could ask him yourself, here he comes."

Ira walked up to us and said, casually enough, "Is this a private meeting or can I join in?"

"Sure, Ira," said Hazel lightly. "We were just walking a little, getting away from all that ruckus up the street." Self-consciously, she put her little hat back on and tied the string under her chin.

Ira's eyes went to all of us, and he paused a little before speaking. What was going through his mind I didn't know. That is, until he casually started to roll a cigarette and, as he lit it, asked, "You three are getting awful chummy in a hurry. You're not holding anything out on us, are you?"

With a smile wider than she felt like making, Hazel said, "Well, yeah, we are, Ira." I wasn't prepared when she put her arm around my shoulders and said, "I knew Jed many years ago. In fact, I used to babysit him for his family."

Ira quickly blew out some smoke and raised his eyebrows at that one. "Do tell?"

"Yep," she nodded, still smiling.

"Well, he's not a baby anymore, so maybe you'd best get your arm off him."

Hazel instantly dropped her smile and quickly took her arm off me. Ty and I shot each other looks. Seeing this, Ira turned away and firmly said, "Let's get back to the others. Finch has another job in mind for us..."

As Ira walked away, he didn't see the looks of dread on our three faces...

CHAPTER TEN

As we followed Ira down the street, at a distance of course, Ty said to me, "When we were talking about Hazel being your babysitter years ago, you said to me, 'You don't know all of it.' What did you mean by that?"

I replied, "It means that our beautiful waitress back there is closer to me than just being a babysitter. And it all happened before my folks were killed and your folks took me in..."

For what little time I had as we walked, I told him the important details of Hazel's turning out to be my big sister, a kind of abbreviated, hop-skip-and-jump version of the story she told me when we were taking our walk in another part of Dentonville.

Ty stared at me, shaking his head.

"She's your *sister*!"

I nodded.

He looked at the ground for some time, trying to make sense of it, trying to accept the fact that he was literally no longer my only sibling.

Then, as he watched the street ahead of him, he said

earnestly, "Jed. I didn't want to say this, but you know I have to."

I had a feeling about what he was going to say.

He paused before he said, "I see the way you look at Hazel. The way you risk a beating defending her. I thought before that it was just a crush on a beautiful older woman. But now, after what you just told me, this is getting to be kind of...ya know..."

"Don't say it, Ty."

"I won't, Jed. It should be obvious what it is..."

Yeah, I thought. *It was.*

To everyone but me...

———

WE HAD all assembled in a closed-off back room of a dump called the Wildkat Saloon—*again* with the misspelling. The other cowboys in the front room steered very clear of us as we literally took over the back and sat around the tables in various chairs, with long legs and booted feet outstretched and settled on other tables and other chairs, opened bottles of whiskey everywhere and much cigarette smoke floating up to the cheap lamp above. The drinks were never paid for, of course and no one in their right mind knocked on the old wooden door or came near us unless it was to get us drinks, much less disturbed us as we discussed our pressing *business*.

Finch sat on a long table, put his boot on a turned-around chair and said, "Hiram over there has informed me that a big payroll is coming through our range any day now."

I looked at Hiram Jessup seated at a table all the way

in the back of the room, conveniently *outside* our circle, gazing at Finch sourly.

After pausing for any reaction, Finch continued, "Our friends who work for the Butterfield stage say it's coming in a strongbox. The money's goin' to Fort Garland..."

One man asked, "That's in New Mexico, ain't it?"

Finch stared at him and the man suddenly found a reason to look at the floor.

"Like I was sayin', it's going to Fort Garland. Now I heard that those bluecoats haven't been paid in a few months so we're talking a haul of at least fifty or sixty thousand dollars, maybe more. Actually, if that money includes officers' pay, and I'm pretty sure it will, we're *really* talking eighty thousand or more. We know the route and we know when it's gonna come through, which'll be sometime in late morning, maybe noon. All in all, it should be easy pickin's..."

Taking Finch's pause as an opportunity for questions, Arch spat some juice on the floor and asked, "How many guards?"

Finch looked at him and paused, not because he was annoyed at the interruption, but because he seemed, for once, uncertain how to answer the question.

"Not sure," Finch responded. "Our contacts still have to get back to us with that information."

Ben remarked, "That's a nice haul."

"Damn right," said Stu. "I wouldn't mind findin' that much money under my Christmas tree."

Others around the group nodded their approval, all except me and Ty, who were horrified by the prospect of attacking a stagecoach under federal guard. However, in the next instant, it seemed someone else agreed with us.

When Finch asked if anyone had any problems with the job, Jessup instantly called out, "Yeah! I do!"

Finch kind of smirked and said wryly, "Well, Uncle Hiram, we're not exactly expecting you to saddle up with us and start fannin' a gun like some old-style desperado. We'll handle the heavy work, if you don't mind..." The remark brought a few laughs from his men, but Jessup stuck to his guns—pardon the expression.

Ignoring the jibe, Jessup said, "You're telling us that you're going to attack a coach going through territory you're not familiar with and guarded by federal troops, of which you don't know the exact number, lift a strongbox and ride twenty or thirty miles back to your home base without getting so much as a scratch? Is that right, Clay?"

Finch wasn't smiling as he stared back at him all the way across the room. It was obvious he didn't appreciate his uncle's sarcastic tone.

Without emotion, Finch answered, "Yeah, Hiram, that's about the size of it."

Jessup said, "Shit!" with such contempt we actually saw spittle fly out of his mouth, belying his usually refined appearance. Everyone looked at each other and I could see that Finch tensed up right away. The Toombs brothers glanced at each other without expression, choosing to stay out of any donnybrook between Finch and his ornery uncle.

Jessup said bluntly, "Finch, you don't know dick about New Mexico Territory and you know it!"

I noticed Finch's face redden briefly. Then he replied, "That's not for you to say, clerk!"

Now it was Jessup's turn to redden with both embarrassment and rage. The *clerk* name must've hit him hard.

"All right!" said Jessup, leaning forward in his chair. His remarks were directed to Finch, but I had a feeling he was also addressing the gang. "I'll talk so plain and simple even *you* can understand me! You're going into this blind! You and your gunslinging sheep over here! The federals may not be able to hit a can at fifty paces, but there'll be enough of 'em to shoot your boys out of the saddle and not even take the time to bury your sorry butts! They'll blow you wide open! And even if you kill some of them and ride away clean, there'll be federal warrants for your arrest from Montana to the Texas border. Before, the government didn't give a damn what you boys did locally, including murder and robbery. But you start taking their money away from them and killing their men to boot, they won't stop until you're all dangling from a rope!"

Finch said loudly, "We'll have enough protection!"

Jessup sighed angrily and shook his head as if he had just been talking to a recalcitrant child.

"Don't you *get it*? The governor and the rest of his bootlickers let you stay where you are and do what you do as long as you stay in your own bailiwick and keep the killings low-profile. They're making a bundle off us, but don't think that they accept graft because they love us. The minute the jobs get out of hand and the public thinks they're soft on outlaws, they'll stab you in the back so deep you'll never recover! And as soon as that happens, the citizens of this wonderful town you've been lording over will finally find their balls and finish you off—like pigs in a slaughterhouse!"

What Jessup said left everybody uncomfortable,

even the Toombs boys. Ty and me looked at each other and knew it was true. We couldn't go back to our home and, according to Jessup's predictions, we couldn't stay either!

Finch was furious, and for a second, his right hand actually brushed the butt of the gun at his hip.

"Then why the hell did you tell me about the job in the first place?"

Jessup replied, "I was warning you that federal troops were going to be on the move south of here and you wanted to know why. I'm sorry now that I told you! I only wanted your boys to stay north of the New Mexico border. I wasn't endorsing the idea of stealing a fucking army payroll!"

Finch just stared at him, like he was trying to make up his mind whether to call him names or just ignore him.

He finally made up his mind.

"Hiram, why don't you wait outside? Get yourself a drink at the bar. Don't worry, you won't have to pay for it..."

Jessup stared back at him, scowling. You could see that the not-paying-for-the-drink jibe insulted him. Rising from his chair, he kept his eyes on Finch and said bitterly, "I don't want any favors from you, nephew. I'll pay for my own..."

And so he left us, slamming the door so hard it was like a gun going off.

Acting as if Jessup wasn't ever in the room, Finch leaned forward, his hands cuffed over his knee, his boot planted on the chair under him.

"I think it's worth a try. We'll keep pressing our contact at Butterfield for information on that troop escort, but overall, I think the rewards are worth the risks."

Ben's voice rumbled. "I'm with ya, Clay."

With a mouthful of tobacco, Arch echoed, "So am I."

Others in the room nodded or voiced their agreement. Seeing themselves outnumbered, the Toombs boys quietly nodded as well, though I got the impression both of them weren't crazy about the plan. Then, with everyone counted, Finch looked down at us—we weren't far from the front—and asked, "And what about our two transplanted farm boys? With this haul, they'll *really* remember you in Beaumont."

With that statement, I instantly knew that Finch had seen the newspaper we had swiped off the table. He figured we were going the outlaw way whether we liked it or not. Under the circumstances, what could we do? The alternative might've been fatal.

We agreed to the robbery...

CHAPTER ELEVEN

WE RODE BACK TO THE DOVER HOUSE. ALL ALONG THE trail, we toyed with the idea of just riding the hell off, getting as far away from the Hennessey Gang as we could, put miles between us and Clay Finch Hennessey's ambitious plan to shoot up an escort of cavalry troops and steal a payroll which would make the gang marked men for every lawman and cavalry trooper in the territory once and for all. Oh yes, we believed every word Hiram Jessup said about the whole plan. We considered riding the hell out of there, but we didn't do it. Indeed, had we just ridden away, and not gotten shot in the back as we did so, where the hell were we going to go? With no money and no one to shelter us, we could've plodded along on the trails hungry, tired, and cold until either some law dog or vigilante shot us from ambush. For what it was worth, with the Hennesseys we had free food, a place to stay and were well-protected from any posse from Beaumont looking to capture the *notorious* young murderers of Old Man Reynolds.

As soon as we arrived at the Dover House and the

horses were unsaddled and cared for, one of the men who had been staying at the house came out on the porch and came up to Finch. He spoke quietly to him. We couldn't catch what he was saying, but his eyes went to me and Ty a couple times and it was obvious he was talking about us. Of course, Finch was far more subtle and never glanced back at us once. He nodded solemnly and put his hand on the other man's arm, gently pushing him to get back inside. Then he turned around and came up to us.

"Couple things I think you should know. One is that Ed Plummer and Jack Foster are here and they're going to help us with the army payroll job."

Ty and me did not feel good about having the two hardcases who beat us up back at the Pellican close by, but there was little we could do about it.

Seeing the concern in our faces, Finch said, "Don't worry. I'll tell both of them that if they dry-gulch either of you, they'll have to answer to me."

We respected Finch's word up to a certain point, but we weren't sure he could control those two.

Then he continued, "Also, Lone finally woke up after you slugged him. He's still mad. But I told them to tell him that I won't stand for him attacking you boys. You're both with us now. And I won't stand for any trouble in this gang. By the same token, I would look on it as bad manners if either of you boys harmed Lone in any way as well. Now is that clear?"

Ty started, "Now wait a minute, Finch—"

But I cut him off. "We *never* harmed Lone except to defend ourselves. *He's* got the problem with *us*, not the other way around."

Finch paused and said, "Yeah, I guess you're right. But I still insist you not provoke him in any way. He's got a good reason to be as angry as he is. After our pa raped that Oglala Sioux squaw, the cavalry wiped out her band and then he deserted and took the woman away. Her baby was born miles away from Dakota Territory so the army wouldn't catch him and hang him for desertion. The squaw died giving birth to Lone and Dad married a saloon gal who couldn't add two and two, but at least she gave him two boys. Needless to say, she kind of favored the white boys over the half-breed. Lone got along with us, but when Mom whipped us, she ended up whipping him a lot harder. So you see what you're dealing with."

Curiously, Ty asked, "Thought you said your dad was a poor farmer."

Warming to his subject, Finch replied, "He *was*. He and my ma moved to Colorado and tried farmin'. But he didn't like starvin' and he didn't like bein' responsible, so he cut loose from my ma and the farm faster than a Kansas twister. Heard somewhere he had his throat cut in some chippie's bedroom by her old man, but I couldn't say for sure."

I asked, "What happened to your ma?"

"She hanged herself..."

As we stood near the stable, the horses being put away and the cool wind coming down from the San Juan Mountains, we both stared at Finch, not saying anything. We weren't a bit moved by his story of why Lone Hennessey was the way he was. We figured his animosity to White people was his own personal problem, not ours. But his tale about his parents was kind of shocking for us to hear. To me and Ty, it explained a lot

—about Finch as well as his devotion to his family, come what may.

But also, I was moved by the fact that Finch would actually take the time to reveal to us some of his family history that was both personal and obviously important to him as well as the fact that, though he could've simply laid down the law to us with no ifs ands or buts, he felt it necessary to seek our understanding.

Suddenly sensing that perhaps he was revealing too much to us, he curtly said, "Get some rest. We got some plannin' to do." He turned and left us where we were as we tried to understand, not the story he had just told us, but the man who was telling it...

———

WHEN WE ENTERED THE HOUSE, we were headed for that front room they had designated as ours. But before we entered it, we saw a woman on her hands and knees in the hallway. In the partial darkness, it looked like she was rocking up and down for some reason. When we curiously moved closer, we saw that she had a bucket of soapy water near her and she was scrubbing the floor at the bottom of the stairs with a hard brush. It was Jill. She was wearing a frumpy apron, a man's old shirt, torn at the shoulder, and a pair of Levis that had seen better days. And though her dark-brown hair was pinned up, it was falling all over her eyes in loose strands. As we approached, she stopped and looked up at us. Even with her mussed hair covering her forehead, we easily saw the resentment in her reddened eyes.

Bitterly, she asked, "What now, boys? You want me to scrub the horses and clean out the stables too?"

We both felt awkward standing there looking down at her.

Innocently, I said, "We don't want you to do anything for us."

"No," she said angrily, "just polish your boots!"

"Listen," said Ty, "we're not with them."

"You're not?" she asked incredulously. Rising up on her knees, she said, "Well, the Hennesseys must be getting awfully generous letting two sodbusters stay with them for no reason."

I remembered her down-home accent, from the deep or mid-south I guessed. When she said sodbusters, I figured she might've been a child of a farming family herself, but I wasn't sure.

Still, I could see by the simmering hatred in her worn face that she totally forgot about Ty being gentlemanly enough to help her into that buckboard. To her, we were now the enemy, no better than the gang who kidnapped her and now forced her to scrub floors and break her back, two things I'm sure she *wasn't* used to.

"Now wait a minute," said Ty, "you got us wrong. We're not Hennesseys."

"No," she said resentfully, "you're just *men*. And that's bad enough!" Then she angrily threw down the brush and stood up to her full height, which was slightly shorter than me and Ty. She faced both of us and said, her voice rising, "If bein' your cook and scullery maid doesn't pay you boys back what you think I owe you, then maybe you want me upstairs in one of those moth-eaten beds like you've got Sherry!"

We looked at each other, now fully understanding how the Hennesseys are having these women *pay back* what Severin took.

Suddenly she threw her arms around my neck and started to pull my head down to her lips. "Is this what you want?" Then she planted one right on my lips as I vainly tried to pull her arms off me. Ty quickly stepped in and pulled her arms off my neck and turned her around. She struggled fiercely to break his hold and that's when she kicked his shins savagely. I looked down and saw that, instead of the high-heels she had worn when we saw her back at Kings, someone had made her wear a pair of men's boots. Therefore, when she kicked Ty's shins, it *really* hurt more than if they had been a woman's shoes.

Ty cried out and then, swinging her around into position, slapped her hard in the left cheek. For a moment, she stopped and felt her cheek, staring at Ty as she did so. Then the rage returned and she hauled off with her right fist, but Ty ducked and the swing merely knocked off his Stetson. Quickly both of us grabbed her and tried to stop her struggling form from doing either of us any harm.

Without thinking, I shouted to Ty, "And you thought she was *decent*? She's as crazy as the other one!"

"Let's get her in the room and quiet her down!"

Hearing that we were trying to quiet her down, she defiantly started screaming, not out of fear that we might harm her, but to make as much noise and grief for everyone that she could.

Hearing the ruckus, two of the boys, smiling from ear to ear, came downstairs from one of the upper floors and watched the scene. During the struggle, I glanced back at them and, to my horror, saw that it was Ed Plummer and Jack Foster.

"Well, well, it's the sodbuster trash," said Jack.

Ed added, "Finch or no Finch, I say we send 'em to hell right now."

Jack said, "Looks like that hellcat is doin' it for us."

Plummer apparently didn't like anyone getting in the way of his killing, which Jill was. Whether he was seriously going to kill us or he was just saying that to scare us, I wasn't sure. Anyway, he moved forward and drawled, "Get this tart outta here."

The two of them came up and shoved us back with such force we both hit the floor. In the narrow confines of the hallway, I fell on top of Ty and rolled over, trying to put my hands under me to get me back on my feet.

In the meantime, the two men grabbed the struggling young woman in their own hands. But they didn't count on Jill's rage, thinking they could just pull her out of the way. She resisted—in spades. Now free of us, she started fighting with *them*, kicking their shins and swinging her fists. Unlike me and Ty, who were trying to be gentlemen about it—except for Ty's slapping her, that is—the two gang members wrestled with her and cursed as she struggled even more. That's when Plummer backhanded her in the face and Jack yanked her arm far back enough to almost break it. Jill cried out as the two rushed her down the hallway and then, after Jack yanked the front door open, pulled her out onto the porch.

After they got outside, I heard Plummer shout to his partner, "This bitch needs some coolin' off!"

As Jill was dragged down the wooden front steps, she bruised both her arms and legs. Then after she hit the ground, they dragged her through the dirt, dead grass, and mud puddles across the front lawn and over to the huge wash basin which was filled with cold water.

The gang members outside the house watching the scene were all laughing. Even Finch and the Toombs brothers were amused, especially Andrew, who loved the scene. I wondered if the Toombs brothers would've been amused had they witnessed her being back-handed inside.

The two men pulled the struggling woman over to the basin. Grabbing Jill by the hair, Jack shoved her head down into the icy-cold water. In fact, he was clearly shoving her head *under* the water as the men around them clapped their hands and roared.

Me and Ty ran out of the house and moved in on them fast. Having tackled pairs of bullies before when we were kids, we immediately knew to separate, with him grabbing one man and me grabbing the other. Remembering the beating we got in the restaurant, it was easy, so I went for Ed and Ty tackled Jack.

But when I grabbed the arm of my target, Plummer instinctively struck back with his elbow and he clipped me good in the nose. I sprawled back on the ground, hat flying off and the area above my lip in pain. Sitting up on my elbows, I felt my upper lip and saw blood dripping down it. As I leaned upward about to spring off the ground, my hand closed around a rock. I glanced at it and knew what I had to do. I'd been knocked around enough by these boys and it was time to play it as they did.

Leaping off the ground, I knocked Plummer's Stetson off and swung the rock while he was still dunking Jill. Slamming it on the back of his head, I felt the sickening crunch through the rock and under my palm as it made impact. In an instant, Plummer crumpled to the ground, his face down in the dirt.

Ty was able to get Jack off Jill and shoved him back. Then he pulled Jill's head up from the water. Gasping for air, her wet brown hair in her face, she coughed loudly and let Ty hold her up. Then, taking her gently by the arm, Ty attempted to walk her away from the basin and back into the house. But he didn't get the chance. Foster came back and swung his fist right at Ty.

He connected with Ty's right cheek and came in fast, using his other arm to knock Jill out of the way. She fell limply to the ground, though she had the presence of mind to throw her hands out to break her fall. Meanwhile, Ty was getting punched around as the big bruiser moved in for the kill.

I stepped forward, ready to throw myself at the man, but that's when I heard the clicking back of a gun hammer and felt the cold barrel of a Colt pressed into my back. Another gang member was behind me. With what sounded like he was chewing tobacco, he said, "Let's just see what your brother's made of, little boy." It was Arch, the tobacco-chewing trash who almost shot me and Bessie at the restaurant. As he pressed the gunsight into my back, he cheerfully said, "Jack'll break his spine if he's able..."

I certainly didn't want to let that happen, but a gun at my back was hard to ignore.

Helplessly watching, I saw Foster belt Ty again, actually knocking him to the ground. I looked around. Finch was watching it all, his expression now blank. I wasn't sure whether he was enjoying the fight or whether he was truly looking to see if Ty would measure up. I spied the Toombs brothers off to the right. Andrew, of course, was enjoying it all, but Ira's reaction was different. He wasn't enjoying the fight like Andrew, but I could see that he had hung back because he had to, not because he wanted to. There were too many of the gang around, and they were, like animals, enjoying themselves. To interfere and spoil their fun wouldn't do. Catching my eye, I could've sworn that he was making a helpless shrug.

I looked back the other way. Wiping the blood off my nose, I saw Jill sitting up on the ground and watching the fight. Shoving the wet hair out of her eyes, she saw Ty get knocked down and her eyes widened in fear.

Foster reached down and punched Ty again as he started to rise.

Knocked back down, Ty was now prone on the ground and he looked like he was making a feeble effort to crawl away. I saw Finch shake his head, as if he expected more from Ty.

I wanted to turn around and belt Arch for pressing a Colt against my back and keeping me from helping my brother. But I figured this man would kill me just as he'd spit his tobacco, which he did often as the fight went on, several times barely missing my face. I heard his laugh every time after he spat.

Then things changed in a hurry. Ty suddenly reached out with both hands and yanked Foster's feet out from under him. Caught off guard, the big man tumbled back onto the ground, arms upraised. After he landed, Ty was on him, striking fast with his right and then following up with his left, all on Jack's face. He had clearly not expected Ty to rebound so quickly—or pull a dirty fighting tactic like that, but it did the trick; it killed the momentum in Foster's attack.

Soon, the two of them rolled over and over across

the lawn as everyone cheered. I have to say, I've seen Ty in fights before—we've had a few ourselves—but I never saw him this angry. The two soon stopped rolling and both of them struggled to rise to their feet, but neither man would let the other up. Furiously, Ty plowed his fist into Foster's stomach and I saw the bigger man grimace in pain. Then he followed up with a few punches to his opponent's head.

As he sat on top of his opponent's prone figure, I heard Ty say, "This time, you haven't got a chair to help you, Foster..."

Looking across the lawn, I saw Jill watching the fight as well. Was I mistaken or did I see her give a kind of weak smile?

The gun suddenly pushed into the small of my back and Arch said, "You better hope your friend don't win this one or I might put one in 'em for fun..."

I turned around for a moment and glimpsed the grizzled, smiling face, missing more than one tooth in a tobacco juice stained mouth. He was not as tall as me, this was emphasized by the low placement of the gun barrel in my back. But I didn't care if he was four feet high or nine, it would've been my great pleasure to clock him in that ugly, yellow-stained teeth smiling thing he called a face.

I turned back in time to see that Jack had shoved Ty over and he had rolled on top again. Pressing his right hand all over Ty's face and pinning his head to the ground, Foster reached across the ground with his free hand for something to clobber him with. In fact, he easily found the very same rock I had used to put Plummer out of the running. He quickly covered it with the long fingers of his free hand and was about to lift it.

Gun or no gun at my back, I *had* to stop this.

I started to rush forward, but on the first step, I felt something pull my foot out from under me and I fell to the ground with my hands breaking my fall just before my face hit the dirt. It was Arch who tripped me. I heard him laughing loudly after I hit the ground. Then a glob of spat tobacco juice struck me behind my right ear. It was hot, wet, and stung a lot. But before I could rise, the action a few feet on the ground in front of me drew my attention.

Ty had used his own fingers to gouge into Jack's eyes. Screaming, he let go of Ty's face and swung with the rock, but by then Ty moved out of position and it struck the ground behind him. Rolling over, Foster was now on the ground and Ty was once again on top. With his right hand, he chopped down on Foster's wrist and forced him to let go of the rock. Then he bashed him in the face with his other hand. In short order, his fists kept smashing into Jack's face until it was bloody as hell. Then he picked his head up by the hair and continued the punching, though he was aiming for his eyes. In just a few seconds, Ty was no longer punching someone who was conscious, but a man who was now beaten, bloody and out cold, though Ty was slow to realize it, he was so enraged.

I smiled at the sight, and when I faced Jill while I was still sprawled on the ground, I saw she was now openly glad at the turnout of the fight.

But the man who held the cocked gun on me wasn't. Arch raised it and had a bead on Ty when I took a page out of his book and used my own long legs to trip him. But after I swept my feet into his legs and they buckled, his gun suddenly fired. Right away I heard a scream from across the lawn.

I looked across the lawn just in time to see Ben grasp his stomach and double over. This happened as I glimpsed the Toombs boys grab Ty and pull him up off of Foster. Then I felt fingers hook into my left shoulder as a gun barrel was swung in my direction. Arch was trying to club me down with his Colt, but I had seen the movement out of the corner of my eye and I blocked him with my hand. With the other, I smashed him in the side of his still-chewing face and we rolled over onto the ground. I was soon on top and I pinned his arm with the gun still in it. I gleefully punched him in the left eye with my other hand, and then, thinking back to the chopping motion I saw Ty do with Foster, I flattened my fingers and chopped him right across the throat. But as my fingers finished the motion, a weird thing happened. His face turned blood red in a second and he opened his mouth helplessly. I stared at him oddly. He was choking on the tobacco that he was chewing—now on his back, and with my neck-chop to aid it, the awful stuff got stuck in his windpipe and stayed there.

Someone, a gang member, yanked me off of him and threw me aside. Then he and another man tried to turn Arch over and induce vomiting, but after a few chaotic seconds they could see it was useless. In fact, the gang was now divided into uselessly helping Ben and uselessly helping Arch who was slowly and painfully choking on his own crud.

Ignoring Arch, I went over to Ty, who was still being held by Ira and Andrew. "You all right?"

"Yeah, for whatever that's worth," he answered

tiredly, still getting his breath after the fight. Gradually, they let him stand on his own.

Andrew said happily, "I knew I was right about you two! You're *both* wildcats!"

Ignoring him, I spied Finch bent over Ben with a few others. I saw him solemnly get to his feet and I heard him say, "He's dead..."

If this weren't shocking enough, the men who were bending over the tobacco-chewer stood back and one of them said, "Arch is a goner too."

Finch stood there and stared at him. Angrily, he said, "What?"

The man said quietly, "The wad o' tobacco and all that juice cut off his air. He's deader than Lincoln..."

The shock on Finch's face was something to see. Slowly he and the others stared at us. The law couldn't get them, but with one fell swoop, two of their own were dead, including Finch's brother.

Finch stared at us for just a moment, and he looked like he was about to explode. Suddenly, he drew his gun. I don't think I was so scared in my life as when he did that. I thought for sure that Finch was going to drill both of us for what happened to his brother. It was an accident and it wouldn't have happened if Arch didn't have a gun in his fist and pulled the trigger when he did.

I wondered if Finch understood that too.

Ignoring us, he suddenly went up to Arch's prone figure and fired at him again and again until his gun was empty.

The man who pronounced Arch dead looked up at Finch and said, "I said he was already dead, Finch..."

Finch just glared at the man with such rage that I actually saw this tough hombre swallow hard and back away. Still, after Finch holstered his gun, I could see that he was trying his damnedest to calm down.

I looked over the grounds. Ed and Jack were both still out cold. Across the way, Ben was dead, and not far from me, Arch, with his bloody chest, head and stomach full of bullets and his throat full of tobacco. Only Jill was missing from the scene. The little minx we had fought and apparently killed men over had flown the coop, probably while everyone's attention was on the various fights taking place all over the front lawn. Certainly, two men dying within seconds of each other because of me and Ty wasn't what we had in mind when we decided to protect this apparently ungrateful young woman.

Damsels in distress, you can't trust 'em...

Andrew made that plain when he said, "Hell, boys, I'm glad the fight stopped when it did or you would've wiped out all of us!" It was meant to be a joke, but I could see that it wasn't funny to Finch and the others.

They started to move toward us when Ty shouted, "Accidents, Finch! They were both freak accidents!"

One of the gang said, "You killed two of our own! Fuck that accident shit!"

I knew I couldn't get the gang to understand me, so my next remark was directed to Finch. But instead of simply explaining, I ended up sounding angrier than I wanted to.

"There was a fight goin' on and no one did anything to stop it! Ty could've gotten his skull crushed in and you boys would've just shrugged it off, saying he couldn't measure up to being in the gang. Well, you got what you wanted. He measured up all right, but you lost two men."

I gradually started to hear the cocking of guns near me and I soon realized that Ira and Andrew had drawn their guns as well, but instead of us, they were training their weapons on the gang. What I said was defiant and might not have been the right thing to say, but it impressed the Toombs brothers enough to back us up.

Ira said, in his usual quiet but firm manner, "He's right, Clay. Hangin' these two out to dry ain't gonna bring Ben back..."

That wasn't exactly what I said, but I kind of expected Ira to say things his own way.

Finch stood there for a moment that seemed to last forever. You could tell the whole thing was heavy on his mind. Through avoidable accidents, he had lost two of his men, including his brother. Hell, they hadn't even been killed during a robbery! And now he had to deal with his own gang who wanted to lynch the two farm boys he happened to like.

Finch stared at the Toombs boys and asked, "You'd shoot us to save them?"

With an eternal twinkle in his eye, Andrew replied, "Well, Clay, it's like this. We just happened to be pointing our iron at you boys and nothin' happens. But if they decide to lay a hand on Ty or Jed, they might suddenly go off."

Ty and me tried to keep a straight face at that one.

Then, in the middle of this impasse, the lanky outlaw named Stu said, "Finch, I think I've got a way of settling this mess..."

Finch asked, "And how's that?"

"It's private..."

And so, as Finch and Stu walked away a few yards and spoke quietly to each other, the rest of the gang watched us. With the Toombs boys drawing a bead on them, they dared not reach for their holstered guns.

Ed and Jack were still out cold on the lawn, their own bruises remained unattended.

Somehow I saw the humor in this standoff and I said to the gang, "Nice weather, ain't it?"

My response was a glob of spit spat onto the ground from a gang member in the forefront of the group.

Andrew, amused, just said, "Some folks don't like discussin' the weather..."

We watched Finch and Stu in the distance. Finch cocking an ear to listen to what the taller man had to say. I wondered what it was.

Then Finch turned around and said, "I think everybody should cool down. What happened were accidents and that's how we're gonna take it."

I could see the anger and disappointment from the others, though I noticed that Ira and Andrew still had their guns out and were just as prepared to use them as ever.

Finch then said, "I want to talk to all of you."

The gang started to follow him as he and Stu started to walk outside the fence.

The four of us started to follow them when Finch said, "Not you boys. I'm just trying to calm down some bad feeling against you so it wouldn't make sense for you to hear what I've got to say." His next words, however, were for me and Ty. "Don't you boys try to leave the property. Not a good idea right now." He then turned to two men and told them to hang around and make sure we didn't leave the grounds. To Ira and Andrew, he said, "Why don't you boys take a ride into town and get a drink or something?" When they paused, Finch said, "You have my word nothing will happen to them..."

They looked at each other and then, hesitantly, they holstered their guns. We looked at them then.

Ira answered our looks. "Finch Hennessey may be a lot of things, but I've never known him to break his word."

Considering that Clay Finch Hennessey robbed and killed, but didn't break his word, wasn't exactly a comfort to me and Ty, but what else were we to do? If this were indeed a time to *cool off*, we welcomed every chance we got not to be killed...

CHAPTER TWELVE

TY AND I WERE LYING DOWN ON OUR MOLDY MATTRESSES, jackets and Stetsons off and using damp rags from the water basin to dab our various wounds from the fights. Ira and Andrew had ridden to town as Finch had advised, and Finch and the rest were nowhere to be seen. Maybe they were around the property, maybe they weren't, I wasn't sure. Ed Plummer and Jack Foster weren't around either, though I assumed that wherever they were, they must've been hurting something awful.

Certainly, if this was a period to *cool down*, then I wasn't anxious to find any of them anyway. But there *were* maybe two or three of them wandering around the property keeping an eye on things_in other words, their job was to make sure me and Ty didn't get to the stables, grab a pair of animals, and ride away from the Hennesseys, never to return. And, wanted dead or alive or not, they couldn't take a chance we'd ride over to some town with a law dog who wasn't on their payroll and spill everything about the gang that was worth spilling.

Trying to get my mind off the trap we were in, I said, "I *never* saw you fight like that, Ty."

He replied, "I never had a bruiser like that to fight, Jed..."

That was when we heard a knock on the door.

We looked at each other.

Ty asked, "Think it's one of 'em lookin' to put a bullet in us?"

I replied, "If it is, then they're being awful polite about it..."

That made sense to him, so he called out, "Come in."

The door hesitantly swung open and who should be standing there, but Jill, the woman we had both fought to protect, especially Ty. Her brown hair down about her shoulders. There was still a huge red blotch on her cheek where Ed had backhanded her and we could plainly see the ugly bruises through rips in her torn man's shirt and pants. Standing there and looking at us, she paused before entering. Vainly she pushed back her still-damp hair out of her eyes.

"Can I come in?" she asked meekly.

Ty answered, "Sure."

She entered and closed the door behind her. Right away that said to both me and Ty that she trusted us. There was no rage at all in her now. She seemed as quiet and docile as a kitten.

She looked down at her scuffed man's boots for a moment, not knowing how to begin.

That's when I said, "You owe us nothing."

In a voice that was barely above a whisper, she said, "I'm not so sure..."

Suddenly realizing that we were addressing a young

woman while lying back on a couple of mattresses, we both sat up. Self-consciously, Ty gestured to a chair with moth-eaten upholstery. Jill looked at it and hesitated, studying the thing as if it were full of worms, which it probably was. Could it be that this former saloon girl *did* have some standards? Seeing her hesitate, Ty quickly pulled off his own sheet and stood up. He draped the thing over the seat of the chair. She looked at him and gave a wan smile; then she sat down on the sheet.

Ty sat back down on the mattress, but he made sure he didn't lie back on it.

He said to her, "Um, just want to say that...I'm sorry about slapping you. It was a stupid thing for me to do..." Ty had already forgotten that she was kicking him in the shins just before he slapped her.

Jill looked at him intently and absently felt her cheek.

"Yes," she said, maybe with a little iron in her voice, "yes, it was."

Then there was an awkward silence, as if we were not only uncomfortable giving apologies, but didn't quite know how to react to them when they were given.

I decided to straighten things out.

"You were kicking Ty in the shins..."

Jill's eyes lit up at my comment.

Ty quickly said to her, "Forget it."

"No, he's right," she said. "I don't like bein' slapped by any man, but I guess you don't like getting bruises on your legs."

"You kick hard," he said.

"In the saloons, when randy men start pawin' you

like you're their personal property, it's best to kick 'em where it hurts."

Ty and I glanced at each other.

Jill added, "Still, there wasn't any excuse for attacking you. I...I guess they were just workin' me too hard and I..." She shrugged helplessly and blurted out, "I just went crazy!"

Ty said, "I'm starting to see that the Hennesseys have that effect on people."

She smiled at what he said, and it was a pretty smile too. Complimented by the blue eyes and down-home accent, she looked—and probably was—pleasant company to a man on a lonely night, or at any other time of the day as well.

She eventually came to the point when she said, "I'm sorry for you boys getting hurt over me."

"We usually get hurt nowadays for a lot less," said Ty.

She smiled briefly, then looked at us and said seriously, "I've heard of the Hennesseys long before they ever came to Telluride and got us fired. For you two to go up against them, I don't think I've ever seen two more brave men since my daddy, and he had a ball in his leg from fightin' in Bull Run and Vicksburg."

We weren't too comfortable being compared to war heroes, even if they were on the losing side.

Suddenly our discomfort was rudely interrupted by a loud cranking noise from above us.

We all looked up at the ceiling. The cranking seemed steady and with a certain rhythm to it, but what we heard wasn't any music accompanying it. Me and Ty knowingly looked at each other when we heard the moans, loud, ecstatic sounds which at times rose to screams. Then we heard them punctuated by small impacts of some kind. It took us a moment or two before we realized they were slaps. We both looked at Jill.

Red-faced, her eyes cast downward, she just said, "Sherry..."

We went back to being uncomfortable, but this time for different reasons.

Then Ty said to Jill, "Maybe I don't have a right to ask this—"

Knowing where he was headed, Jill cut him off with, "Go ahead, *ask*."

Ty used his index finger and indicated the ceiling. "Do they have *you* doing that?"

Jill looked at him intently and asked, "Would it make a difference to you if they did?"

Ty hesitated and looked at the floor. I could see how awkward the question was for him, though he felt it was something he had to ask. At the same time, he also knew it was none of his business.

Jill saved him the trouble of answering when she said gently, "No, Ty, they don't have me doing what Sherry's doin'..."

We both took a moment to think about that. But without our prompting, Jill added, "They've got me doing all the cooking and the housework, and they've got Sherry doing...what she does best." She gave a weak smile to that last remark.

Then, as if she knew we were talking about her, Sherry gave a loud shout which, though muffled through the floorboards above, still hurt our ears.

I said, "Too bad we can't go somewhere else to talk."

Jill said, "Our movements are kinda what you call

restricted. They're hanging around watching us, making sure we don't pull a getaway. Anyway, this is the only time I've had to relax since they kidnapped us."

I scanned the ceiling. Suddenly the creaking and the other noises stopped.

Jill sighed and said, "Sherry and whoever's ridin' her are done..."

Ty said wryly, "Paul Revere would be proud..."

Jill looked at both of us and said, "You're not like the others. You both look like you actually give a damn about people. I heard one of 'em even call you farm boys."

"'Cause that's what we are," I said.

Then we told her who we are and how we got in this mess.

"Jesus," she said. "I've seen a bad shuffle of the cards before, but not like this."

We both didn't say anything to that. It was obvious she was right.

"Let me ask you something, Ty."

Ty said to her, "Sure."

After a slight pause, she asked, "Do you like me?"

I started to rise and said, "Maybe I better leave..."

She quickly said, "No, Jed, stay..."

I sat back down.

Jill then stared at Ty and said, "I ask that because I remember while you two were trying to get me to calm down, Jed said to you, 'And you thought she was decent. She's as crazy as the other one.'"

We both remembered now. You'd think she was too busy fighting with us to remember a comment like that. For a saloon gal, this one had a good memory for little details that had nothing to do with playing cards or randy patrons.

I admitted I said it.

She smiled then and looked at him. She said gently, "Thanks, Ty. I think you're decent too." Turning a shade of bright red, he avoided her eyes.

Jill got up then.

"Now I don't feel so alone. Hopefully, we'll all find a way to get out of here."

She turned to leave, but Ty said, "Don't go."

"I have to. Sun's setting and I'm pretty sure they want me to fix 'em dinner. What I wouldn't give for a bottle of poison..."

We said our goodbyes and she left.

I said, "She likes you."

"She likes both of us."

"Yeah, but I'm younger than her. You're closer to her age."

Changing the subject, he asked, "What do you think they have in mind for us?"

"I don't know," I replied, "but I have a feeling we might not survive the experience..."

CHAPTER THIRTEEN

MOST OF THE TIME, THE GANG ATE THEIR DINNER IN town, but of course now that they had an actual woman with them doing the cooking, things were a little different. Only this time, to keep up the *cooling off* order issued by Finch, just a couple of men sat at the table with me and Ty as Jill served us. They were our guards who were tasked to see that we didn't stray too far from home base. Jill's cooking wasn't bad, considering what she had to work with, which wasn't much—the Hennesseys were not big on shopping for foodstuffs— but at least we were fed. Unfortunately, we had to sit there and watch poor Jill get her butt pinched more than once by one or the other man who sat on the other side of the table. It seemed every time she passed them, they grinned and gave her a squeeze with one of their paws. You could tell by the crestfallen look on her face that she felt humiliated as she passed quickly through with another empty tray she had to scrub clean in the already dirty sink. It was hard not to ignore them grinning widely in our direction after one or the other pinched Jill, like they were purposely trying to provoke us into doing something about it.

We said nothing to them, but the tension was definitely there. Through their conversation with each other—possibly said for our benefit—we learned that Ed Plummer now has frequent headaches and vision problems, thanks to my conking him with that rock, and that Jack Foster, who was beaten so badly by Ty, will survive. But just to make it clear to Ty, they insisted that Jack could still fan a gun—as if we really cared at this point.

We also heard from them that Lone Hennessey had gone to town with them. They also guessed that while in town Lone might even have a drink or two—and we all knew what a wild man *the chief* could be with some booze in his system. Of course, as they said this, their eyes were sneaking little peaks at us as they smiled playfully. I wanted badly to slam my plate into their faces.

They weren't wearing their guns, but they were lying on the table before them within easy reach. You could tell they were just itching to use them on me and Ty should we decide to interfere with their molesting of Jill. I didn't like seeing her getting pinched, but it must've been infuriating for Ty to sit there and watch it. I figured he was really starting to like her. Of course, that meant nothing if these guys killed us, so he had to keep his peace.

Still, we waited until they were finished and left the room before we left Jill alone.

After they left, she said quietly, "I know what you boys are doin' and I appreciate it, but those two are clearly tryin' to provoke you."

Before we could deny it, she added, "Listen, I've

been fightin' off randy men at Kings, so I can take care of myself. Anyway, if they hurt me seriously, Finch would be mad at 'em because I couldn't work off my *debt*."

She smiled at us, then turned around and focused her attention on the dishes.

Satisfied, we wandered out to the front porch.

The night was cool and a full moon cast a bright light onto the surrounding forest. The front of the house was facing the moon and Ty and I saw each other clearly, but there was still darkness and shadows beneath the porch's overhang.

For us, it was a much-needed break from fights and beatings and seeing others beaten as well. We both seemed relaxed and comfortable as we stood on the top step and looked out into the night. Then we both glanced back at the stables not far from the right side of the house.

Ty said, "So close, yet so far..."

"It's quiet out here."

Actually, it wasn't *that* quiet, with small animals and birds making their usual racket close by.

I asked him, "Think we should make a break for the horses?"

"No," he replied.

"Why?"

As if to answer me, a cough was suddenly heard from the direction of the stables.

I looked at him. Either the horses were getting a cold or our watchdogs were hovering near the stables, just to make sure Ty and me didn't suddenly decide to take a spur-of-the-moment night ride.

Ty said, "I saw the moon cast their long shadows

near the stables. I wouldn't be surprised if those two slept with the horses."

"Looking at 'em, that somehow makes sense."

We stood there for a while breathing in the cool, fresh Southern Colorado air and saying nothing, both of us lost in our own thoughts. I assumed his might've been on Jill since he glanced back at the house a few times, clearly worried about her. He also kept looking toward the stables to see if the two outlaws wandered off and abandoned their posts.

As for me, my mind wandered to thoughts of Bessie. The two words that came to mind when I thought of her were stubborn and infuriating. But even I had to admit it took guts for her to wade right in and stand up to those outlaws bullying little John.

In fact, we were both so preoccupied with our problems that it took a long time before we started to smell cigarette smoke hovering in the cool air around us. We looked at each other with a question on our faces.

"Them?" I asked.

"I've been keeping an eye on 'em. They're still back there guarding the stable."

"Then who's smoking that awful tobacco?"

Then we heard a deep, drawling voice say, "I am..."

We glanced at each other and then turned back toward the end of the porch. The spot we were looking at was in total darkness, but for a red pinhole wandering back and forth to where a man's mouth would be, the pinhole glowing brighter every time the figure inhaled.

Curiously, we walked over to the figure, who was apparently seated in one of the porch chairs. As we got closer, we saw more of the man, with some spill of moonlight reflected off his hands and shoulders as he sat forward every once in a while. I saw the shape of the head and there was something familiar about him, though I was certain I'd never met the man.

"Go ahead," he said, gesturing to two chairs. "Sit down."

Instinctively, both of us not trusting him, we instead decided to sit on the porch railing, positioning ourselves on either side of him. This also allowed some of the moon to show him more so we'd know what he was doing.

"Don't trust me too much, huh?" We didn't answer him. Then he said, "It's really me who shouldn't trust *you*—especially after what you did to me."

Ty gave a wry smile and asked, "And just what did we do to you?"

The figure took a drag from his cigarette and answered, "It's not you particularly, but your friend…"

I said, "Me?"

We saw him nod. Then he said, "I had Finch Hennessey in my sights and you spoiled it."

We both got up from the railing as I exclaimed, "Severin!"

"Yeah," he answered bitterly. "Severin, the worst of the Hennessey Gang!"

We didn't know what he meant by that since it was hard to imagine a Hennessey Gang member worse than the examples we'd already seen.

He tried to take another drag from his cigarette, but he looked at it and said, "Shit!" It was true, the pinhole light had gone out. Ty reached into his pocket and quickly lit a match on the wooden post. Then he bent forward, offering to light his cigarette, but Severin leaned back.

Seeing him not holding up his cigarette, Ty said, "I just want to light your cigarette. What's wrong?"

"Nothing!" Severin said, perhaps too loudly.

I suspected something was wrong. So on impulse, I took Ty's already outstretched hand and moved it closer to Severin. He said, "No!" just as the light from the match illuminated his face.

Both me and Ty jumped back in horror and I exclaimed, "Jesus!"

As Ty held the match forward, we saw the scars, some done by a razor, some by a knife, with what was left of his nose covered by some barely clean bandage wrapped around his head. In fact, much of his black hair was missing and in that second-long glimpse, we could clearly see stubble where his hair used to be.

Suddenly the match burned down to Ty's fingers and he quickly dropped it to the porch and stepped on it. Then we both stared at what we could see of the distorted face in the darkness.

We didn't know what to say. We had never been faced with such a frightening example of brutality before and I could tell it was making both of us physically ill, but admirably, we found the strength *not* to run off into the bushes and vomit. Why make this man feel worse than he already did?

I faced Severin and said, "I came into the upstairs room the other day and saw them beating you up. You didn't look like...like this."

Severin's voice, deep, sad and bitter, replied, "After you boys went to town, they untied Lone and let him go to work."

Appalled, we both found ourselves shaking our heads in unison.

"You like it?" he asked us gravely. "A little present from the chief! Out of all the Hennesseys, he's the one who knows all the Indian tortures. Like scalping, Lone did a good job, as you can see." He pointed a gnarled finger at his nose and said, "And this is what the Apaches do to their women when they cheat on them. Cut their noses off so no other man will have them. So this is how they punished me for squandering their stolen money on drinks and women—make sure no woman will ever look at me again..."

I was already starting to regret saving Finch's life and indirectly harming Severin's.

"What will you do now?"

"What can I do?" he asked. "I dare not leave here, not lookin' like this. They'll feed me and give me a place to sleep and plenty of liquor to drink. The Hennesseys are loyal that way..."

We knew he was being sarcastic. Still, no matter how low a man he was, no one deserved what he was now going through.

"Or maybe," he said, "when they're busy and not looking, I'll go down to the stream not far from here and jump in and never come up..."

Sitting back onto the railing, Ty said firmly, "I wouldn't do that if I were you, Samuel."

I stared at Ty.

Severin asked, "What did you call me?"

Ty said, "Samuel. Samuel Dover, whose family disappeared five years ago."

Severin said accusingly, "How did you find out? Someone told you!"

Ty shook his head and said, "I'll admit it was a shot in the dark. But this whole deal where the Hennesseys suddenly take over a house where the family mysteriously *disappeared* didn't make sense. Also, something Finch said before he brought you back here while you were out cold and tied to your horse. 'Sev, we're takin' you back to home sweet home.' I don't think he was just being ironic."

I cut in and said, "That's right! Finch said to me, 'I'd sooner trust Satan with a Gatling gun than that low-rent, drunken little rich boy...'" I wondered if I should've said that because I could see Severin wince in the semi-darkness.

"Yeah," he said, "I was rich *once*—but I can still drink..."

Ty folded his arms and asked, "What happened to your family?"

There was a long pause before Severin answered, and when he did he pulled his head back into the darkness, as if he didn't want us to see anything in his busted eyes that might reveal something.

"The Hennesseys murdered them! What do you think?"

Curiously, I asked, "Did the Toombs brothers kill them too?"

Even in the slight spill of moonlight, I could tell he was shaking his head.

"My family was killed long before the Toombs brothers joined the gang."

Ty went back to quizzing Severin. "I don't understand. Finch and the others murdered your family, yet you joined them?"

"What could I do?" cried the figure in the darkness.

"They had already murdered my mother and father and baby sister before I arrived home. I was young. I could ride and shoot and they needed men. So they gave me a choice. Join them or die..."

We thought about that one. It sounded reasonable up to a point, remembering that Severin was naturally weak, devoid of morals and a lush to boot, that he would help the murderers of his family rob and kill and thrive throughout the territory. But I know that if it were me or Ty, we would've gladly given our lives to kill the bastards who murdered *our* family, come what may.

Ty asked, "What happened to their bodies?"

"They forced me to bury them somewhere on this property."

Suddenly from behind us, we heard a gruff question, "What's goin' on here?" It was one of our two watchdogs. They were standing on the lawn and staring at us talking to Severin. We turned back and looked at them, not bothering to answer.

One of them said, "Maybe you boys better turn in. You've got a long day tomorrow."

We didn't know what he meant by that, but we could see the other outlaw with his hand on his gun-butt and we quickly got the idea. We left the porch and headed inside for bed.

But as we entered the house, I heard one of them say to Severin, "That goes for you too, freak!" Then we heard both of them laugh loudly. God knew how Severin felt.

CHAPTER FOURTEEN

WITH MORNING CAME A BRIGHT, SUNNY DAY, THOUGH THE cheerful weather made no difference to Jill. They forced her to cook us breakfast, which, alone and unassisted by anyone else, she did with flying colors. She used old pans, rusty pots, rags which used to be torn shirts to use in order to grip hot pot handles, used up whatever supply of flour, eggs, biscuits and coffee that the boys were freely given by merchants in town—did these folks have a choice to refuse—and served about all of us whatever we wanted.

Needless to say, me and Ty just had what we needed to survive through the day, not wanting to overwork the poor woman more than she was. It was different than when she was cooking for me, Ty and the two *watchdogs* the other night. This time it was about a dozen or so gang members, all with their own loud demands for more—always more. How this woman held up is beyond me, but there was certainly something in her greater than whatever surface charms she used to make cowboys buy her drinks at Kings.

We watched her as she was frying the next batch of eggs she was cooking, buttering the next biscuit, or boiling the next pot of coffee. Always looking down, sweat appearing on her forehead, shoving back the damp hair falling into her eyes and keeping her man's shirt buttoned up to the neck and not giving any of them a chance to get a better look at her. Jill was something to see. If there was any consolation for her hard work, it was the fact that now Finch was at the table as well, and the gang seemed better behaved, if that was possible, while he was in the room, so any pinching of Jill's butt was now out of the question. Me and Ty were grateful for that.

We looked around but didn't see Severin. Maybe he felt uncomfortable eating with the gang—now we knew he really wasn't a Hennessey—and ate alone because of his facial mutilation. It was a sure thing they'd make fun of his appearance. Unfortunately, Lone Hennessey was there. It was the first time we'd seen him since he tried to jump me a couple nights before. Thank God he didn't sit opposite us at the long table. Instead, he sat at the opposite end of it. Still, his black eyes glared at us from all the way down there. At times, we glared back. Both of us were more angry at him than afraid—which is what he wanted us to be—especially after learning of his torturing Severin. Lord knows, Severin, or Samuel Dover, wasn't our friend, but no man deserved punishment like that, and it galled both of us that Lone Hennessey felt he was entitled to ruin a man for life, even if it might have been on Finch's orders.

I could tell that Ira and Andrew were watching Lone carefully to make sure he didn't pull anything on us. I'm sure Lone wasn't afraid of the Toombs boys either, and that it was only his younger stepbrother Finch who was able to ride herd on him. It didn't surprise me that, in his own way, Finch loved Lone as much as he had Ben, though seeing what a disgusting human being he was, I couldn't for the life of me figure out why. To me, Ty was my brother. He was not of my blood but I couldn't find a better brother, companion, and friend than him. I'd probably kill for him, and I think he'd do the same for me. We got ornery and sometimes rowdy and fought with each other, but at least we weren't the Hennesseys.

And then there were the Toombs brothers. I wondered, were they as bad as they appeared? I knew that Andrew would use his gun at the drop of a hat, but would Ira? He seemed to be the more mature of the two, and though he'd definitely done his share of lawbreaking, I wondered if his crimes stopped short of cold-blooded killing. After all, he was never wanted outside the state, and when he was wanted it was never for murder. But from what Ty had previously read of him, when they called Ira a killer, he never disputed the label, he just let everyone think that he was much worse than he may have been. I had a strong feeling that, to the prying eyes of some out-of-town reporter looking for a big story, Ira allowed himself to be portrayed as some ornery, trigger-happy badman—or at least that's what I wanted to think. But I had to be realistic. He and Andrew were still part of the Hennesseys, and how could anyone have anything to do with them and still be on the side of the angels?

Then I got a sobering thought. Me and Ty were with them. Me and Ty had planned to rob a store. Me and Ty

openly admitted to liking Finch Hennessey and I actually saved his life. Me and Ty were poor farm boys who
wanted to strike back by breaking the law—according to
Finch, so were the Hennesseys, though they were far
more successful at lawbreaking than we'd ever be. Their
family was bad, rotten to the core, and whether we were
considered their prisoners or not, we were with them,
eating their food, sleeping in their hideout and running
from the law, just as they were. All in all, the hangman's
noose doesn't care whether it hangs a poor farm boy
who robbed and murdered for a living or the poor farm
boy who reluctantly rode with the murderers, but
grudgingly admired one of them from afar. The
Hennesseys were rotten, and since we were with them,
we were rotten as well.

Who was I to judge?

———

WE RODE INTO TOWN. As we came in, I scanned the faces
of the townspeople on the boardwalks and in the
streets. They never once looked at us, never once gave
us any eye contact. It was as if we were just a bunch of
fellows who were riding in for a drink or a smoke at the
local saloon—which was exactly what the gang did. I
say the gang because Finch rode back to where we were
—they had us riding in the center as usual, with gang
members all around us as we rode in—and told us to
just hang around town. We all dismounted at the
Pellican and tied our horses to the tie rails.

"Just meet us here in about an hour," Finch said,
and then he followed the gang into the saloon. No
reason was given why he wanted us to just hang around.

With nothing to do, we just walked down the street.

"You know," I said quietly, "now's our chance."

Ty said, just as quietly, "Think again."

"Hmm?"

With his head, he indicated the two watchdogs following us down the street.

Wryly, I said, "Maybe we should have Ma and Pa adopt them..."

"Personally I'd like to drop 'em over the edge of a cliff."

"I'm with ya there."

Ty and I glanced back at them and we saw one of them playfully lift his gun just a little up out of the holster and then drop it back, smiling as he did so.

Ty said, "They're just looking for an excuse. They can taste it."

"And with no law around here but those beholden to the Hennesseys, they can get away with it too."

"Um-hm..."

We walked down the street, wondering how to kill time and trying to keep our minds off the fact that what we really wanted was to kill our escorts.

It was another minute or so before we spotted them. They were coming across the street. Hazel, and this surprised me, Bessie was with her. Hazel had on her little hat and light jacket and Bessie was hatless, but wore a shawl, her blouse and long skirt showing some of the wear of the back kitchen she worked in.

They waved at us, actually, only Hazel did, and we crossed the street and came up to them.

Hazel said, "I'm glad you boys are here. I saw them all ride into town. Is something up?"

Ty answered, "If something is, they're not saying it to us."

"This is our break. We have to be back in a few minutes."

"Yeah, we were told to kill an hour and then meet them back at the saloon."

"Why?"

"They didn't let us know that either."

Through this conversation I noticed Bessie staring at me, her sharp blue eyes studying me intently. When I faced her, she suddenly averted her eyes. I wondered if she was still angry or she had calmed down long enough to stop being a maddening pain-in-the-ass. When I looked at her, I could definitely see a few changes since I last saw her at the Pellican. Her dark-brown hair seemed neater somehow, brushed and in place and not falling in her eyes as I always saw when she was in the restaurant's back kitchen. She also seemed more fair-skinned and her cheeks seemed to have more color now that she was outdoors in the bright sunlight.

Hazel said, "I wish I could get you boys out of this fix. Maybe I could talk to Ira or something and he can find a way to help get you out of here..."

I stared at her and said, "Why is it so important that *Ira* get us out of this?"

Hazel blinked her beautiful eyes innocently and said, "Why, I just thought between him and Andrew, Ira's the more level-headed one and he'd come up with some way to get you away from the gang."

"Yeah," I said resentfully, "especially since the Toombs brothers got us into this mess by bringing us here. A posse was chasing Ira and they saw us with him. He's one of the reasons we're wanted."

"Jed, you're being unfair to Ira. He rode in the other day with Andrew and they told me—that is, after I got it out of them—that their guns are keeping you boys alive, as they did the other day during that fight."

Churlishly, I ignored her very good point and repeated, "'Unfair to Ira'? What're you, his admirer?"

At the time, it never dawned on me that my anger was based on something that had nothing to do with the fact that the Toombs brothers brought us to the Hennesseys.

All through this conversation, Ty just watched me as if he didn't recognize me.

But it was Bessie who couldn't stand anymore.

"Who the hell do you think you are?" she asked me accusingly.

"Stay out of it," I said.

"No, I won't stay out of it! You've been giving this poor girl a tongue-lashing and all she's trying to do is help you. And in my opinion, you're hardly worth it! You're a young hooligan and you always will be!"

Hazel said, "Please, Bessie!"

"Please, my foot! My mother would've planted one right in your face if she knew you even *thought* of bein' an outlaw! You're no better than my own brother, God rest his soul! He thought with a gun in his hand, he could own the world! Just like that bunch you ride with!"

"I'm glad I'm not in your family!" I said, my voice rising. "Now could you butt out while I try to talk some sense into *mine*?"

Both Ty and Hazel almost winced when I said that.

"Listen, Jed," Ty started and he put his hand on my arm.

I shook him off and focused on Bessie as she stared at me incredulously.

"Your *family*?" she said. "What is Hazel to you? Is she your wife? What in the Lord's name did you mean by *that*?"

I was getting riled. With people passing by, glancing at us but not interfering—we were, after all, with the Hennesseys—I was still feeling a little self-conscious arguing with this young woman in the streets.

I glared at Bessie and in an unusually rough voice, I said, "This doesn't concern you, so why don't you go back to that dirty kitchen where your kind belongs!"

Bessie's slap came fast and hard. I barely rolled with it, and though it stung, I even found myself giving her a little smirk after she did it. Maybe all the beatings I'd gone through lately had toughened me up. A woman's slap was nothing compared to a kick in the face by a lunatic like Lone Hennessey.

But when I looked back at her, I was taken aback by her reaction. Instead of her reaching back to slap me again or getting ready to give me a good tongue-lashing, her face crumpled in despair and she suddenly looked like she was on the verge of crying.

Before I could take another breath, she turned around and ran away back down the street before tears started to form. We heard her sobs even as she ran, and she was fast too, having covered the block in seconds.

Angrily, Hazel said, "That was *disgusting*, Jed! She was only concerned about you!"

"Concerned?" I said, disbelieving. "She's been tearing me down ever since she met me!"

Hazel sighed in exasperation and said, "Men! They should be cooked in dried fat!"

Then she turned and walked back down the street, angry and frustrated and perhaps having lost faith in the young man she thought of as her little brother, a young man who sure as hell didn't look on her as a big sister...

CHAPTER FIFTEEN

TY LOOKED IN THE DIRECTION BESSIE RAN. THEN HE looked back in the direction Hazel stalked off.

He said, "That was...interesting, Jed."

"Was it?"

"Yeah, you just drove off two beautiful women who cared about you in less than ten seconds..."

I looked at him oddly. "Bessie? Beautiful?"

"Yep," he said. "But right now you're too preoccupied to notice."

"Oh, don't you start with me!"

"I wouldn't think of it now. We've got our own prob..."

Ty stopped and stared at Hazel down the street. I followed his look and I saw the two watchdogs coming up to her. In fact, she had to stop when they blocked her path. They were a few yards away from us, but I could hear one of them say, "Forget those two saddle-tramps, honey. Won't we do?"

The old jealous rage came to me when I saw them

accosting Hazel. In a heartbeat, I ran toward them as Ty cried out, "Jed, no!"

The one on the right saw me rushing toward them and quickly pulled out his gun just as I ducked and my head hit his stomach. The impact knocked the wind out of him and he grunted painfully as we both flew backward, hitting the ground and rolling over each other. The gun flew out of his hand and landed somewhere on the ground. From what I could see, the other one drew his gun and was ready to aim it at me when I saw Ty run up to him and grab his gun arm. But the outlaw was able to pull back the hammer of the Colt with his thumb as he tried to wrench his arm free of Ty's hold.

I didn't see her as I wrestled on the ground with the other man, but I heard Hazel scream. While I was on my back on the hard-packed ground, the man popped me across the mouth and I felt blood on my lip with the blow. Angry, I put my spread fingers in his face and shoved hard. He went over and my fist flew into his eye as his head hit the ground.

But the man Ty was struggling with was strong, and like a persistent snake, his outstretched arm continued to aim at me and the other man as we were rolling around the street. That's when Ty finally wrapped his free arm around the man's head. The hold was tight and Ty's forearm pressed hard against the man's eyes and nose, blocking his vision. In reflex action, the man fired and a second later, I heard Hazel scream.

Thinking he shot Hazel, I quickly punched my opponent hard in the nose and mouth, hoping to get him out of the way and see what happened to her. But he wouldn't let me see much daylight, slugging me in the head and using his body to block my view of the street. From what I could see, Ty's man still had his gun and he tried hard to aim it in my direction. A hard punch in the forehead made me dizzy for a moment and the man above me—his unwashed body with its awful smell an added pain I had to endure—tried to put his hands on my throat to strangle me. Thanks to my long neck I was able to raise my head slightly and bite him hard on the lower thumb and part of the wrist of his right hand. He cried out in pain and angrily backhanded me in the mouth with his other hand.

That's when I heard two shots real close. One bullet tore the left shoulder of my jacket and veered off the ground into God-knew-where, barely missing my collarbone. But I knew where the other bullet went when my opponent suddenly stiffened and blood quickly appeared on his mouth. I pushed the dead man off me. By the puddle of blood spreading on the back of his light-colored jacket, I could tell *exactly* where the bullet went.

The man Ty was struggling with quickly saw his error and maybe that gave him a little more strength. He had been using his free elbow to slam Ty in the ribs whenever he could, and this time he was able to knock him back, causing Ty to loosen his arm-hold around his head. Then the man punched Ty hard in the head with his other hand, knocking him to the street.

Sitting up on my elbows, I frantically searched the ground. It was closer than I thought. I had felt the pain when I had rolled over it during the fight, idly wondering what it was as its hard metal cylinder almost embedded itself into my hip. I grabbed it, my hand wrapping around its hard ivory grip. In that moment, I thought, *Fancy, fits the Hennessey Gang perfectly.*

While still on the ground, I turned around and aimed it at the other man just as he was pointing his gun at Ty. Dizzy from the blow, but not unconscious, Ty was rising up to attack the man just as I fired.

When the smoke cleared, I saw the outlaw double over. Glimpsing Ty, I could see that he dropped and flattened himself on the ground as soon as he saw me aim the gun. The man was still holding his gun and when he slowly turned and lifted it toward me, I fired again. The bullet's impact made him bend over double and he fell forward, hitting the ground and rolling over once and then no more.

As Ty cautiously rose off the ground, I could tell that he was all right. Suddenly, thinking of Hazel, I remembered that one of the outlaws' gunshots went off and made her scream. Still on the ground, I quickly turned around and saw a crowd of people bent over someone lying on the ground. I rose fast and, still with the gun in my hand, I headed toward the crowd.

Using my free hand, I shoved a couple people out of the way and looked down.

Lying on the ground, his derby hat next to his head and his glasses broken, was John, the mousy clerk at the hotel. His eyes were shut and his face calm. He looked like he was asleep, or more likely finally at peace, never again to be bullied by the Hennessey Gang.

When I felt a woman's hand come around my neck, I turned and saw Hazel standing there, her eyes reddened and her anguish plain on her face. She embraced me then, tightly, her head on my chest and her tears on my jacket.

"Oh, my little brother!" she said through her tears. "My dear little brother! I thought they got you…"

I held her close, my thoughts far away. With a dead man at my feet and a growing crowd right there around us, it felt like time had stopped and I was totally cut off from the events happening around me. I had already killed a man, but that was an accident. Now I killed a man on purpose, shooting him down like a mad dog, and I did it like an expert. And despite the fact that I was saving Ty's life, I felt that, had that not been the case, I *still* would not have been sorry about it. These men tried to kill us, and they ended up killing poor John. No, I'm sorry to say I have no regrets about it.

But the thing that hit me even more than my killing another man were the words of the woman I loved. *My little brother, my dear little brother...*

CHAPTER SIXTEEN

THE CROWD HAD PULLED BACK FOR SOME REASON. TY joined us, and when we looked up, we saw the reason why. The gang was standing there with their guns drawn and pointed at us. By now, Ty had grabbed the dead outlaw's gun and so we were both armed. Hesitantly, we pointed our guns back at the gang. The crowd had already fully backed out of the way. In fact, they basically got off the street and let us have it. Every one of them drifted away and disappeared behind closed doors and shades were pulled over windows. If any of them *were* around, fearing flying bullets, they only watched us from afar.

Finch and the rest stood there with guns pointed in our direction. Even the Toombs brothers, suddenly realizing like the rest that we were armed, were pointing their guns at us. Having gotten there first, the two of them were standing in front of Finch and the others. They were watching us intently, but then I saw Ira's eyes widen when he saw Hazel standing with us.

"Hazel!" he called out. "Get away from them!"

She answered defiantly, "*No*, Ira!"

"Hazel, please!"

"No! You and this pack of animals won't murder them like they did so many others!"

Ty said, "Better do as he says, Hazel! Just step out of the way."

"He's right, Hazel," I said.

"No!" she said stubbornly. "As soon as I step out of the way, they'll riddle you! I'm staying put until the two of you grab a pair of horses and light out of here!"

Ira said, "Don't be a fool, Hazel! They can't get away from us!"

Bitterly, Hazel said, "*You're* the fool, Ira! All right, so your brother's a killer, that didn't mean you had to join him! And when Andrew joined these maniacs, you *had* to join up too? Oh, god, why couldn't you be the man I wanted you to be!"

Ira was stunned when he heard her confession. Andrew stared at her. The rest of the gang, including Finch, was momentarily held speechless by her words.

Serious for the first time I'd ever seen him, Andrew said to his brother, "You didn't have to join up with me three years ago. If you refused, I would've understood..."

I saw Ira swallow uncomfortably and he said, "You're my brother, Andy. Where you go, I go..."

Nobody knew what to say after that, with the gang as plainly surprised that Ira Toombs might not have been as murderous as his fearsome reputation implied. But apparently he *was* a hell of a loyal brother.

This rather tense conversation in the middle of a Dentonville street also brought home to me and my own narrow, closed little mind something else: Hazel may been the object of Lone Hennessey's attentions every once in a while, and I may have had certain desires about her myself, but it was Ira Toombs who had captured her heart.

But Hazel wasn't through yet. Ignoring the others, her words were still meant for Ira.

"When Ty decided to rob Reynolds's store, Jed went with him. Just like when Andrew robbed his first store, you *had* to join him. They're just like you. Can't you find it in you to let them go?"

Finally, Finch decided to join in the conversation.

"All this airing of family laundry is very touching," he said, "but I'm dead serious. I don't want you hurt, Hazel, so why don't you just step aside?"

That's when I saw Ira and Andrew give each other a little look that only they understood. Already standing a few feet in front of the rest, they simply took a few steps forward and swung around. Suddenly they were pointing their guns at the gang. The movement was so quick and graceful it stunned me and Ty into not pulling the hair triggers of our own guns.

Finch said, "What the hell kind of fast shuffle is this?"

Ira said, "She's right, Clay."

Andrew added, "I like a good fightin' man, and these two are real men who should be fightin' their own battles for themselves, not scum like us."

"Boys," said Finch to the Toombs brothers with slowly ebbing patience, "I know you kind of admire these two, but they're not your family. You rode with us. *We're* your family!"

Ira answered quietly, "Not anymore, Clay..."

Hazel smiled when she heard them. She looked

with admiration at Ira. It was as if she found someone she had lost long ago.

"Fine," Finch said as anger grew within him. "You and Andrew want to leave us, we're not gonna stop you. But Ty and Jed are a different matter. They're young, they can scrap, and I need good men. For the first time in their lives, these two poor farm boys have a chance to make something of themselves, and I aim to give 'em that chance. Their alternative is a hangman's rope."

We all stood and stared at him, thinking about what he said. We didn't want the Law to hang us, but we also knew we didn't want to be with them either. We were at a stalemate. We couldn't stand there and we couldn't move, not very far.

That's when Finch's next comment made up our minds for us.

"By the way, have you boys seen Lone?"

It was true. Lone was not there to be seen. We all wondered why, during this tense standoff, he would bring him up. Cautiously, me and Ty looked around, thinking the "chief" had snuck around behind us, but there was no one there. If there was anyone behind us, it was only frightened townspeople cowering behind locked doors.

Ira asked, "What's up, Clay? Why'd you ask that?"

Now Finch dropped the mask. He stopped playing with us and he was all business.

"Just this, Ira. Jill is back at the Dover House and Lone, Ed Plummer, and Jack Foster are with her. Our late friends on the ground over here told me that you two ran into Severin on the porch. So you know what the chief could do to a man when he's drunk and angry. Think of what he'd do to a woman..."

I saw Ty tense up. Hazel just stared at the gang, frightened.

Finch continued, "There aren't enough of you to get all of us. So if any of my boys survive, *any of 'em*, they'll have enough time to ride back to the Dover and tell the chief to go to work..."

We all stared at him. Now I was truly sorry I hadn't allowed Severin to shoot Finch. But then I realized that that wouldn't have made much of a difference. With Finch in the lead, the Hennessey Gang was a bunch of animals with a purpose and had the ability to perform their evil deeds like a well-oiled machine. Without him, all restraints would be off and only the animals would remain.

"And who knows what'll happen if we all shoot each other to pieces and no one survives to ride back to the Dover?" Finch asked without humor. "If we don't show up, Lone might take it upon himself to do something to Jill on his own. And the way he is, he could do something far worse to her than just ruin her face..."

We all absorbed what Finch said; he didn't have to paint us a picture.

"So what's your play?" asked Ira.

"Just this," replied Finch. "We need more men to get that army payroll. I just got word it'll go out tomorrow around noon along the Butterfield southern route. That means we'll have enough time to ride for the New Mexican border first thing in the morning and be there just in time to head off the stage. Thanks to your farm boys, I'm out four men! But I'm willing to forget about this little family squabble if all of you joined us on this job."

Andrew asked, "After we all pointed our hog-legs at you for the second time, you'd take us back?"

Finch answered, "Like I said, I need the men. What's the problem anyway? A favor for a favor. You boys join us and I promise that neither Lone nor anyone else will lay a hand on Jill. And anyway, when we're through, you boys will end up with more money than you know what to do with."

The four of us hesitated at his offer, really thinking about it. Our guns suddenly seemed to gain weight and without realizing it, we gradually started to point them to the ground.

Seeing this, Hazel said, "Don't do it! You'll only get yourselves in deeper!"

Ty said gravely, "Yeah, but there's Jill's life to consider too."

That did it. Our guns were down.

Finch said, "Put up your hardware, boys."

A few gang members protested, but Finch insisted, telling them he gave his word. His *word* again. I loved that.

"Come on, boys," he said to us, as well as the rest of them, "let's ride back to the Dover and do some plannin'..." He faced me and Ty and said, "You boys look good with guns in your hands. You can keep 'em. You'll need 'em with you tomorrow." Then he said to Hazel, "You know, Hazel, you're a very nice girl, but honestly, I don't think I'd want you to serve us anymore..." He turned away to join the others, detailing one of his men to ride over to the undertaker and handle the burials—for free, of course.

Meanwhile, none of us were feeling very good about the devil's bargain we had just made. But with Jill in their hands, Finch knew full well that we'd all follow them and not make any trouble.

"Sorry, boys," Ira said to us.

"Yeah," said Andrew sullenly, "I'll be damned if some innocent woman has to suffer because of me. But if I ever got that damn red son-of-a-bitch in my sights..."

On that note, he headed for his horse.

Concerned for Jill, Ty said, "We'd better get back with 'em, Jed. But first..."

He went over to one of the outlaws and, with some difficulty, pulled off his holster. Following his lead, I went to the other dead man whose gun I had and did the same. Now at least we had bullets along with our guns. As we tied the holsters around our waists and tied the strings down around our legs to keep them from bouncing around, Hazel stared at us with no expression. She knew we had to put them on whether we liked it or not.

After he was finished, Ty walked back to the Pellican to pick up his horse.

Ira wanted to talk to Hazel, but I asked him if I could speak privately to her first. Reluctantly, he walked away a little bit from us.

"Hazel..."

"I know, Jed..."

"Ty and me won't let anything happen to us."

"Promise me, Jed!"

"I promise. After all, I'm your brother..."

She embraced me then, as she did before, like her little brother.

After the hug, I stepped back and said, "You can do me a favor."

"Anything!"

"Tell Bessie I was one stupid jackass..."

With tears coming in her eyes, she asked, "Anything else?"

"Yeah," I answered. "Tell her I'm sorry. Tell her I'm sorry I didn't meet someone like her under better circumstances..."

And with that last comment, I picked my hat up off the ground and walked away.

I didn't know if I was going to ever see her *or Bessie* again...

CHAPTER SEVENTEEN

WE WERE ALL QUIET AS WE RODE BACK TO THE DOVER. OF course, certain gang members shot us dirty looks—we figured they'd like to shoot us something else. We were indirectly responsible for the deaths of two of their own; then we were *directly* responsible for killing two more. In fact, Ty and me figured it would only be a matter of time before these men would wait for our backs to be turned before they blew us away. It was Finch who kept them in line, but how long would it be before they would buck his authority and end it for us once and for all?

Hell, we never robbed a stagecoach. What would we do? Wave our guns and bark demands, suffocate ourselves and feel downright silly in dirty cloth masks? And if anyone even *thought* of reaching for a gun, would we pistol-whip them? Or worse, kill them? Hazel was right; we'd be getting ourselves in deeper. Before, we were suspected of robbery and murder. This time, we wouldn't be suspects any longer, we *would* be robbers and murderers. At this point, we had to participate; as

long as Jill was being held hostage, we had to do what
Finch wanted.

But how long would we do that? One way or the
other, we had to get Jill out of there.

When we rode in, we saw Severin sitting on the
porch, as we saw him the other night. He was hatless,
with patches of mottled skin sticking out horribly in his
scalp, his scars and swollen lips more prominent in the
daylight.

A few of the gang laughed when they saw him and
some just gave knowing smirks to each other, with
smart-ass comments said loudly for Severin's benefit.

"Hey, Finch, could you keep him inside or somethin'? He's scarin' the horses..."

"Damn it, I didn't know we kept any pets on the
property!"

Finch didn't join in when they started their cruel
jibes, but he didn't stop them either. It was obvious he
didn't give a damn about Severin's feelings one way or
the other. In his mind, he saw Severin's squandering the
gang's profits on the robbery as a betrayal—which it
most definitely *was*. From what I'd gathered, Severin
had pulled off this kind of thing more than once, but
Finch always stood in the way of the gang's wrath,
protecting his drunken brother, and allowing Severin to
call himself a Hennessey to keep the gang from getting
rid of him once and for all. I suspected there was something else about why Finch was protecting him, but I
couldn't put my finger on it. But then, Finch was also
pissed off by Severin's attempt to kill him; it might've
had something to do with his allowing the chief to
disfigure him. Lord knows, we witnessed Finch's wrath

more than once now, with his riddling the corpse of the man who killed his brother still fresh in my mind.

We were in a goddamn nest of snakes, all right—and no one was throwing us a rope.

Finch rode up to Severin and asked him, "What're you doing out here? I thought you were so ashamed of your face that you didn't want to see daylight ever again."

Here, Finch might have been quoting something Severin said to him after his disfigurement, I wasn't sure.

Taking a labored breath before he spoke, Severin said, "I did too, but I'm not gonna be in there with the chief now, not the way he is."

Ty rode up beside Finch and asked, "*How* is the chief now? What happened?"

Severin answered, "He got a little frisky with the girl. Tried something with her and she grabbed a knife and slashed him across the face, got his nose too..." Then, through his own mutilated face, he gave a wicked little smile. No doubt he saw this as some kind of poetic justice.

But Ty didn't give a damn about Severin's sense of poetic justice. Anxiously, he leaned forward in the saddle and asked, "What happened to the girl?"

There was a long pause before Severin answered.

"Lone broke her neck..."

Ty leaped off his horse and hit the porch on all fours. Then he rose and headed for the front door.

Severin quickly got up from his chair and rushed forward, tripping Ty just as he opened the front door, but before he could enter Ty fell flat on his face but quickly rose and tried to rush forward. Severin tried to hold him back, but Ty was far stronger.

Seeing this, Finch said only, "Boys."

Three of his men rushed over and they all helped Severin grab onto Ty and pull him back out of the house.

Then, from inside, we all heard a loud, terrifying roar. It might have come from a man, but it sounded more like that of an angry, wounded animal.

One of the men holding Ty said, "Lord, I never heard him sound like that."

As it turned out, the horrible cry was nothing compared to what came right after that.

We heard a loud, terrible shattering of glass from above and the bloodcurdling scream of a man which got closer and closer. We all turned around and saw, amid a free shower of glass shards and splintered wood that used to be a window, a man's body plunge to the front lawn and hit the sod with a loud impact, his scream cut short and his head now covered in blood. Even from where I stood with the rest, I could tell that the dead man used to be Ed Plummer.

Also witnessing the fall, Ty was now filled with a new urgency to get into the house and see what happened to Jill. "Let me go!" he cried. Struggling with the men holding him, he was so anxious to move himself forward that he was starting to drag the others into the house with him.

That's when Finch stepped before Ty and punched twice in the face, a right and a left in quick succession. Ty's hat flew off and he crumpled in their arms. He'd be out for a little while.

Angrily, I rushed forward, but Stu ran up and grabbed me before I could get to Ty.

Seeing my rage, Finch said, "I had to, Jed! The way he is now, the chief would've torn Ty into little pieces, gun or no gun."

I was still angry, but I relaxed after hearing that. I realized that in knocking out Ty—he could've, after all, hit him with the butt of his gun, which could've given Ty permanent damage—Finch was really saving his life. Blinded by his own anger, had Ty tried to tackle Lone in his present state, God knows what that crazy Indian would've done to him. We saw the results of his rage on the lawn right behind us.

"Okay, I got it!" I said, and then angrily shook myself out of Stu's hold.

Finch glanced back at the front hallway. We heard Lone yell again, louder this time.

He said, "I'll go in there. I know how to talk to him."

He started to enter the hallway when I said, "Finch, I'm going with you."

"Can't, kid, it's too dangerous."

"That's my choice. Ty's my brother. He wanted to know what happened to the girl and I want to find out myself and tell him. He liked her. And if I see what happened and tell him later, I might make it easier for him."

Finch stood there thinking about it. Somehow, he had this incredible calm while deeper inside the house, a madman was howling like a wolf at a non-existent moon.

"All right," he said. "But keep behind me and follow my lead. He's my brother, so if you pull that gun on him, I'll kill you."

I didn't like being threatened, but I found myself saying, "I understand..."

Finch nodded and then, with him in the lead, we went down the hallway.

Needless to say, none of Finch's men volunteered to go with us.

Another howl came from the room on the third floor where Ed's body had been flung out of. Slowly we climbed the stairs, and I followed Finch with some apprehension.

When we got to the second-floor landing, we heard another howl and right after that, a loud gunshot exploded from the floor above us. Then we heard some scattered footfalls from the hallway ceiling and a thud, as if a human body had just staggered around and then hit the floor. Finch and I glanced at each other. His eyes were admonishing me, as if he could read my mind. He *knew* I wanted to reach for my gun, but his stern look stopped me from exploring the idea any further. Then he moved forward again. We passed the second-floor hallway, rounded the banister, and started to climb up the next flight of stairs. We heard more crashes, as if Lone, with no one else to murder, now started to break up the furniture.

We finally hit the third-floor landing and went down the hallway. As we moved closer to the small window at the end of the hall, the sunlight coming in revealed a man's body on the floor in front of an open doorway. He was on his back with his arms spread out and we could tell that he still had his unfired gun in his right hand. I peered over at him, and by his clothes I could see that it was Jack Foster, but it was hard to say for sure since a bullet had practically torn the man's face off.

There was *no way* I was going to keep my word on this one. Quietly I put my right hand on the butt of my gun and was about to lift it when Finch, already knowing what I was going to do, roughly shoved me back into the wall behind me. If he wanted me to quit going for my gun, it worked because I let go of it and put up both hands to block his shove. But it was too late. So powerful was his push that I hit the wall, knocking a picture to the ground and I lost my balance and fell to the carpeted floor, my hat rolling off somewhere and my head pounding. Painfully, I rolled over and stared down the hallway.

I saw Finch, his gun now in his hand, leap before the open doorway and hit the hallway floor, firing one shot as he did so. It was a quick shot, and the man who fired it would have to be able to take in the whole room and place where his target was in a split second, an amazing feat for anyone, but apparently an easy one for a man of Finch Hennessey's peculiar talents.

Forgetting my own pain, I rose off the floor quickly, drew my gun and went to the open doorway. But as I did, Finch got up quickly and the barrel of his gun went into my belly.

A moan from inside the room made us both turn and look inside. Lone Hennessey was on the floor, a now-empty gun lying nearby. The bullet had gone exactly where Finch had wanted it to go, into the half-breed's right leg. Finch removed the gun from my belly and we both slowly entered the room.

A cool breeze blew in from the now huge hole where the room's window used to be. Furniture and bric-a-brac of all kinds, chairs, vases, a full mirror, the drawers of a large bureau, and even parts of a bed, were strewn across the floor. Blood was everywhere, though I wasn't sure whose it was at the time. We looked down at Lone, his howling now gone and in its place the chief was whimpering like a hungry dog. Tears formed in his black eyes and he cried without shame. His face was covered with blood, deep scars on both cheeks and one large gash across the bridge of his nose and straight down to his top lip. If there was some kind of rugged handsomeness about him, it was all gone now. I would've been sorry for him had he not been the bully and mass murderer he was.

With his gun still in his hand, Finch ordered, "Put it away, Jed..."

Seeing that the chief wasn't armed anymore, I holstered my gun.

Finch then put away his own gun. As he started to lift Lone up to a sitting position, he said, "Help me get him into a chair."

"Ohhh no," I said stubbornly. "That maniac is *your* brother, not mine. You deal with him..."

Finch didn't like hearing that, but in a way, he also seemed to understand my anger. I let him try to lift Lone by himself as I turned around and scanned the room. *What a mess!* Obviously the two men Finch left with the chief, the late Ed Plummer and Jack Foster, couldn't control him, either his appetites or his rages, and paid for it with their lives. Looking across the room where most of the broken bed was, I saw it then.

A milky white arm under a torn mattress in the far corner.

I quickly moved across the room, stepping over a headboard and the broken-off legs of chairs and scattered porcelain. I got to the arm and looked down at it, taking a deep breath before I squatted down and lifted up the mattress, tossing it aside far enough to view the body.

I had mentally prepared myself for it, but I still gasped at the sight.

There she was lying on her back with her eyes wide open and staring sightlessly at the ceiling. She looked like a broken doll, with her arms and legs in crazy, abnormal positions. But one thing was still clutched in her right hand, her fingers tightly wrapped around its bone handle—a razor-sharp kitchen knife.

Sherry's neck was indeed broken, and her head was certainly far from being in any kind of normal position. In fact, it looked like Lone had pretty much almost literally tried to tear her head off. But his rage hadn't stopped there, and from what I could tell, it looked like he had literally broken every bone in her body, I assume, long *after* he murdered her.

And still, as I looked down at her now lifeless face, I could almost detect a little smile. Pain and ecstatic joy came to her at the same time. She gave violence and she received it, but the game had gone too far. One last thrill to a sick little life.

There was nothing to even stand there for. I turned around and looked at Finch as he tore a blanket to shreds for a tourniquet. Lone was still on the floor, his big hands covering what it could of his face. Hell, he wasn't even thinking of his bleeding leg with a bullet having gone completely through it. Finch didn't look at me as I tramped past him and his brother and left the room.

I stepped over the dead body lying in the hallway, picked up my hat and kept on going down the stairs. By the time I reached the second floor, Ty had intercepted me and asked urgently, "Did you find her?"

"Yeah," I answered, "I found her all right."

Furiously, he said, "I'll kill that fucking Indian!"

He was about to move past me, but I put my hands on his shoulders and stopped him.

"He killed *Sherry*..."

Ty stared at me and all the rage that was there went out of him in an instant.

"Sherry!" he said, realizing. "Then where's—"

"Let's find her," I said gently.

We separated and searched the second floor, then the first floor, even thinking that she would flee to our room when the trouble started, but she wasn't there either. The gang was still outside, not planning to go anywhere near the front door.

Frustrated, we both went back up to the third floor. Then Ty said something to me that made sense after we couldn't find her on all the other floors.

"Jill would've run out of the house if she had the chance. But if Lone and those two men were watching her, they all had to be in that third-floor room with together."

I said, "But she *wasn't* in the room. I only found Sherry—"

"Plummer and Foster were probably out in the hallway when Lone tried to rape Sherry."

"Do you think Jill saw what he did to her?"

"I don't know, Jed. I hope to God she didn't. That's a sight I wouldn't want anyone to live with."

I nodded, unconsciously shivering.

He continued, "But when Sherry scarred him and he killed her, then he started screaming. Maybe he looked at himself in the mirror before he screamed, I don't know, but as soon as he started acting up, those two men burst into the room. One got thrown through the window and the other got shot. Jill clearly took a chance during the confusion and she was able to make it out of the room."

"Then where is she?"

Ty simply pointed down the hall. The stairway went up another flight. When we got to it, we saw just thirty or so feet up, a door to an attic. As we mounted the steps, we definitely heard movement inside. We looked at each other, and then we rushed up to the door and put our shoulders to it.

But right after our first thrust at it, I heard a bolt suddenly being thrown from within and the door swung open. I couldn't stop myself from rushing into the room, tripping on something I couldn't see and hitting the floor. When I turned to look back at who had opened the door, I saw Jill in Ty's arms, her hands gripping him tightly and she was crying on his chest. She was pale and haggard, her already ripped men's clothes ripped even further. She still had her pants on, but I could clearly see her naked back, with her man's shirt now torn into rags. In fact, as she cried against Ty's chest, her breasts were barely covered and her right forearm had a huge bruise on it as if it had been yanked real hard. Seeing her nakedness, I decided not to get off the floor and instead just stayed where I was and looked off toward the attic window.

Knowing he had to do something, Ty pulled her off him and held her at arm's length for a moment, carefully averting his eyes. Self-conscious, holding back tears, Jill covered her breasts with her arms. Her eyes were downcast as she patiently stood there and waited while Ty took off his jacket and gave it to her. She quickly put it on and buttoned the front up to the collar.

"Thanks, Ty."

"That's okay," he replied, though I got the impression he would've preferred *not* covering her up.

Then a sudden chill came to her as she said, "He... he tried to..."

"You don't have to say it," said Ty grimly. "We got the idea."

"But Sherry got angry and she interfered. She said, 'What do you want her for when you've got me?' So he smiled and shoved me aside. Sherry thought she was gonna have her usual fun, but she didn't know how crazy that damn Injun was! As soon as he attacked her and those two men ran in to stop him, I got the hell out of there!"

Ty asked gently, "So you ran up here?"

She said, "I didn't know how many of them were outside! So I ran up here and locked myself in!" Nervously running her hands back through her hair and trying to calm down, she asked, "Where's Sherry? Is she all right?"

Ty looked off at me, and I returned his look.

Jill saw us and realized what happened.

"No!" She fell against Ty's chest and her tears returned. "No!" she wailed. "Poor Sherry! Lord knows, she was crazy out-of-her-mind, but she didn't deserve that!"

Ty just stroked her hair and tried to comfort her, not knowing what to say.

Meanwhile, I was still on the floor in a far corner of the attic. All around me was the usual old furniture or rolled-up rugs or musty framed paintings of boats or once prominent men and women now long dead, with what seemed like a foot of dust covering their faces. The place reeked of dirt and debris. Cobwebs were scattered all over; there didn't seem to be one corner or foot of space of that room that wasn't covered with the sticky stuff. I even had to brush some of it off my jacket after I fell. But then, when I finally made a move to get up, an old cast-iron coat-tree that was standing against the wall tipped over and smashed through some thin wooden boards. So aged was the wood that it broke apart as soon as the coat-tree hit it.

When I turned back to see what it fell into, I froze. The light wasn't that good in the attic, but some daylight spilled in from a dust-covered skylight, just enough for all of us to see what was beneath the smashed-up boards.

Also staring at where the coat-tree fell, Jill gasped and hugged Ty even tighter. Ty himself stood there with his mouth open until he was finally able to say, "What the hell?"

Still on the floor, I was the closest to it, and my heart jumped when I saw it.

Three skeletons were sitting up against the back wall, with the skulls facing our direction.

They almost looked like they were laughing at us...

CHAPTER EIGHTEEN

I SHOT OFF THE FLOOR LIKE A CANNONBALL AND STOOD back near them.

Scared, Jill asked, "Ty, what does it mean?"

Ty said wryly, "It means that either the Hennesseys are too lazy to bury their victims, or..."

His voice trailed off and his face changed, as if he came to some sudden realization.

He gently pulled Jill off him and approached the area. Bending over, with some effort he yanked the remaining broken boards away and threw them aside. Curiously, Jill and I came up behind him and peered at them.

Ty said, "These skeletons were shoved into this crawlspace and covered with those boards. Kind of a quick burial, as if the person who did this didn't give a damn about giving any respect to the departed."

"But why?" I asked.

"Take a look at 'em, Jed," Ty insisted. "Take a *good* look at 'em."

I peered inside at the three skeletons. Two large ones and one much smaller one.

I turned and looked up at Ty, a question on my face.

Ty nodded and said, "The Dovers."

Jill asked, "Who?"

Ty answered, "The family that used to own this house. There's the mother and father and that's the little girl."

"What happened to them?"

"They were murdered by the Hennesseys..."

But then Ty stopped, his eyes fixed on one of the skeletons. I could tell that he spotted something.

"What is it?" I asked him.

He didn't answer me. He just leaned in and stretched his hand toward the larger of the

two skeletons. His fingers touched the nearest shoulder blade. It looked like he was trying to move the thing, horrible as it was.

"Ty, what the hell are you doing?" I said. "Leave the damn thing alone!"

Too late. As soon as he moved the shoulder-bone, the rotted thing fell apart and the bones, grinning skull included, shattered to the floor. Jill and I leaped back, not wanting those bones to come near us, but Ty saw something shiny and metallic fall to the ground.

He bent over and picked it up.

It had once been a good knife with an eight-inch blade and an ivory-bone handle. Now though, its once-shiny blade had been dulled and corroded by what had once been blood, the blood of the man whose skeleton it was put into. Only it wasn't a skeleton when it was put there.

Ty said, "The bigger skeleton is that of a man, the

patriarch of the Dover family—and he was stabbed in the back, twixt the shoulder blades."

Jill said gravely, "That's another killin' the Hennesseys have to answer for."

"Do they?" asked Ty.

I didn't know what he meant by that, but I said urgently, "I've seen enough for one day. Come on, let's get out of this graveyard..."

———

SOME THINGS HAD TAKEN place while we were up in the attic.

Finch had some of the boys take Lone to the doctor in town by buckboard for some free medical treatment. The other gang members took the two dead men and proceeded to bury them somewhere on the property.

Going downstairs, we were about to pass the third floor when Jill wanted to go in the room and see Sherry's body. They had already removed Foster's body and taken it away for burial, so we didn't have to pass it on the way down.

Ty said to her, "You sure you want to do this?"

"I'm sure," she said. And she went into the room while we waited outside. From where I stood, I saw her as she stepped over the wreckage and stopped at the place where I told her Sherry's body was. Then Ty reminded me to give her some privacy; after all, Sherry was her friend. But as it turned out, her body wasn't there. The gang had already removed it with all the others for burial. After all, they were experts at this sort of thing.

It took a couple minutes before she came out of the

room and joined us. If the body wasn't there, I wondered what she was doing in all that time.

When we got downstairs, a few men were around; some were in the living room, some outside. They looked at us when we came downstairs, but didn't say or do anything. Maybe they had also seen too much for one day. Too much death, too many of their own ranks taken from them, too much madness. Several of them had either flasks or bottles and they were taking good swigs every once in a while.

We left the house and stepped outside into the warm mid-afternoon air. We found more of them seemingly wandering about just keeping an eye on things—and on us. Just because Finch now trusted us and took back the Toombs boys, but it didn't mean that *they* had to trust us as well.

The Toombs brothers were on the porch. Ira sat on one of the chairs, his long legs stretched out and his boots resting on the wooden railing. Andrew was seated comfortably on another chair smoking a cigarette and quietly blowing curls of smoke into the once—fresh air.

When Jill appeared, both of them suddenly moved to get up, but she said, "Thanks, boys. But the railing's all right..." They obediently sat back on their chairs as Jill sat on the railing. Ty and I sat on either side of her.

Andrew looked at Jill and said, "Heard you've been through a lot, ma'am."

Jill didn't say anything right away. She threw her hair back and ran her fingers back through it. Then she looked at him with reddened eyes and said, "Sherry went through worse..."

Andrew looked down and didn't say anything to

that. He and Ira had already seen her body being brought out.

"Yeah," he said, with unusual maturity, "sorry about that."

Again, Jill paused before responding. At first, it looked like she didn't hear him. She was looking off somewhere, her eyes fixed on some place none of us could see. And when she did speak, her lovely face took on an ugliness that put a chill in me.

"I swear," she said bitterly, "I'll get that Injun. One way or the other, I'll get 'em..."

The Toombs boys looked at each other.

Andrew asked, "Sure you don't want to sit down?"

"I'm fine, thank you."

Ty said, "We all have a score to settle with the chief, but takin' him on is not a good idea."

"He's right, ma'am," said Ira. "Gettin' even is a losing game. Especially for a woman."

Jill stopped looking at nothing and turned to stare at Ira.

"Oh? You mean only *men* can seek vengeance? Is that it?"

Andrew said, "Let's say that men...got more experience at it."

Ira then turned to his brother and idly said, "But there was that randy cowpoke in Grand Junction a couple months ago. He was beatin' the tar out of this dancehall girl up in her room."

Andrew piped up, "Right! I remember. Two weeks later her sister invites him up and she was able to take out a knife and cut off his—" Suddenly he realized a young lady was present and he stopped talking.

I turned around and looked at the others on the

property. Attempting to change a subject I personally found disgusting, I said, "Doesn't look like they're inviting us into their circle, does it? Not that I'd want to be..."

Andrew said, "The four of us are just hired guns now, livin' on borrowed time. They'll use us for the robbery and then..." He shrugged as if it all didn't matter to him, but me and Ty filled in the picture quite well of what would happen to us after the big payroll job tomorrow. Maybe the gang wouldn't be good enough to go against the Toombs boys, but me and Ty were another matter. Our mere presence was a thorn in their collective sides. One way or the other, thanks to us, the gang lost a few of their own. And for all we knew, if Finch was looking the other way, the two of us might be the victims of some *accident*.

I said quietly, "So I guess we can't take Jill, get a couple horses and ride out of here before anyone notices, can we?"

Andrew grinned at me and shook his head.

"Which of these impossible things do you think we should do first, Jed?"

Ty said, "How about all of them at once? We have guns now."

Without looking at us, Ira said, "There are too many of 'em to fight."

"Then let's just get Jill out of here. At least so they won't be able to use her as a hostage."

"Still too many of 'em." Then he looked steadily at both of us. "And even if you have guns, the kind of guns I figure you boys never fired before, that doesn't mean either of you are good shots."

I said, "You forgot. I already killed one of the gang

with this gun." I patted the gun at my hip for emphasis —and instantly felt stupid as soon as I did it.

Ira smiled wryly and said, "He wasn't even ten feet away from you and ya got 'em in broad daylight. Added to those little details, *no one* was shooting at you when you killed him, *especially* the man you were shooting. He was aiming his gun at Ty, *not you!*"

"But that doesn't mean—"

"Oh please!" Ira shook his head as if he were talking to a child. Looking up at me and Ty, he continued, warming to his subject as he spoke. "The Hennessey Gang has been killing men while you two were still in long knickers. Most of these boys would be able to get off five shots to your one—or be able to empty their guns while you're still pawin' your holster. No, Jed. Neither of you are going to beat them face to face. The only way we're all gonna be clear of this mess is during the robbery itself, when there'll be so much confusion, they wouldn't be able to watch us."

"Confusion?" said Ty. "I thought the Hennesseys did this kind of thing as second nature."

Andrew grinned again and Ira quietly shook his head.

"It's all bullshit," said Ira, not with contempt, but as a statement of fact. "When you're committing a robbery in a very public place, nine times out of ten you'll fail. And if you're committing a robbery and a gunfight occurs, the odds are even *less* you'll be able to ride out of it the same way you rode in. Look at the James-Younger Gang at Northfield! Went against the odds and got shot to pieces because of it. Usually with a gang on one side and the Law and the townsmen on the other, you're *beggin'* for a situation where one hand don't know what the other's doin' on *both sides*. A gunfight is a little war that neither side declared and without political ideology of any kind. Both townsmen and robbers shoot each other to death during all the gunsmoke and wild horses dancing around in a panic, and most of the time both sides end up killing their own men! It's *just* like a war! Sure, you kill the enemy once in a while, but you'd be getting off a lucky shot. Most of the time, you're runnin' back and forth trying not to be hit.

"Yeah, the Hennesseys are good robbers and killers. But I don't care how good you are, when you're on the battlefield, you'll be lucky keeping yourself alive much less shootin' the other guy out of the saddle..."

Ty and me stared at Ira with some surprise. That's the *most* either of us ever heard him say.

After he finished, he looked at the ground, embarrassed and uncomfortable, as if he'd suddenly realized he'd said too much. Then Andrew did something unusual; that is, for him. He reached out and touched his brother's shoulder tenderly.

For Ira, that seemed to be the last straw. He shook off Andrew's hand and rose to his feet.

"I'm headin' to town for some grub," he said sullenly. "You comin'?"

Andrew replied, "Sure."

Ira stalked off, heading for the stables.

We all looked at Andrew.

Seeing the unasked question on our faces, he said, "Don't tell him I told you this, but Ira was a bluebelly once. Fought the Navajo in New Mexico Territory. He was probably in more scrapes than Custer, Meade, and Hallock put together..."

Ty said quietly, "That's why he knows so much about men under fire..."

"More than you know, Ty. During one Navajo raid, one of the soldiers panicked and blew off the head of his best friend."

"Jesus!" I said.

"Yeah," Andrew replied. "He never mentions his army service. 'Specially the battles..."

Ira was calling from the stables. "Hey, Andrew, ya comin'?"

Andrew called back, "In two shakes, big brother!"

He gave us that infectious grin of his for a last time and then got up and headed for the stables. No one stopped them as they rode out. The Toombs boys were still part of the gang *we* were the ones they had to watch out for and we knew it.

After they rode off, we were sitting on that porch quietly for a few minutes when one of the outlaws stood on the lawn and called to Jill.

"Hey!" We all turned around. "I want some grub!"

Ty said, "Get it yourself!"

Jill put her hand on Ty's arm and said gently, "Ty, please. It's all right. I'll do it..."

The man smiled crookedly as Jill got up and headed inside. He stared at us as he passed and followed her in.

I asked, "Think she'll be all right?"

"Well," he replied, "if they kill her, she can't cook for 'em."

"True..."

"And they need her alive if they're going to keep stringing us along."

"True again."

"Anyway, after all the killing they've seen of their

own lately, I have a feeling they're not going to pull anything for a while that might bring on more killing. Though I know if we push things, they'll blow us away in two seconds."

"True a third time."

"Jed, there's one thing I want you to do that would make me feel better."

"What's that?"

"Call me a liar..."

CHAPTER NINETEEN

THE NIGHT WAS QUIET AND, FOR THIS GANG, UNEVENTFUL.

So was dinner. As we sat at the long table, Jill served what few gang members were there; and again, unusual for them, they were quiet. Not only was Jill given a new man's shirt and pants to replace the torn clothes she had worn, but no one tried to grab her butt or make her feel uncomfortable. And except for the usual rude demands for seconds that Jill had to stretch to be fair to everyone who wanted them, she was not insulted and there were not the usual leering smiles. Maybe seeing Ed Plummer thrown through a third-floor window and falling to his death had something to do with it. Or maybe seeing the corpses of Sherry or Jack Foster made them sit back and see what a thin string they were *all* held by, I didn't know. After all, it was everyone fighting over Jill, or trying to molest her, that brought on all the killings that lessened their numbers. Maybe they finally got it in them—especially after Finch's orders—to just let Jill serve the meals and, for now anyway, stay the hell away from her. He couldn't afford to lose any more men.

Inside, Finch and his men planned for the next day's raid. And, for obvious reasons, we were told not to participate in the meeting. Instead, Finch just told us to trust him and that if all went well, we could take our share and do whatever we wanted—even take Jill with us—and never return. Though I suspect that Finch actually believed, even after what we'd been through, that the money and the sheer thrill of robbing and killing would intoxicate us and we'd stay with the gang.

The moon was full again that night, and though the outlaws were wandering about the grounds, they didn't bother us when me, Ty and Jill wandered outside. Maybe they were thinking about the big job the next day to be too concerned, I wasn't sure. But after we went outside, I told Ty and Jill I'd just relax on the porch before turning in. Ty looked at me again, probably wondering why I just wanted to sit on the porch in the shadows alone.

I knew why. This allowed him and Jill to wander around the lawn by themselves for a change. Hell, every time those two were together, I'd always be with them. Well, this time, I was giving nature a little push, that's all.

They were not too far from where I was sitting so I could still see them, even in the shadows. Maybe they thought I couldn't hear them, but I caught most of what they said too. Quiet as the night was, and even with the voices lowered, their words were clear.

Jill drawled, "I can't thank you boys enough for all you've done for me."

Ty looked at her and said, "My pleasure..."

She walked a little ways and looked up at the moon. Ty followed her.

"A young man and a young woman walkin' in the moonlight," she said. "Anywhere else, it'd be…"

"Yeah," he said quietly, "I know what it'd be."

Jill looked back at him, her eyes suddenly moist. "Why didn't I meet you years ago?"

Ty answered, "You're meeting me now."

"Yeah. I am at that…"

It wasn't a second before they were in each other's arms.

She was about to say something else, but the passionate kiss the two of them shared got in the way of her words. As if on cue, dark clouds passed over the moon and the two were in the dark, which I was glad for, not only for their privacy, but if any gang members were passing by, they couldn't spy on them at that moment.

The clouds passed over and I saw them again in each other's arms, hugging tightly. Then they separated a little and she looked up at him.

"Some things you've got to know about me, Ty."

"Like *what*?"

"I haven't always been…well, the kind of girl you can bring home to your ma."

He shook his head and said, "Let me be the judge of that…"

"I've danced in saloons. I've sat on men's laps and drank hard liquor with them."

"That's because your job dictated that you had to make them comfortable."

"I'm—I'm not—"

The words were stuck in her throat. But Ty just cupped her chin up to him and said, "Look me in the eye when you say it."

"I'm—I'm not pure!"

"You're pure enough."

"But I've slept with other men!"

"Often?"

"Well...here and there. There was that whiskey drummer in Grand Junction. And then there was that saddle-maker in Glenwood Springs. And Crowley used to push us to...you know, treat his friends special..."

"That wasn't you."

"All right, then who was it?"

"Okay, it *was* you. But that kind of life wasn't what you always wanted, was it?"

Jill paused and bit her lower lip. Then she looked at him and said, "I *did* those things. Isn't that bad enough?"

"You ever kick dogs or beat horses? Murder someone? Vote for Samuel Tilden?"

She smiled up at him. "*No to all of it*! And how about *you*?"

"The only girls I ever loved were in my schoolhouse."

"Aww, schoolyard crushes."

Ty cleared his throat and said, "Well, sometimes they went beyond just bein' crushes..."

Jill grinned and her eyes lit up when she said, "So you *really* learned something at school, huh?"

Ty smiled and said, "You're the first one I told that to. I never even told Jed, and he's my best friend."

Jill glanced over my way and I quickly dropped my head as if I was fast asleep.

"Can he hear us?" she asked.

I assume Ty took a quick look at me because he said, "Doesn't look like it."

It was quiet then. I wasn't sure what was happening

until I chanced a peek at them and saw them kissing again—much longer this time.

They embraced afterward.

Jill said, "Am I gonna see you again after tomorrow?"

"You can bet on it."

"Oh, god I hope so! I want all of us to get the hell away from these lunatics."

"It'll happen. I promise..."

I didn't hear them say anything again after that, but my imagination could fill in what they were doing anyway.

Then I heard their footsteps getting closer and they were both climbing the porch.

Ty gently shook me *awake* I pretended to be waking up, including looking like I was yawning and stretching. When I opened my eyes, I saw the two of them holding hands.

"Eh, sleepyhead..."

"Oh, what time is it?"

"Time to sleep indoors."

"I'll be inside in a moment. Just want to sit out here a little while longer."

"In that case," Jill said, "I'll see you boys tomorrow morning. Good night."

They thought I wasn't looking, but I sneaked a peek and saw them look lovingly at each other and even blow kisses. I couldn't help but smile. Yet I also felt some sadness.

I was losing my big brother.

She left us alone and Ty finally turned to me and said, "You heard every word, didn't you?"

"Yes, I did."

"And?"

"You've got to be alive to marry her, Ty."

"I know it."

"We've got a lot to think about. To consider what Ira said about getting away during the robbery."

"I won't leave without her, Jed."

"I wouldn't want you to. Neither would I. There's just got to be some way we can all get out clean. And maybe after that, try to prove to everyone that we're innocent of murdering Old Man Reynolds."

"It's been a long, crazy day, Jed. Let's sleep on it. Maybe we'll come up with something tomorrow."

"Okay, I'll see you inside."

Ty was about to head inside when at the last minute I stopped him and said, "And you've been sparkin' with some of the gals at school and never told me?"

He stopped and I could tell his face was redder than a beet even in the shadows.

After a moment, he finally said, "There are some things a man doesn't spout off to his little brother—not for a while anyway..."

I smiled and said, "Go to bed, you ol' dog..."

He grinned back and went inside to our little room with the moldy mattresses.

I sat there for a little while, just thinking about what I had witnessed. Ty and Jill sparking in the moonlight. I liked her. She didn't fold up and let it all get to her as some other woman might've. She had strength; not something you find every day in these crazy times. And I was proud of my big brother for the way he expertly shot down all her reasons that they couldn't be together.

After a while, I started thinking about Hazel, how much I still loved her, how much I *had* wanted her. And then, whether I was conscious of it or not, Bessie started to drift into my thoughts. I knew she wasn't as hard-nosed as she appeared. That was clinched earlier today when I saw her run off in tears. Was she crying because of me? Was that possible?

And then there's her outward appearance, the mussed-up brown hair always falling out of its bun, the sparkling blue eyes that looked right into you, the long, sleek neck, the proud way she carried herself beneath the dirty apron and worn blouse, the expressive hands that were always covered with grease and grime.

Ty was right. No matter how unkempt she appeared, she *was* beautiful.

I glanced back at the house. It was time to get to sleep.

But before I went inside, I thought about what I had witnessed between Ty and Jill; how the two of them were kissing each other with such passion, such longing.

They were both kissing each other as if there would be no tomorrow...

CHAPTER TWENTY

W<small>E BOTH SLEPT WELL THAT NIGHT</small>—OR AS WELL AS ONE could sleep knowing he was going to be in the middle of a stagecoach robbery the next day.

At first, I dreamed of nice things; soft meadows, lush grass, and the front lawns of fine old houses situated in beautiful forests. Places where lovers met and kissed in the moonlight the night before facing an uncertain future. Then things turned bad and I saw men being flung through windows and hitting the ground hard. Visions of people being shot in the streets in broad daylight and men dying by choking to death on their own chewing tobacco. And then things turned again and a face came to dominate my dreams. At this point, it didn't surprise me that the face belonged to a young Irish brunette with blue eyes, her smile shining down at me like the rays of the sun.

The rays of the sun. They started to come into our room through that goddamn torn shade over our dirty window. My eyes opened and I looked over at Ty. He was sitting up on his elbow and his eyes were looking ahead at nothing. How long he had been up, I couldn't say. I wondered what he was thinking of, but I could imagine.

He knew I was up. I knew it because he started talking before he even glanced in my direction.

"I'll tell ya one thing, Jed."

I said nothing, just waited.

"I don't care if they kill me for it, but I'm not shooting any soldiers."

I looked at him and said, just as decisively, "I feel the way you do, Ty. I'm not shooting any soldiers either."

He looked at me without smiling. Then he sat up and reached out with his right hand.

We shook hands then, me and my brother. We didn't know if this was going to be the last morning we'd ever spend together...

———

It was decided that we'd have breakfast in town.

But before we headed out, we assembled on the front lawn and some men were already on their horses. Jill stood on the porch watching us. A man had been ordered to stay behind and watch her. In fact, he had strict orders not to let her out of his sight. He was even ordered to follow her to the small outhouse in the back and make sure she didn't spend more than a couple minutes inside. The man was an ugly cuss, with a mouth too wide, a black beard too thick and eyebrows that knotted together at the top and almost joined with some more coarse hairs growing out of his forehead. He smelled like a dead cat and his slovenly clothes complimented the rest of him.

Finch said that if she behaved herself, the man wouldn't lay a hand on her. And if he did try, Finch told him he'd personally put a bullet through him.

Leading his horse, Ty stopped for a moment and he and Jill looked at each other. The man who was supposed to be watching her was standing behind her on the porch. He saw the looks they gave each other and then, as if he were testing the waters, he gave a leering smile and put his hands on Jill's shoulders. Jill tried to shake him off and I saw Ty tense up. But before he could take any action, Finch came up and shouted angrily at the man.

"Hagel! What the hell did I tell you before? Now keep your goddamn paws to yourself or I'll put one in your thick skull right now and have someone else watch her!"

Suddenly sobered by the threat, Hagel quickly took his dirty fingers off Jill's shoulders and fearfully backed away from her.

Then Finch said to Jill, "After we come back, you tell me if he mistreats you."

Jill said, "All right, Finch, I will..."

Finch nodded and then turned and walked back to his horse.

Ty and Jill gave each other a last look and then he was about to mount his horse when he spotted Severin. The disfigured man was coming across the lawn and was about to pass him when Ty suddenly dropped the reins in his right hand and punched Severin in the face. After he fell to the ground, he looked up at Ty, hate coming through clearly even in that distorted face of his.

Finch rushed over as the Toombs brothers grabbed Ty and held him back.

The gang stopped whatever they were doing and stared at us, not knowing what to make of the scene, but also not interfering. They had no need for either me or Ty, true, but I can safely say that none of them regretted seeing Severin get knocked on his ass.

"What the hell's wrong now?" Finch demanded.

Ty said, "Sorry, Finch, but I *had* to do it! Didn't know if I'd get another chance..."

Finch said wryly, "Lord knows, none of us here admire Severin very much, but you've got me curious, Ty. What suddenly put you in the club?"

I came over and said, "I know why he hit 'em, Finch. And you can put me in that club too."

Finch said to the Toombs boys, "Let 'em go." They did so as Severin slowly got up of the ground. We noticed no one helped him. Then Finch asked Ty, "Okay, why'd you do it?"

Ty said, "Something about skeletons in the family closet."

Finch looked at him oddly and asked, "You been drinkin'?"

Jill said from the porch, "He's right, Finch. Up in the attic we found three skeletons. That of a man, a woman, and a little girl. The man had a knife in his back..."

Finch turned to look back at Ty, his expression demanding an explanation. If Finch was pretending not to know what was going on, he did a damn good job of it. In fact, I realized right then and there that he *didn't know*. He had absolutely no idea that the skeletons of a murdered family were hidden in the attic of the house he and his gang slept in and used as a hideout.

Answering Finch's look, Ty said, "What was left of the Dover family." Then he turned to Severin and said bitterly, "Maybe your parents were big enough to take care of themselves, but to murder your own sister, to murder that little girl!" He started toward Severin, but again the Toombs boys grabbed him.

Severin cried out, "He's lying!"

Ty said to him, "Am I? You told us that the Hennessey Gang murdered your family and then forced you to bury them somewhere on the property. Then what were they doing in that crawlspace in the attic? And the old man with a knife in his back? The Hennessey Gang *could* have done that, but a bullet in the guts is more their style." God bless Ty; he didn't hesitate for a second to say that out loud right in front of the gang as they were listening to us.

Finch turned around and faced Severin. I could see that the rest of his face was perfectly calm, but his eyes turned mean so fast, it was frightening to see.

"You told me your family went to Europe, and we were free to take over the house as long as we wanted. You even wanted me to call you my brother so none of the others would push you around..."

Severin stepped back and stared at him fearfully, fully realizing that Finch was wearing a gun and he wasn't. It was said that Clay Finch Hennessey never shot down an unarmed man, but by the look I saw on his face at that moment, I was sure he'd break that rule.

Finch said angrily, "We're pressed for time, Severin! Now what did you do with your family?"

Severin blurted out, "Don't you see, Finch? I wanted to ride with you boys! I'd have done *anything* to be one of you! To be one of the feared Hennessey Gang and strut around this pathetic little burg you call a town and not have any of 'em lay a hand on me. I was sick of being looked on like some pampered rich boy. I wanted to be treated like a man!

"My father wouldn't let me ride with you. So one night we had a fight about it. And when the old bastard—"

Finch finished the sentence for him. "So when the old man turned his back, you put a knife in it. And what about the woman and the little girl?"

Severin said, "You said you and the boys needed the house. And I wanted so badly to join up with you that—"

"So you killed your own mother and little sister just to *join us*?"

Finch was as shocked as the rest of us standing around, hardened outlaws to boot.

Ty stared at Severin and said, "You poisoned them, didn't you?"

Severin didn't answer Ty or face him, but under Finch's withering stare, he was forced to nod his head reluctantly.

Severin had already pushed Finch too far by double-crossing the gang after the Beaumont robbery and then attempting to back-shoot him in that whorehouse; therefore, Finch allowed Lone to mutilate his face. And now, there was a new reason for him to get angry at Severin all over again.

For the price of having the Dover House, Finch had allowed their only son to ride with the gang and even tell the others he was a Hennessey as well to give him a special status within the gang. But it came at a cost. Samuel Dover, alias Severin Hennessey, was a weak man with an ego that needed constant reminders of how wonderful he was. He did this by drinking constantly, dallying with women all the time and, the ultimate challenge for someone like him, joining the gang on robberies, running off with the loot and spending it all before they could make him give it back. It didn't happen all that often, but when it did, Severin had a savior in the man he called his *brother*. Finch had stood for it all and reluctantly protected him to boot. In fact, he was treating this pathetic man as if he *was* his own brother, with all the loyalties that came with it. But now Severin had crossed a line Finch wouldn't have dared approached: Severin had destroyed his own family. To a man like Finch who valued family allegiance above all else, Severin had not only shook hands with Satan, but he joined him for a few drinks as well.

Looking from one gang member to another, Severin was starting to tremble like a tree branch swaying in the wind.

"Please, Finch, don't do anything to me! You protected me all those years. I mean, I'm your *brother*!"

"Not anymore..." When Finch said it, the normal down-home drawl sounded like sandpaper.

The clicks of Colt hammers were heard and me and Ty glanced back and saw several men with their guns out, all wanting to be the first one to end Severin's life for all time. The Toombs boys, I was glad to see, weren't among them.

"Say the word, Finch," said one of the gun-toting men.

I looked at the gang boss and he seemed to be thinking real hard about it. As yet, he had not even put his hand on his own gun.

Severin took a few steps back in fear. "Don't let 'em kill me, Clay!" He didn't exactly burst into tears, nor did he relieve himself, but still, I almost felt sorry for this man who came into the world as a child of privilege and would leave it as an outlaw and a coward. Looking the way he did, he could never move among so-called polite society like everyone else without someone feeling horror and disgust. Now he couldn't even hide among society's outcasts either. But then I remembered how he murdered his family, especially that little girl, and all sympathy drained out of me like pus out of an open wound.

Finch finally said, "You're comin' with us, Sev. You always wanted to be an outlaw like us. Now you can die like one..."

"No!" screamed Severin. "You can't take *me* with you! I won't do it!"

I had thought of Severin as having average intelligence, but *stupid* was definitely the first word that came to my mind when I heard him say he wouldn't go with them. As if he had a choice.

A few quiet orders from Finch and two men came up to Severin as he backed away fearfully. Before I could blink, one of them took out his pistol and knocked Severin across the head with it; not enough to kill him, but just enough to knock him out. They caught the collapsing man and then dragged him across the lawn, not caring how violently they did it.

"Tie him to his horse," was Finch's last order. He then turned and headed back to his horse. His back seemed stiffer somehow. You could see that he had become more stubborn than ever, more unwilling to compromise. One way or the other, Finch Hennessey was going to make absolutely sure that we rode to town, had our breakfast, then rode to New Mexico Territory and robbed that damn stagecoach even if it killed him—and probably us as well...

———

THE RIDE to town was uneventful and unusually quiet.

Severin was out cold and tied hand and foot to his horse, which was being led by one of the gang. During the ride, I heard that Lone was coming with us as well, and all we had to do was pick him up at the doctor's office after we ate. Me and Ty were *not* looking forward to the occasion.

As usual, folks around town made themselves scarce when we rode in.

There was one person I saw who didn't make himself scarce. Hiram Jessup stood ramrod straight on the boardwalk outside his office. As we rode by, he glared at every one of us. There was no greeting, not even for Finch, who rode by as if his uncle wasn't even there. Jessup knew where we would be going after our meal, and the anger we witnessed the other day didn't disappear; it still burned in the man. I could tell as me and Ty rode by him, that he especially seemed to reserve his hostility for us, because as we passed, he shook his head as if we were either sorry, misguided idiots or greedy young roughnecks. I was glad when we got past him.

We ate at the Pellican. But there were some changes. Word had gotten back to the people who managed the hotel, who, of course, also managed the restaurant. Hazel was sacked on Finch's orders. He had already said as much to her back on the street that morning when she tactlessly sided with us over the gang. Instead, they had a new woman working in the kitchen while Bessie served us in the restaurant.

Actually, since the whole gang was there, both she and this other woman served us, taking turns running back in the kitchen and cooking as well. Lord, we were lucky this new woman didn't spill whole pots of coffee on us. Either serving the Hennessey Gang made her nervous or she'd never been a waitress in her life—or maybe both.

Bessie went around the table and poured our second and third cups of coffee, but she paused when she saw me. I thought she'd still be mad at me from the other day, but the look on her face when she saw me wasn't hostile at all. In fact, except for being preoccupied serving the gang, she almost looked friendly. After serving a couple more men, she took the empty pot and was about to pass me when she stopped and said my name in a harsh whisper.

I looked up at her.

"Can you meet me in the kitchen in ten minutes?"

I nodded. Then she nodded and moved away quickly.

At least she didn't seem mad as she was before. I didn't see Hazel anywhere around, but at that point I didn't even care. I had my own problems.

Breakfast was quiet, at least quiet for the Hennessey Gang anyway.

Ty noticed Bessie's quick visit to my part of the table and I could detect a little smile on his face, though he was looking down when I saw it.

I finished my food quickly, and after about ten

minutes, I got up and headed for the kitchen. I noticed Finch saw me as I went across the room, but then he must've thought nothing of it because he quickly returned his attention to his meal.

When I entered, Bessie was at the sink, scrubbing a pan.

The new waitress, whose name was Zelda, asked me what I wanted and I told her I was here to see Bessie.

At the sound of my voice, Bessie turned around and saw me. She self-consciously shoved her hair back out of her eyes and wiped her hands on her already stained apron.

"It's all right, Zelda," she said in her usual light brogue. "Uh, could you leave us for a moment?"

"Why?" Zelda asked.

She wasn't very bright.

Bessie said patiently, "Zelda, please."

"Oh, all right," Zelda said, tossing a rag on a counter. Then she went out of the kitchen and slammed the door.

I faced Bessie then. Even in this harsh kitchen light and covered in grease, she looked good. I stepped closer to her.

I asked, "Did Hazel give you my message?"

"Yes," she said, coming closer to me. "Yes, she did..."

Then she paused for a moment, as if she didn't know what to say.

"And?" I asked.

"And I'm sorry I got mad at you."

"No, you had every right. I shouldn't have said what I did."

"Well, I shouldn't have slapped you. Not that hard anyway..."

I put a hand to my cheek and said, "I'll agree with ya there..."

She smiled then, a wonderful grin that I had a feeling you rarely saw from her.

Then her expression turned serious and she said, "Are you still going to go through with that robbery?"

I sighed in exasperation and said, "Yeah. We have to."

"Ira was in town last night visiting Hazel. He told her why you're doing it, and she told me. It's fine of you to be concerned for that girl they're holding at the house."

"Finch promised to let her go after the robbery."

"Maybe," she said with some resentment. "But in the meantime, you and Ty will get yourselves in *deeper*."

"I know..."

"What will you do when the robbery happens?"

"Well, Ty and me know what we *won't* do. We won't try to shoot any soldiers. Maybe...maybe during the confusion we'll get away and ride back here. Somehow get Jill out of there. We're kind of playing it by ear right now..."

Then Bessie surprised me by leaning forward and gently putting her hand on my forearm. It felt good having it there.

"You're a good person, Jed. You and Ty don't deserve this."

"Yeah," I said gravely, "tell me something I *don't* know."

Removing her arm, she said, "I'm sorry."

I faced her and said, "No, Bessie, *I'm* the one that's sorry. It's just that...I'm so goddamn riled! *Everything's* been going wrong lately! Everything in my life for the past week had been going wrong! I've been in too many fights, been beaten senseless, kicked in the face, had guns pointed at me and now I'm wanted for murder and robbery along with my big brother and I don't know if I'm comin' or goin' or if I'm a righteous man or an outlaw. Outside of Ty, I've been living with savages. Not the kind that wear war paint and scream like a bunch of idiots, but home-grown, all-American white boys who act like animals in a damn jungle. All I've known for the past few days is beatings and seeing people die and I'm goddamn sick of it!"

My tirade had about reached a climax. And when I stopped, I suddenly realized that I was close to tears. I didn't know what Bessie thought of it, and I didn't care. Still, I quickly wiped my eyes and pretended to look around the room to avoid her seeing them.

But when I looked at her again, I saw the compassion in her face, and maybe I imagined there was something more in her eyes when they looked up at me.

I continued, "All I want is for someone to say to me that they understand everything I've done, someone to say they're on my side and maybe pat me on the back and say keep up the good work because I know you'll do the right thing in the long run." I paused then and looked into her eyes without realizing it.

"Someone to care about whether I live or die... maybe I'm asking too much. I'm no prize. I'm just a poor farm boy who's not too bright and—"

She blurted out, "You've got *me!*"

"You?"

She gave me a quick little nod.

I said, "You hate me."

"I hate *what I thought you were*. I know better now."

"How do you know?"

"*Your sister* told me all about you."

"So you know..."

"She told me the whole story. Now I see why you called her your family the other day. She told me who you were, where you and Ty came from, the wonderful parents you have and what you're doin' with the Hennesseys. Your actions told me the rest..."

"Did she even tell you how stupidly we got into this mess?"

She gave that quick, little nod again.

"And you still want someone like—"

She came to me then and embraced me tightly.

With her arms around me and her head against my chest, she looked up at me and asked, "Does this answer your question?"

I put my arms around her then. After a moment my head reached down and I kissed her on the forehead. She smiled as she held on to me.

"You're a hell of a girl, Bessie."

"I like to think I'm a hell of a *woman*."

"You're that in spades."

We heard the sound of the kitchen door opening and we both looked at it. Stu was standing there looking at us with a typically wicked smile on his face.

"All right, lover boy," he said. "Finch said we're movin' out. So get your last feels from 'er and meet us outside." Then he left, closing the door.

I tensed up and started to move out of her embrace and toward the door when she stopped me.

"No, Jed," Bessie said. "His kind aren't worth it. At least not right now."

I turned and looked at her.

I said, "I don't want to go with them. I want to stay with *you*."

"And you *will*! I promise."

I didn't want to sound like some corny, old romance novel, but I suddenly felt warm all over. It could've been all those pots of boiling water on the stove, but I doubted it.

"You mean, if I live through this, I could see you?"

"Well," she said good-naturedly, "hopefully, you could do more than just *see me...*"

I glanced back at the door; then I took a couple steps toward it. "I better get goin'."

She moved with me, as if we were in some kind of slow dance.

"Jed, please live through this! Do it for me if not for yourself!"

"I promise," I said.

I wanted to come closer to her, but then I heard the sounds of boots headed toward the kitchen door and without another word I ducked through it, almost colliding with Stu as he was about to enter.

He stopped short and gave me a nasty look. "Just in time! Finch told me to get you outta there if I had to drag you out by your ass."

"Yeah," I said. "You're the kind that'd probably like doin' that..."

By the anger on his face, I could see that the crack had gotten to him, but with some difficulty he restrained himself. I followed him outside where everyone else was already on his horse, including Ty. He and I gave each other a final look before I went over to my horse and mounted up.

Then we all started to follow Finch's horse down the street.

I took a look at the restaurant window. Sure enough, with complaining customers around her now demanding service, Bessie had her face almost pressed against the window watching me as we rode away.

I looked back at her and our eyes locked from a distance for a moment.

Then I turned around and faced the street as we all made our way out of town and took the trail to New Mexico.

I didn't know what would happen at the end of that trail...

CHAPTER TWENTY-ONE

WE SET OUT ON OUR JOURNEY, A COUPLE HOURS RIDE down to the New Mexican border.

We heard that the army was using the Butterfield stage line to get the payroll across, and better still—according to Hennessey standards anyway—the army would only be sending a skeleton crew to escort the coach. Maybe they didn't realize how the Hennesseys were going to make the words skeleton crew very real.

It wasn't all that far to our destination, but it wasn't exactly in the next town either.

Lone Hennessey had joined us sometime on the route before we rode out of town. He joined us so quietly that I didn't realize until long after we passed the town limits that he was with us. When we got a chance, we glanced back and saw him. He was riding his horse as tall and steady as you'd expect him to, and he was wearing the same clothes he had before, but his pants leg had been torn short just below the knee by Doc Elder, and a heavy cloth bandage was wrapped around where Finch had been forced to shoot him in the leg. How Lone had been able to mount his horse was testament to his crazed desire to wipe out the white-eyes in blue uniforms, pain be damned. His head was entirely covered in some old burlap sack with eye-slits carved into it. I imagined that his face was probably covered in bandages beneath the sack itself. On the one hand, Ty and me wanted to laugh at the picture of him wearing that silly getup, but on the other it kind of sent a chill up my spine. He reminded us of drawings of southern bushwhackers and redlegs we had read about in books and newspapers on the war. They looked ridiculous in those sacks and pillowcases they wore during their raids, but there was nothing funny about their sick acts of violence. We immediately saw a parallel between those night-riding madmen and Lone Hennessey's particular brand of hate.

The sun got warmer as we rode, and it beat down on us the closer we came to the border. Eventually, me and Ty took off our jackets and folded them under our pommels as sweat started to form on our faces—or was it the sweat of fear at what tasks we had to perform to stay alive. I noticed that the others—maybe about a dozen or so—were also mopping their foreheads and taking off their jackets and vests. Some of these men were clearly too young to have fought in the war, but I had the impression their sympathies would've been with the South. It gave them an added initiative for attacking federal troops—the so-called skeleton crew—and take some measure of revenge on them while stealing that payroll. And for Lone, he would've had no problem attacking any white man in a cavalry uniform.

As for Severin, by the time we had gotten close to the Butterfield Road, he had regained consciousness. But his freedom of movement was restricted. First of all his legs were tied under the horse's belly so that he couldn't jump off his mount and run even if he wanted to—and we were pretty sure he wanted to. His hands were tied in front of him just enough so that he could hold the horse's reins, but not enough so that he could do anything else. Another man led his horse on a long rope. Needless to say, he was given no gun. Also, tightly tied around his mouth was a large dirty neckerchief which doubled as a gag in case Severin should have the gall to shout out a warning to any approaching rider, bluebelly or not. Therefore, Finch's prediction that Severin was going to die like an outlaw was going to come true. For without any freedom of movement except to ride forward with his wrists tied, the only thing Severin could accomplish was to ride into the cavalry's skirmish line and that's it. He couldn't defend himself. He couldn't shoot back for he had no gun. He was only there to put up a delaying action and then die while he did it, that's it. Were Finch and his men being cruel by setting Severin up as a sacrificial lamb, or were they meting out their own twisted brand of justice to a child-murderer? Hard to come up with the right answer sometimes.

I glanced back at the Toombs boys all the way in the rear. Andrew, of course, had a big grin on his face and even waved at us. To him, it was all a lark, as if he was riding to a barn dance with several nubile young ladies and a bowl full of spiked punch waiting for him at the end of his journey. I then turned to look at Ira. He was the total opposite. He was his usual quiet self, even dare I say glum and morose. To him, it was another battle he had to ride into and didn't want to. Regardless, he'd do his best. Fighting was serious business to him.

It was getting closer to noon as we approached the rim of Southern Colorado. Ty and I had never been to New Mexico, but this was certainly *not* the way we wanted to be there.

Quietly, we had made our pact; no shooting of soldiers even to defend ourselves. Probably better to die than to take an innocent life alongside the Hennessey Gang. We were already fugitives, but to be caught guilty of murdering soldiers would *really* shame our folks, and we had to think of them as well.

Then, as we neared a clearing, we saw that the road we were on opened up onto a fork, with our road continuing west and the new opening going east. The stage was going to be coming from the east. The cavalry would have flankers and outriders spread out ahead of the approaching coach. According to snatches of conversation we were able to pick up, Finch was going to let the detachment pass by, then hit the coach and knock off the guards as it came abreast of our trail. The firefight would, of course, turn the outriders back in our direction, but before they could hit the first group, *another* group would come out of the trees before they got to us and wipe out the rest of the soldiers. Pretty simple. It didn't take a Sherman or Sheridan to come up with that. Unfortunately, despite our repeated questions, we were not told which group we were going to be in.

Finally, Finch called a halt to the ride. We could

clearly see the new road and its fork ahead of us. Finch must've had men scout the place before choosing it as an ambush point. It seemed all-too perfect. The lush overgrowth of trees on both sides of our trail covered our appearance from the view of anyone coming up the main road, like, for instance, those cavalry outriders. It wasn't going to be hard keeping a dozen to fifteen men on horseback quiet, but if there was any sound, they'd know of our presence and that was the end of any element of surprise. When it looked like their approach was close, we were to put our hands over our horses' muzzles; otherwise, the presence of other horses would make the cavalry mounts get excited, something that would put any good horseman on his guard.

We didn't have too long to wait. In the quiet of those desolate woods, we easily heard the clip-clop of horses a half mile away. And behind them the rolling of wheels of some conveyance—and it wasn't a freighter with a spring wagon either. Seems we got to the ambush point just in time. Finch's calculations timed to the moment. No wonder he insisted that Stu get me out of the kitchen and away from Bessie and got us moving.

My Bessie. Dare I call her *my* Bessie? Or my beautiful Bessie? Hell, sitting on my horse waiting for those bluebellies to show up, I was drowning in such tension and fear that I vowed that if I survived this mess, I'd swear off all infantile crushes on unattainable women like Hazel and be happy with a girl like Bessie the rest of my days. So help me God...

I glanced at Ty. He was sweating as much as I was. We were both reluctant to start reaching for our guns, but as time painfully dragged on and the clopping sound of the cavalry mounts got louder, we both couldn't help fingering the butts of our .45s, if only to defend ourselves. Nevertheless, the plan, if that's what it could be called, was to survive, somehow ride back ahead of the surviving gang members, if any, and somehow rescue Jill.

The horses' hooves of the soldiers got louder and louder, coming closer and closer.

And soon there they were, big as blue-coated life. There were half a dozen of them. I had never seen soldiers before. I was surprised at how young and fresh-faced they were, with curly mustaches grown on their upper lips to give them maturity, their blue blouses all shiny and clean in the mid-afternoon sun. They rode stiffly and upright in the saddle, ramrod straight and proud of who they were, not out of arrogance, but because they damn well had a right to be. It looked like they were almost on parade. Their appearance almost took my breath away. Perhaps had I been born forty years ago instead of almost twenty, I would've been one of them, taking back Georgia, laying waste to the Shenandoah Valley and the Confederacy's ability to make war, marching to South Carolina, being one of thousands of white men—and negroes—in an army of liberation.

But now they rode by and the only cause they were fighting for was guarding a coach full of their pay. And if the Hennesseys' plan came to be, these young boys would be every bit as dead as the ones who came before them who fought at Chancellorsville and Fredericks-burg and Falls Church.

They were walking their horses past us so calmly it was like they were all asleep. What kind of flankers were they anyway? Didn't they know a trap was being set?

They passed us as if they were just on routine patrol and the danger was somewhere way ahead of them in another state. We were so close to them; the clouds of dust that rose in their wake almost choked us as we sat our horses. Ty and me had to hold down our impulse to cough as we watched them pass, one hand over our horses' snouts, the other on the butts of our guns.

Then, after maybe ten minutes, the rolling of the wheels got louder and the shadow of the coach came into view. Finally, after what seemed like another hour, the stagecoach crossed in front of us. Finch saw it and raised his hand to signal the attack.

But before he could drop his arm, all hell—as it could do in those usually special instances of uncontrollable chaos and calamity—broke loose.

First of all, the driver atop the coach wasn't a Butterfield man, but a soldier. A soldier with a Springfield rifle that was now aimed at us. As soon as we saw him, other bluebellies appeared from within the coach and aimed their own rifles at us through the windows.

As soon as Ty spotted them, he yelled at me, "Hit the ground!"

He didn't have to tell me twice. Despite the fact that our horses stood several yards back from the front of our column, Ty and I both kicked our feet out of our stirrups, dove off our horses and hit the dirt.

Ty's warning couldn't have come any sooner than it did. Seconds after we dropped from our horses, the soldiers in the coach and the trooper on top of it opened fire. Gang members toppled from their horses as if they were suddenly swept from their saddles by a giant, invisible hand. Only Finch seemed to be smart enough to follow our lead and also drop from his mount. After hitting the ground, he rose and scrambled for the trees, finally ducking behind some bushes and firing at the soldiers from cover. Unfortunately, his own rifle was still on his now-riderless horse, and his Colt wasn't very effective against the combined firepower of a dozen Springfields.

At least the troopers valued good horseflesh, if not outlaws. They aimed high at the riders, not the animals. From the ground, me and Ty also scrambled over to the trees, though in a different area than where Finch was firing from. Instinctively, we knew not to go near him because we didn't want to look like we were also resisting them.

From the ground, I looked up and saw Severin. Tied to his horse, he couldn't leap off of it and he took a bullet in his right shoulder. A muffled scream was heard from under the neckerchief tied around his mouth. Bending low in the saddle, he turned his mount so that its left side faced the soldiers' bullets. Needless to say, several shots hit the poor horse and he started to fall. Unfortunately for Severin, since he was tied to his horse, he went down with it. Therefore, when the poor thing hit the ground, the man still in the saddle screamed when his left leg was crushed underneath the horse's side.

Lone took a different tack. Despite the fact that he was covered in that copperhead mask, he howled as if he were at the Little Big Horn or raiding some settler family's cabin or God knows where else. He howled as if this was his last attack on his hated enemies, and Lord knew, it sure seemed it. As soon as he rode forward, firing his own rifle pistol-style, the troopers wasted little time before they opened fire on him. A rifle slug hit him in the right torso, then another pierced his bull-neck throat and actually glanced off it, a third hit his right side and a fourth punctured the outline of the burlap hood and shot off his right ear. His Indian howl suddenly turned into a scream of pain as soon as blood and cartilage and the large piece of flesh that used to be an ear flew off and landed, without ceremony, somewhere on some New Mexico soil. Another bullet hit his left ribcage and we could clearly see him weaken. He rode within a few feet of them when he finally rolled off his horse and hit the ground with a loud thud, a cloud of dust rising in his wake.

Most of the others in the gang were dead. But there were a few of them who got up from the ground and opened fire on the soldiers as they were leaving the coach—being stationary restricted their fire, so their leaving it was understandable. Unfortunately, in those few seconds it took for them to jump out of the coach they were forced to hold their fire. Several of them were hit by bullets fired by two gang members who sprang off the ground.

Me and Ty looked at each other then, knowing what we had to do. It was now time for us to stop being helpless victims pushed back and forth by fate; and start being men again.

We sprang from our hiding place in the trees, drew our guns and opened fire on the two gang members shooting at the soldiers. Not being gunmen and knowing just where to aim to kill an enemy, we both ended up emptying our pistols at the two. I was glad to see that one of them was Stu, the one who interrupted me and Bessie back at the restaurant. Still, I took no pleasure in killing him, but I did take some gratification that I had helped save a few soldiers' lives. After emptying our pistols, they both lay crumbled on the ground, with our gunsmoke hovering over their bodies in the slight spring breeze of New Mexico.

Three of the soldiers who sprang from the coach were dead, but at least we paid their murderers back for it. A sudden click of a gun from behind us made us turn around. Finch was aiming his pistol right at us as we stood there, our guns smoking and empty. We heard the soldiers come up behind us and aim their weapons at him.

"No!" I shouted. "I'll talk to him."

"Jed, he'll kill you!" Ty said.

Ignoring him, I slowly walked toward him.

Finch said, "You knew about this!"

I shook my head. "We never knew. But we would never have fired on these men either."

"You haven't changed," he said bitterly. "Neither of you! You still want to be poor sodbusters the rest of your lives!"

I asked him, "And what are you now gonna be the rest of *your* life? Or Severin? Or Lone? Look at what the outlaw life has done for you boys!"

Not having an immediate answer, Finch just aimed that .45 right at me.

A sergeant behind me said, "Get out of the way, son! We've got him in our sights!"

I didn't answer him. I was unarmed and facing a man who sure as hell was.

I said, "Put it down, Finch."

He was still aiming at me.

"Please!"

It was another thirty seconds, maybe forty, before he suddenly uncocked the hammer and threw the gun to the ground.

Irritably, he glared at us and said, "Farm boys! Damn sentimental farm boys!"

The big raid was over.

CHAPTER TWENTY-TWO

The soldiers got to mending the wounded, and burying their dead, theirs as well as ours. Though they had lost three or four compared to the Hennessey Gang losing everyone but three. Severin was pulled out from under his dead horse and he and Lone were patched up as well as possible under the circumstances. Unfortunately for them, with no doctor there, the soldiers were forced to bandage them up with torn strips of clothing from dead outlaws until army doctors could perform surgery on them. Finch had his hands tied tightly behind his back and he was mounted on a lead horse. Then we both noticed that the Toombs boys were not around. Being all the way in the rear, they were easily warned of the ambush while at a safe distance and, as quietly as they could, high-tailed it away from there as fast as their mounts would carry them.

I was glad for them. But I wondered if we had seen the last of them.

Needless to say, the trooper-filled stagecoach wasn't

carrying any payroll. This made me curious about the whole counter-ambush.

After Ty and I handed our empty guns over to the sergeant, a lieutenant approached us. He was also young, but a bushy blonde mustache on his upper lip helped him compensate for his youth.

He touched his hand on his hat-brim and said, "I'm Lieutenant Durkin. And you must be Jed and Tyrone?"

We stared at him.

I asked, "We're wanted by the federal government too?"

Ty asked the lieutenant, "Who told you about us?"

We saw the young officer smile for the first time.

"We got a telegraph message from a trio of young ladies, apparently. Can't say we get those every day. Their names were..." He snapped his fingers, trying to remember. "Hazel..."

I piped in. "Bessie?"

"Yes," he admitted, "that's the second one. And..."

Ty was in suspense.

Finally, the young man said, "Jill! It was on the tip of my tongue."

I saw the relief on Ty's face. "She got away!"

Durkin looked oddly at him. "Got away?"

I explained, "The gang was holding her hostage so we would join them on the raid."

The lieutenant nodded and said, "Yes, they explained that. They also said that you two were innocent of any murder committed in Beaumont and that you were both forced to join the gang."

"Now if only the law believed us," Ty said gravely.

Durkin said sternly, "There's still got to be an accounting, a clearing-up of what really happened from the point you two joined the gang to now, as well as who was really responsible for the murder of Mr. Reynolds. But it seems we shot him out of his horse. It was the Indian. The one named Severin said as much..."

I said, "We've still got to face our folks, our town."

"If I were you, Jed, I wouldn't worry. By the showing you two made today, gunning down those two outlaws probably saved some more of my men. You boys have already got our vote if it ever comes to a trial. And as representatives of the federal government, that still counts for *something* in this state."

Ty and me couldn't hide our joy.

"Now come on," Durkin said. "We've got a long ride back. The least we can do is have a skeleton crew escort you back to Dentonville. We know that there isn't any law there that isn't controlled by the Hennesseys, so a few of my men will ride along until the government can appoint a lawman there. At least, the Hennessey Gang is broken up—for good." He started to leave, but then he turned back and said, "Oh, by the way. Maybe his word isn't any good, maybe it is. But you two have one more witness who said the gang forced you to ride with them."

"Who?"

"The gang's leader. The one you call Finch..."

―――――

THE RIDE WAS UNEVENTFUL, though it wasn't every day that you saw a caravan that looked like us.

Lieutenant Durkin took the bulk of his men and continued down the trail they originally had taken. We even passed the *real* coach with the payroll as we rode back. It was several miles behind us at a safe distance while the gang was getting shot to pieces. There were now twelve of us headed to Dentonville; me, Ty, the wounded Severin, and Lone, Finch, and half a dozen troopers led by a crusty sergeant named Nyby. Severin was tied down atop the phony stagecoach, stretched out there with a broken leg. The bullet wound to his shoulder, awkwardly bandaged up with an outlaw's torn shirt. Lone's hood was ripped off so a couple troopers could somehow bandage the location where his ear used to be. But in the process, the slight bandages covering his facial scars came off and the soldiers gaped at his disfigured face. They tried to find something else to cover him up with but failed. They settled for a dead outlaw's hat jammed onto Lone's head. He tried to make an ugly face to frighten the soldiers, but it still pained him to move his features. It didn't matter; the troopers were repelled by him anyway. With all his bullet wounds, clumsily covered by torn clothes and tourniquets, he was also tied atop the stagecoach. Ironically, he was alongside Severin, whose own face was disfigured thanks to the murderer strapped down beside him.

Having no wounds at all, Finch was the luckiest of the three surviving gang members. His hands were tied behind him and his horse was led by another trooper. He spoke little. Lord only knew what he was thinking.

Soon, Fraternitas, a.k.a. Dentonville, came into view. The sun was going down and as we climbed over a short hill, we could see the lights of the town flickering below.

Nyby called a halt, and then asked Finch where they would find a doctor for his men atop the coach.

Finch told where Doc Elder was and we proceeded down the hill and rode into town.

For some reason, the streets were empty. Though the sun had set by the time we rode in, it wasn't *that* late. Ty and I looked at each other.

I asked, "Everyone's at dinner?"

Ty looked around the main street worriedly and said, "Must be a hell of a meal to keep folks indoors all this time—"

Nyby asked, "Finch, you know this town. Where is everybody?"

Finch didn't answer him. Looking around the empty street, it was obvious that even he was baffled by the town's sudden desolation. I thought of the other day, when me and Ty grabbed the dead outlaws' guns and the Toombs boys and us held off the Hennessey Gang while we protected Hazel. The crowds that had formed earlier vanished in seconds when the townsmen saw that there would be a shootout or any other kind of trouble.

I had that same feeling now. Somehow the people in the town knew there was going to be trouble, but *we* didn't.

And that's when they appeared. At first, it was preceded by a fiery glow. It came from up a side street we had stopped in front of; and as we focused our eyes in the darkness, we saw the scene much clearer.

Horsemen, about twenty of them, all wearing pillowcases on their heads with eye-slits in them and carrying, believe it or not, flaming torches, drifted out of a side street like weirdly-intruding ghosts and rode up to us. Except for the pillowcases, they were all dressed like anyone else who lived in a small town; overalls, Levis, calico shirts, and besides their long guns, every one of them wore a Colt or some such firearm on his hip.

One of them, a tall man who was riding in the rear of the column, was holding a rope. As we looked closer, we could see a man, a beaten, bloodied man, tied to the end of it. He was now being dragged into view. The rider came to the head of the column and the man was forced to go with him until the man on horseback whipped out the rope and the figure dropped to the ground on his face. When he looked up, we saw it was the bloody face of Hiram Jessup. Whether he had been dragged through the street facedown or he had been beaten by the mob beforehand, we didn't know. All we did know was that all were appalled by the sight.

In unison, the troopers jacked down the levers of their rifles and started to raise them, but the hooded riders already had their own rifles raised and pointed at us.

"Throw 'em down!" one of them commanded.

Nyby may have ordinarily been a tough soldier, but he was no fool. There was no choice. There were too many of them and they had too many guns.

He ordered, "Drop 'em, boys."

The troopers paused only slightly before they dropped their long guns to the ground.

"The Dragoons too," said the tall rider gruffly.

Reluctantly, and not exactly in unison, the troopers drew their pistols from their holsters and also dropped them to the street.

Then, as a weird kind of *greeting*, the tall one announced, *"Salus populi suprema est lex!"*

No one knew what the hell that meant, until I heard Nyby, who must've been a practicing Catholic and knew his Latin far better than the rest of us, muttered, "'The safety of the people is the supreme law...'"

At a signal from the head man who had dragged Jessup, four men left the column and rode over to the coach. One stayed in the saddle and the other three then climbed atop the roof and found the two wounded outlaws.

One of them called down, "Two of them tied to the top. Both wounded. In fact, they're still bleedin' through the bandages."

The tall, hooded man replied gravely, "We'll save 'em the trouble of bleedin' to death..."

Then he pointed to Finch and said, "There's the leader."

Finch said nothing. You could tell he was enraged when he saw his uncle being dragged through the streets, but his look of contempt said it all. He would give these men nothing, not even fear.

However, Jessup still had some words left in him. Weakly, he gazed up at his nephew and, between labored breaths, said, "You see, Clay? I told you that you boys rolled over these people too much. I told you they were like a bomb waitin' to go off! So one of 'em called these boys in." He had the strength to turn his head and glare at them as he continued, "They ride the counties lookin' for anyone they consider *the outlaw menace*!" He exhaled a tired breath and added bitterly, "A bunch of cheap killers with pillowcases for faces!"

Angry at Jessup's withering condemnation of what they considered a Holy Mission, the tall one straightened himself in the saddle as he faced us. Raising his torch for emphasis, he announced, "We are the People's

Court! We enforce the law around here when the real one is in the pockets of outlaws and killers!"

"People's Court, my ass!" Nyby said bluntly. And then he asked, "Do you know what the hell you're doing? These men are under the protection of the federal government!"

As if in response to this, the hooded leader pulled out a Colt, aimed it at Jessup lying half-conscious on the ground and pulled the trigger. The bullet went right into the old man's forehead as we watched helplessly.

Finch didn't react at first. Then he suddenly turned the horse with his legs and spurred him forward. He was heading right for the nightriders when one of them raised a pistol and shot Finch right out of the saddle. He hit the street and rolled over, his hands still tied behind his back. He was still alive, having just been shot in the side, but his horse continued hurtling himself toward the vigilantes.

They didn't even bother to get out of the way. In unison, they raised their rifles and opened fire on the helpless animal. As it still hurtled itself toward the hooded men, the horse's legs quickly buckled and its huge carcass collapsed just a few feet before it got to them.

In the confusion that followed, I saw a trooper pull out a small handgun from inside his blouse—apparently a backup gun—aim it straight at the tall man who was the group's leader, and open fire twice.

I saw the hooded man stiffen and then topple off his horse and hit the street, his body as dead as Hiram Jessup's. The troopers scattered. Their horses flew in all directions and angry clouds of dust rose from the street and just about choked us as we paused there.

I knew where I was going to go, and so did Ty. I leaped off my horse and ran for Finch lying in the street as cavalry mounts galloped around him. Ty was right behind me. With some effort, we both picked up the outlaw leader and ran for the nearest alley. As we did this, rifle bullets bounced off the street around us. Through the pandemonium, we pulled Finch across the wide street and headed for the mouth of that alley, his boot heels dragging in the dirt. We didn't know what happened to Nyby or the soldiers. I couldn't blame them if they had ridden out of town and fled for reinforcements.

We finally made it to the mouth of the alley and pulled Finch into the shadow of a wall.

Breathing fast, he said, "You boys don't have to do this. I pay my own debts!"

I looked at him and said, "Shut up, Clay!" It was the first time I called him by his name, which surprised him.

Echoing this new camaraderie, Ty added, "You may not be a model citizen, Clay, but we'll be damned if we hand you over to that bunch of ghouls!"

Suddenly we heard gunshots from the opposite side of the street. Looking out from the alley, we saw the Toombs brothers spurring their horses in from the opposite end of the street, firing as they rode. A few of the hooded riders were hit, though I didn't know how seriously, but I *did* see several of them topple from their horses, cutting down their numbers.

But their help wasn't enough.

The horsemen that didn't fall returned fire with renewed hate. I saw Ira hit, and he fell from his saddle to the street. He rolled over in pain and just laid there, face up, his Stetson lying several feet away and his gun having landed on one of the sidewalks somewhere.

Andrew was a different story. He rode right into them and gave a loud rebel yell, a Colt in each hand, firing as he rode. He looked like every cowboy hellion in every penny-dreadful Western novel I had ever read from the usually unknowledgeable east. He fired one gun and then another and he hit several of them as he plunged into their hastily formed skirmish line.

Certainly, if ever pure sand won the day, Andrew Toombs would have wiped these hooded outlaws off the face of the earth and he still would've had bullets to spare for half a dozen posse members who had the gall to challenge him. But that was what you read in story-books, not what you witness, with so much horror, in the real world.

Rifle and pistol bullets hit him all over his body, the chest, the stomach, the arms, his legs. Amazingly, no bullet touched his head, though one shot his Stetson off. Hatless and with a defiant sneer, Andrew continued to charge their line and he crashed right through it, like a knife slicing through a loaf of bread, killing more of them as he came out the other end of the street.

But the firing of the hooded men continued, and their bullets started to take their toll. Andrew looked weak as he turned his horse back for another charge. Then, as I expected, he fell from his horse and hit the ground, his horse flying down the street far away from the bullets and gun smoke.

Then something amazing happened. Andrew rose off the ground, slowly and painfully. And with bullet-riddled arms, he weakly raised his guns. One shot, then another, felled one of the hooded men and he fell from *his* horse to the street. Then, painfully making himself stand fully erect, Andrew kept firing until both of his guns were empty and we heard only the clicks as he continued to pull the triggers. That's when the hooded men lined up and, aiming their rifles and pistols, opened fire with a last, final volley. Andrew was literally blown off the street, his boots flying in the air and his body hitting the street flat on his back.

He died game, the way I knew Andrew Toombs was going to die.

Seeing this from the alley, Finch cursed and said, "Cut me loose and find me a gun!"

I looked around frantically and suddenly spotted a garbage can piled to the rim with trash. And I found what I figured would be there; an empty bottle. Quickly I went over and smashed it against the adobe wall and took the jagged neck. I said loudly to Finch, "Turn around!"

He did so and I got to work on the ropes, but whichever of the soldiers tied them did it so well I had to be careful not to cut Finch's wrists.

But then Ty looked up toward the opposite end of the alley and shouted, "Jed!"

I looked up and saw a huge white horse careening down the other end of the alley. I dropped the broken bottleneck and we quickly pulled Finch and ourselves out of the alley and onto the boardwalk before that hooded rider ran us down. That's when the few hooded horsemen still left alive after Andrew's charge rode right up to us and pointed their rifles practically in our faces.

One of them said, "We don't want you two! We want him! We already have the other two at the jail."

The *other two* had to be the wounded Severin and

Lone, whom they were obviously able to take down off the coach without resistance and drag, badly treated bullet wounds and all, into the nearby jail.

Something Ty pointed out when he said bitterly, "They need a doctor, not a jail!"

"They won't when we get through with them!"

The rest of them, maybe five or six left, dragged me and Ty to the jailhouse along with the still tied-up and bleeding Finch. We were roughly pulled through the empty marshal's office into the back rooms with the cells. The corridor which divided the two rows of cells was wide and it held us all with plenty of room to spare. But in their own contempt for the trappings of the law, the Hennesseys had turned the building into a giant warehouse, with useless boxes and old furniture spread all over the place.

But when we were dragged into the back room, the sight before me and Ty chilled us.

Both Severin and Lone, with their wounds now open and bleeding in plain sight, had nooses around their necks, with the ropes tossed over a thick cross-beam in the ceiling high above us. They were also mounted on a couple old wooden barrels, their bootheels barely scraping the rims. In fact, considering their own leg wounds, they weren't really standing on the barrels as much as being stretched taut in upright positions. It was the ropes tightening around their necks holding them up rather than their own legs, but then what did I expect? These nightriders were experts at what they did, and sadistic ones at that.

A third barrel and a third noose, this one empty and dangling loosely over it, stood waiting for the third man. Severin was shedding tears without shame, and Lone tried to look like the fearsome Indian he imagined he was, but his attempts to be proud and defiant were kind of pathetic. He too was scared of death, and it showed pretty plainly when he soiled his pants right in front of us, just as Severin had when Finch caught him back at the Angel House. To Lone's thinking, he certainly had further reason to fear death by hanging. To an Indian, being hanged and cutting off the air of life from his throat was the worst way possible for him to die.

With a nod from their new surviving leader, a little man in grubby overalls and a dirty pillowcase, the struggling Finch was dragged over and, with some difficulty, mounted on the third barrel. He tried to kick them away, but they held his legs as they knocked off his hat and draped the noose around his neck, then tightened it.

Ty and I were held back by two or three men. I forgot how many. We struggled to break free and stop the damn thing, but it was like trying to push an elephant to the ground. My arms were wrenched back so far they were hurting.

The head man spoke, "We saw you two stand against the Hennesseys a couple days ago. Now you will witness what happens when our county is used as a haven for the outlaw element!"

Ty shouted, "Outlaw element! Why don't you all look at yourselves? You're no better than the Hennesseys!"

One of the hooded men came over and punched Ty across the face. His Stetson spun off his head and blood appeared on his mouth as I struggled to get to the man and return the favor.

"Silence!" the leader shouted. "Or you boys will join these three felons on the scaffold!"

It wasn't a scaffold, it was three dirty wooden barrels. Still, the effect was the same. Kick them out from under the three men and it was all over.

Severin cried and begged for mercy, blaming it all on the Hennesseys, the gang he had murdered his family to join and be so much a part of. A trembling Lone was too scared to move or speak, but he tried vainly to look like a proud Indian defying his white persecutors. As for Finch, he spat a huge glob into the face of the head man. Taken aback, the man wiped it off his hood—and out of the eye holes—Then he nodded to the hooded men standing behind the barrels.

Finch looked at me and Ty and said, "Bye-bye, boys! If you ever find yourselves goin' South, look me up!"

The barrels were kicked over, and the three men, whether crying, frightened or defiant—dropped into the musty air of that old jailhouse, their booted feet dancing around and around, spinning endlessly into space with no stopping in sight. It was obvious that Lone and Severin, by their gagging and their faces turning dark blue, were slowly strangling to death. However, an angel—maybe even a dark one—must've been hovering over Clay Finch Hennessey. That's because his neck broke quick and clean as soon as he dropped. A death he no doubt preferred to the agonizing kind that his brothers were now going through.

Me and Ty watched the horror with widened eyes. Then, when Severin and Lone's bodies stopped gagging and finally hung still and lifeless in the suddenly airless room, we both turned our heads as far away as we could from the sight. My brother and I had seen men shot down before our eyes far too many times, but now we had witnessed a hanging—a lynching really—and up close too. The sight of it, not to mention the travesty of justice behind it, was something we weren't going to forget for a long time.

The crash of the door being broken in behind us made us look up and a volley of rifle shots followed. The vise-like grip of the hooded man who held me loosened and I turned to my right and saw the man who punched Ty fall, grasping his bloody chest. We dropped to the ground then. Looking up just long enough to see the two men who kicked the barrels riddled with bullets as Nyby and the troopers, now backed up by ordinary citizens, entered the room and spread out, looking for more hooded men, but it looked like our rescuers had gotten them all.

Nyby rushed over to us, helping us to our feet.

"We scattered," he explained. "And when they came in here, we ran back for our guns. Some of the townspeople helped us."

Then he caught the sight before him and winced.

"Lord Jesus! Only animals would do this!"

Ty looked at the hanging bodies and said, "Now the Hennesseys really are finished."

Nyby said, "So are a lot of useless men in dirty pillowcases. Some might be clerks and shopkeepers in this town; some might be outsiders who rode the county hangin' outlaws. One thing's for sure, they won't ride down anyone ever again..."

———

THE FIRST THING Ty insisted upon was for Nyby to have his troopers find Jill. She was one of the three women who sent the telegram to Fort Garland warning the soldiers of the Hennesssys' attempt to rob the stage.

Outside of that, however, Nyby and his men basically had us under house arrest. With all the doings between our involvement with the Hennessey Gang, the sudden appearance of the vigilantes, and who were these mysterious women who wired the fort about the planned robbery, he knew that his CO, Lieutenant Durkin, would want to quiz us about the whole sad story from the beginning. He couldn't take a chance that we'd ride away and leave them without any information on what led up to the robbery and how we could clear ourselves, so we had no choice but to stick around. We slept at the jailhouse that night; that is, after his men removed all the bodies there and on the street and took them to Haskin's Funeral Parlor to await a quick, no-frills mass burial in the next day or so. I heard that old man Haskins was fit to be tied when Nyby's men woke him up and forcibly had him open his parlor. Though how he slept through the carnage is anyone's guess; I also heard that he and his wife had a home far from the center of town—and he slept with cotton in his ears as well. He was shocked to find that Finch was one of the bodies he'd be burying. Suddenly, he was no longer, like so many others in the town, at the Hennesseys' beck and call. Overnight, he and the town's other merchants were back to being what they called in the east independent contractors.

For me and Ty, we had no choice. We slept in a couple cells, of course, with the doors wide open. All I can say is that the bedbugs were only *slightly* better than what the Hennesseys provided us.

As it turned out, though Andrew was dead, and in

my opinion, died a hero, Ira was still alive, the bullet having missed his lung and clipped off a piece of skin on his left side. A trooper woke a doctor out of bed and had him patch up Ira. He was pretty weak, but he would recover eventually. Unfortunately, Nyby ordered his men to prevent us from leaving the jail and going anywhere; therefore, we couldn't see Ira, much less find Bessie, Jill, or Hazel and tell them we were safe.

We had just a few hours of blessed sleep; and though we both slept deeply, we got up at sunrise. Part of that was due to the bright haze of a spring sun shining in through our cell windows. How prisoners could deal with it, pre-Hennessey, is anyone's guess.

Another reason was that Nyby ordered a trooper to bang on the bars and wake us up. Lieutenant Durkin had arrived. When we staggered tiredly into the marshal's office, two chairs were set up for us and a breakfast was waiting for us with eggs, fried potatoes, buttered toast, and two mugs with hot black coffee. Durkin was sitting in the swivel chair that used to belong to the town's marshal. An Army stenographer was at his elbow with reams of notepaper, a pen and ink to take everything down. The young officer was himself red-eyed and a bit haggard. After depositing the payroll at Fort Garland, he got a quick couple hours' sleep and then was ordered by his captain to get the whole story of our involvement with the gang before we were allowed to go on our way. He also arrived with a detail of fifteen men and quickly put Dentonville under martial law until the government could appoint a federal marshal and deputies to enforce the law. And that was going to end when a special election for marshal would be held.

After we told our whole story, from the point when Ty woke me up in the middle of the night to the moment when the last vigilante was shot dead in the jailhouse, it was already early evening, with the sun starting to set outside those same bars from which we were awakened. We ate our free lunch and free dinner at the jail and then after they all shook our hands and wished us well, we were allowed to leave that damned place and get on with our lives. The lieutenant also told us that his CO, an army brass-hat named Colonel Fulton, had a couple of his men ride to Beaumont and issue a federal order to Marshal Clell that Ty and me were *not* to be arrested or harmed in any way; and that a local trial—of course, presided over by the army—would officially clear us in a few days. I also heard that if Clell violated that order, he could find himself arrested and jailed for several years. As it turned out, we didn't have to worry much on that score. Just the other day, Clell was shot dead by one of his own former posse men who couldn't forget a nasty remark the marshal had made about his wife while they were tracking us through the woods that night.

Ty asked about Jill, but neither Durkin or Nyby knew where she was. What they *were* able to tell us was where Ira was. Apparently, he was resting comfortably at Doc Elder's house.

We finally left the jail in the early evening and found ourselves gazing at the setting sun. And waiting for us at the tie rails were the two horses we took from Pa to start our journey. We both looked at each other and didn't wait; we mounted our horses and headed to Doc Elder's.

As it turned out, before we got to Elder's house, two

soldiers hailed us and we stopped our mounts. They were two of the original six soldiers we had ridden into town with the other night. After shaking our hands and thanking us for helping to save their buddies, they told us that no one was at Doc Elder's house and that they were headed back to the jail to see Durkin. It seemed that, since Ira and Andrew attacked the vigilantes, no one thought of them as belonging to the Hennessey Gang; or for that matter, did Durkin and his men recognize them as wanted outlaws. Andrew was dead, but Ira was still wanted for robbery. But when we asked where Ira was, we were told that his wife had come with a buckboard and had taken him home.

Ty asked, "What did his wife look like?"

"Oh," answered one of them, a soft-spoken, lanky southerner, "I'd say she was kind of on the tall side. Honey-blonde hair, hazel eyes, very pretty. She and Elder helped carry him to the buckboard and he winked at 'em both and promised to see the wounded man at their home the next day."

Ty looked at me, but my expression was blank.

Then the soldier said, "Oh, yeah, Jed, I almost forgot. I was gonna give this to you at the jailhouse when we got there." He fumbled in his blouse and finally pulled out an envelope. "That woman, his wife, that is, said to give this to you."

I leaned down in the saddle and took it from him.

"Thank you," I said, my voice like a whisper.

"Thank *you!*" said the other one, a mid-westerner with a corn shuck drawl. "You boys helped save our hides. Well, take care."

"So long."

We all shook hands again and they went on their way.

After they left, Ty stared at me.

"You going to open it?"

"Not right now," I said.

"Okay."

"But when I do, I'll let you read it too. After all, we're both her *family*. And I have a feeling that'll include Ira now."

Ty admitted, "I like Ira. Andrew too. God rest his soul."

"Yeah. Well, we've got our own lives to live now."

Ty reached out and put his hand on my shoulder, squeezing it affectionately.

I didn't say anything after that. Then suddenly, I felt Ty's hand come off my shoulder and I heard a small voice from far away calling us. Before I could turn, Ty had leaped off his horse and ran down the now-darkened street. I had to quickly grab his horse's reins so he wouldn't wander off.

Then I looked off to where Ty had run and I saw them. He and Jill were in a tight embrace and kissing in the middle of the street as if the rest of the town wasn't there.

I rode over to them, pulling his horse behind me.

When I got to them, they looked up at me, smiling.

"I see you got away."

Jill nodded happily.

Ty held her at arm's length and asked, "How'd you do it?"

She said, "Remember when I spent a little too much time in that room at the Dover House? I was supposed to be viewing Sherry's body."

"Yeah," I replied. "We were wondering why you took so long if they already took her body out."

"Well, I was lookin' for something that I had a feeling would still be there."

Jill reached into the waistband under the man's pants she was wearing and pulled out a gun. Then she handed it to an astonished Ty. He took the heavy gun and stared at it, and then back at her.

She said, "They never found Ed Plummer's gun, but I did..."

I asked, "So you used it to get away from Hagel."

"I had it hidden under my shirt. Despite Finch's threat, Hagel thought he was going to have his way with me anyway. He cornered me as soon as I left the outhouse."

Ty asked, "You killed him?"

Jill gave a little smile and said, "Let's say he won't be forcing himself on young women for a while. That is, *if ever*! Not where I plugged him..."

"So I grabbed a horse and rode to town. I figured to use the gun to force the telegraph operator to wire the nearest fort and tell 'em about the gang's raid and about you two being forced to go along with them. But guess what? Hazel and Bessie had the same idea. I was surprised they knew who I was, so I figured they were friends of yours. That poor man had *three women* pointing guns at him. Though the two of them had the usual ladies' pocket guns, they kill just as fast as the one I had, and that telegraph operator knew it. I never saw anyone sweat so much—he was so scared. None of us women knew the Morse code, but that man *knew* he'd better not pull a fast one on us."

Then she turned and looked at Ty, especially his

eyes. "I knew that if one of ya didn't come back, it would've been death for me, and that's a fact." They kissed again. I knew then and there that we'd have to get used to having an ex-saloon girl around our home from now on.

I interrupted them. I was sorry for it, but I had to.

"Hey!"

They stopped kissing and looked up at me.

I tossed the reins to Ty, who caught them.

"I'll join you two a little later, but I'm kinda hungry myself right now."

Still in Jill's arms, Ty smiled up at me.

He knew where I wanted to go.

He said, "Good luck, little brother..."

————

WHEN I ENTERED THE PELLICAN, the place was packed with customers. Zelda was waiting on a couple at a table in the rear and it was a miracle they escaped with their lives. She was dropping things practically in their laps. Irritably, she called out to Bessie to help her.

When I appeared under the archway, I didn't have to call Bessie. She saw me as soon as I entered and quickly put down her tray full of food on the table of two middle-aged women who complained loudly about her manners. They were followed by a chorus of customers who couldn't stand Zelda and demanded proper service.

Bessie didn't hear any of them. She just ran into my arms and hugged me as tightly as a person could hug anyone.

Then, as patrons screamed at Bessie with their

demands, we kissed right under that archway, for a *long* time. Her lips pressed against mine as hungrily and full of longing as I'd ever felt in my life.

Afterward, with her arms still around my neck, she looked up at me.

"I didn't sleep at all last night. Then I found out today that you came back, but the soldiers wouldn't let me or Jill see either of you. And you know that Hazel had to take Ira away before they recognized him."

"Yes, I know."

As she looked at me, tears started to come and she embraced me again.

"Oh, darlin', darlin'! I didn't know if I was ever going to see you again!"

By this time, the patrons had about given up on us, and several of them started to get

up and leave the restaurant. A few of them gave us nasty looks as they passed by, hats and coats in hand. And then Zelda looked at us as she passed by, tossing her apron on the ground in disgust. After a few moments, we looked around and the place was empty.

But we didn't care.

I said to her, "Now with the Hennesseys gone, this town'll be ready to get back to normal."

"Not soon enough to suit me!"

I paused and looked down at my boots for a moment.

Then I faced her and asked, "Are you going to stay here? Continue serving folks at the good ol' Pellican?"

Curiously, she asked, "Why?"

"Well...our folks are old now...and...and my mom could use some...help around the house. You know, cooking and other things. We have a spare room. And I was thinking, if it's all right with you—"

She cut me off. "I grew up on a farm in Donegal."

"Did you now?"

She smiled up at me and gave that little nod.

I said, "I can't wait for you to meet our folks."

"Neither can I."

Then I thought of something.

"Ya know, it's kinda funny."

"What is?"

"A couple mornings ago, our parents got up and found their two sons missing. Now we're going to come back and bring them two daughters..."

Bessie smiled at me. I would never get tired of looking at that smile.

————

As we were all outside Bessie's rooming house with a newly purchased buckboard waiting for her to pack, I leaned back against the tie-gate and took Hazel's letter out of my pocket.

I ripped open the envelope and unfolded it. It was a few pages, but Hazel's handwriting was large enough to read easy.

Dear Jed,

If you're reading this, it means that my prayers have been answered and that you came back from your harrowing journey alive, as I hope Ty did as well. If there's any sin I feel guilty of to this day, it's that I felt I abandoned you as a child when you needed a family to help you get through the heartache of your parents' deaths. I was happy when Ty's family took you in, and though I did what I could to help you get through your pain when I and others told you of their deaths, I always felt that I should've stayed. Even when I didn't know then that you were my little brother, I had wished you actually were, for no sister could wish for a more delightful and loving little brother than you. When I found you again, I was in Heaven. For along with the rest of this town, I had gone through the usual outrages associated with being under the thumb of the Hennessey Gang. To top it all off, I had fallen in love with one of them, Ira Toombs, himself a tormented man who sometimes has problems revealing his feelings. But he's a good man, as you yourself have seen. Knowing of my love for him and being forced to fend for myself after my mom died, you can imagine my joy in having found you again. For my brother was back and I was no longer alone.

But now, I have to leave you again. Ira and I have had a long talk in the past couple days. After witnessing you get beaten up a few times defending me and me publicly indicting him that day in the street for not facing his own feelings, Ira had finally admitted that he cares for me and that his usual taciturn manner when he was around me was done to spare me the grief of hooking up with a wanted outlaw. He did love me enough to not want me to share the life of a criminal on the run all the time. I suppose I should be grateful for his concern, but it would've been easier for me had he dropped his usual male restraint and just been honest with me and honest with his emotions.

Andrew's dead now, and gradually it's dawning on him that maybe he has no further reason to live the dead-end life of a wanted "desperado" and instead try to make some kind of living like most folks. Now that the gang is no more and Ira is "out of commission," we also agreed that I would take him far away from this territory, to some place where they never heard of Ira Toombs or the Hennessey Gang. We've already made the first moves in that direction. By the time you read this, we will have left the state. And by the end of the month, we figure to have a new start somewhere in Southern California. I'm not sure what we'll do, but as long as we love each other and are honest with each other, we'll survive.

I'm glad you found Bessie. She was raised on a farm in Ireland and because of British harassment, she and her family came to this country to make a living. But after her folks died, her big brother became attracted to the outlaw life and he did some horrible things to make a name for himself—that is, until a group of men hanged him after he beat up an old man. Bessie has taken a lot of guff from the Hennessey Gang, and when you appeared, she was all mixed up. She knew she was attracted to you, but she also thought you and Ty were young outlaws out to make names for themselves like her brother. If you allow me to play Matchmaker here, I can never say enough that Bessie is a good woman of strong character who would make a great wife.

When you return to your home, Jed, whether you decide to bring Bessie back with you or Ty decides to bring Jill back with him and you both start your own families, remember that you have a chance to make up for the sins and perversions of those like the Hennesseys who hurt so many folks and had taken so many lives. In his own way, Finch Hennessey sought to have his own twisted version of a family through his gang, but it was never that because it was based on greed and cruelty. Ty, Jill, Bessie, you and so many others have proven that one doesn't have to be of the same blood to be a family. I hope you always remember this.

The buckboard will be ready at the stables soon and I'll be picking up Ira for our new journey together. Let's hope I can put one over on these soldiers long enough to get us far away from this territory and onto a new life.

I'll write to you and your new families at your parents' farm. I still remember where it is. Perhaps one day, you and yours can visit us in California. Let it not be goodbye, Jed. Let it not be the end of our family ties.

God bless you always.

Love,
Your sister, Hazel Carney

As promised, I showed the letter to Ty. Then, after Bessie arrived with her bags and the four of us were on our way, I showed her the letter as well.

After she finished it, she looked at me with compassion in her eyes. We both didn't say a word for a few moments. We just stared at each other as the buckboard climbed the trail.

Then I heard water rushing over rocks and something made me turn around.

And there it was, the same jagged rock in the same stream at the bottom of that hill where that reporter's head had been hooked onto. Then, as I looked at it, a sudden rush of water washed over the rock, and with a snap, it broke the piece away and carried it down the river.

Ty saw it also, and with a shout, he shook the reins and the horses jerked the buckboard forward and further down the trail, as far away from the spot as we could get.

I put my arms around Bessie then, and Ty kept Jill close to him as he drove the horses.

We stayed that way until we all arrived home.

A LOOK AT: BORDERLINE

He will uphold the law, even if it costs him everything...

Shortly after the turn of the century on a Colorado range near the town of Sage, Will Landry—an African American land agent enforcing the Van Wyck Fence Law—finds himself in a precarious position. When he discovers the body of a lynched nester swinging out on the prairie, Landry realizes he's stumbled upon a sinister plot orchestrated by German immigrant cattle baron, Joachim Lang—a man steeped in darkness if there ever was one.

To bring Lang to justice, Landry must confront not only the rampant racism of the era but also a town bureaucracy resistant to change. Yet, amidst the adversity, Landry forges unexpected alliances with outcasts and those nursing personal vendettas against a common enemy.

As Landry's unwavering dedication and commitment to the law chip away at Lang's facade, tensions escalate toward a dramatic climax—a showdown that will test Landry's courage and resilience like never before.

AVAILABLE NOW

ABOUT THE AUTHOR

Born in Brooklyn, New York, Bob Herzberg is a cultural historian, Western author, actor, and comedian. He has authored a dozen books, including *The FBI and the Movies*, *The Third Reich on Screen*, and *Hollywood and the Military Bureaucracy*, as well as the Western *Borderline*, the Civil War tale *Sidearm*, and the range war *The McDermott Fifty*.

A member of the Western Writers of America and a previous student of acting teacher extraordinaire William Hickey, Bob has shuttled between New York and Hollywood on various projects and continues to research American history to inspire both his Western writing, as well as his books on film.

Both his book and cinema reviews have appeared in *The Roundup*, as well as other periodicals. His most recent book is *Imperial Japan on Screen*, 1930-2022. As a performer, he's acted on stage and done standup comedy, improvisation, and murder mysteries. He lives with his wife, actress, poet, and horror film fan Colleen Herzberg in New York City.